FERAL

JOE HOPE

HOPE PUBLISHING

CONTENTS

ISBN 978-0-6485622-0-7

To Janet, James and Jenny.

Thanks for waiting, and occasionally cheering.

Chapter 1

OUT?

The glass broke cleanly and easily, giving me a sudden and rather dramatic exit from the building. That was the first surprise. I had been expecting something closer to a loud crack as I bounced off the window, and then a chance to express my own feelings on the matter. But instead I was getting my first breath of fresh air in many months.

Many years previously I'd heard that drunk people sometimes misjudge jumps off the top of buildings and balconies. The pool looks close to the building from way up high, and they think they can land in it. Turns out you don't get much extra time in the air from the increased height, so you don't get much extra distance. The practical upshot being that if you can't jump all the way into the pool from the front door, you're still probably not going to make it that far from the third storey.

Now I knew from experience that it was a deep pool, with a ten metre diving platform and everything. So, as the meme goes, I had that going for me. Plus, my starting point was the fourth storey, so I had a little extra time. Unfortunately, knowing that the common error is to *overestimate* how far you're going to fall just makes it worse as you become increasingly convinced that your landing point is on the short side.

So the second surprise was more welcome, at least for a few seconds. Things were obviously a lot more advanced inside the building than I'd thought, as the explosion blew out the top two floors simultaneously. The pain was presumably immense or whatever, but shock can be highly adaptive on occasion. I still suspect that the little push from the explosion helped me miss the pool's edge as I rag-dolled into the hard, hard water and sank, too stunned to be scared.

You might know how it is when you take a big, big hit. Reality comes back in odd-shaped pieces. I became aware of a crushing pressure on my chest. A sense of overwhelming urgency. My eyes opened to tendrils and murk, like the whole world was as confused as me. Then as everything arranged itself, as it does indeed seem to do, I was surprised about everything all over again. I realised that I was looking at the world from the bottom of a pool with a torso-sized piece of concrete pinning my shoulder. The final surprise was the fact that I was waking up at all; but it wasn't clear whether that state was particularly sustainable, so just like the other surprises, I couldn't pay it much attention at the time.

My arm didn't work well. My head was swimming even more than the rest of me, and that thrice-damned piece of debris was not just heavy, but sharp! So, bleeding internally and externally, with broken bones, I discovered I was much heavier than I remembered, and could not float up when I freed myself. So after a desperate swim/crawl to the side of the pool, I finally got a lungful of sweet, sweet, nasty-smelling, cough-inducing smoke-tinged air. I pulled myself over the edge and crawled away, coughing. There were a lot of building shards all over the area, but the rest of it didn't seem to have actually toppled over in this direction. Although I knew for a fact that it hadn't, for a moment it looked like it had been dropped professionally, all five stories neatly piled on top of each other in a tight package. At least on this side. Thick black smoke covered the rest.

Things dimmed a little as I heaved myself across the street. I heard some voices and felt some hands. My knees buckled, and the dirty concrete lurched up to my face. I coughed weakly, and blood beaded in front of me, dust-covered spheres sagging under their own weight. I heard sirens, and then the lights really went out.

LUCK like that doesn't last, of course. Neither does shock-induced anaesthesia. I woke in so much pain, I couldn't quite manage a scream. Every one of my new muscles tried to clench, and I heard something metallic complaining.

"What the hell, he's conscious!" she exclaimed.

"Put him out. If he moves at all, I could kill him," she said. Different she, deeper voice.

My eyes were covered along with more than half of my head, so I didn't see much past the featureless white of backlit bandage. There was a hiss, and someone quietly muttering to herself about how much she'd already used, and the heart seemed strong, but these something something something...

WAKING WAS WORSE, again. It was quiet and dark, both of

which I instinctively liked. There was a regular beep, like the one you might hear in a hospital scene in a movie. It could have made me worry about my condition, but instead it just reassured me that someone was worrying about it for me.

My vision was still completely blocked by the bandage, but a few tender experiments told me I couldn't move my head anyway. I seemed to be strapped there. A couple of gentle movements later, I resolved that extensive testing could wait until it did not involve searing pain lancing down my neck. Some primitive part of me wanted everything just to stay away for a little longer. Stay away, the pain. Stay away, the thoughts. Stay away, the anger. The beeps went a little irregular there for a moment, and then...

THE NEXT TIME, I came back sharp. The bandages were still on my head and face, but I smelled hospital and I thought "hospital." I also smelled leather. I could feel it too, strapping me down from ankle to forehead. I was fairly heavily sedated as well - not only was the pain an ambient whine instead of its former jet-engine scream, but it had dimmed the frantic urgency that had been writhing in my gut and worming its way down my spine ever since the 'therapy'.

I wasn't alone. Can't say exactly how I knew, but my hackles were up, even though I was lying on them. He was about three metres away in the direction of my left knee, sitting. Probably armed, he smelled confident, alert, alpha. I hated him instantly. Thought he had me under control, did he? Smug asshole. Just because I was strapped down and he...

It was about that point when my pre-therapy brain

managed to wrest some control. Considering the straps and so forth, SmugAss might actually be right to be confident. Also, who was I to judge? If I fronted up once more to a jury of my peers, I could imagine that they might find that the main asshole in the room was strapped down on my bed. Images of some of the recent fighting came back to me. Some of that wouldn't get past ethics clearance, but I... I frowned, and it hurt. Why did all of that seem so natural? What was I thinking? The more my brain tried to make sense of what had happened, the more confused I became.

I heard the footsteps first. Then SmugAss did, and he shifted his weight around. The door opened, and three women entered on a wave of three very different scents.

"Marko," said one, voice firm and strong. I smiled, and it hurt.

"Sandy," he acknowledged. They were companions, used to relying on each other. I hated him.

One of the others came towards me. "Ok, let's see, here," she said. It was the deeper voice from the pain and the bright.

"Hello, doctor," I said, and it hurt. "It all hurts, which seems to be a good sign." My lips were numb, and my tongue felt hard to control.

She took in a quick breath. "You shouldn't be... It seems you are as hard to medicate as you are to move and feed."

The third one spoke from where she had stayed in the doorway, saying, "I told you they heal fast. If you get enough nutrients into them, their metabolism goes off the charts."

"Let's take a look," the doctor said, her hands moving sheets. She grunted a couple of times, and fussed a little with bandages for a while, which hurt.

"Well, Mr..." she said.

"Patrick," I offered.

"Well, Patrick," she said, "you are quite the exception to all the rules I know. It looks like you're over a month into what I would have predicted would have been a long recovery, and I've only slept once."

She sounded tired, though. That single sleep probably represented more than a single day.

"Well, Dr..." I prompted, voice a little raspy.

"Pembleton," she supplied.

"Well, Dr. Pembleton, maybe we can put that down to the skill and efforts of my surgeon." I tried to put my hand on hers. Which hurt, and made the shackles creak. A few seconds later there was a little puff of fear from the doorway, from the third one. I hated that, and the hate had some guilt behind it. She must know about the therapy, and what happened when... Confusion, again.

Sandy walked over to the bedside. "You said your name was Patrick?" she inquired. Formal tone, hint of police, but a bit more power. I liked her.

"Yes, special agent..." I tried to smile winningly, but the bandage probably ruined it.

"Hastings," she offered after a pause. "And are you Patrick Arthurs?"

"I am," I said, "...tied on a bed with a bandage over my eyes." Creaking as I feebly demonstrated my point. "Feeling quite vulnerable, and if we're going to have a polite conversation, can we do something about that?"

"Don't," said voice number three, with another puff of fear. She'd come in a lot closer. "The Ferals aren't safe - they go hyper-violent without warning."

"Doctor?" asked Sandy, just as I said "Ferals?" I tried very hard not to growl it. I'm pretty sure it came out at least a little amiable and encouraging.

There were a few seconds of silence. I pictured a four-way non-verbal conversation. Sandy won.

"We can talk about that once we get to it. First I'd like to do introductions." She moved across the room, towards Marko. "Patrick Arthurs?"

"Yes," I said. "How about just the bandages?"

The good doctor hadn't moved away. Her fingers started working on the least painful side of my head, saying "Good idea to at least change these, anyway. If the rest of you is any indication, you might be..." The bandage started coming off. Doctors are often a lot worse than nurses at those things, but her hands were good. Deft.

Marko whispered very softly in Sandy's ear in the corner. Almost didn't hear over the bandage fuss: "He's the manslaughter. Apparently he discovered a man standing over his wife's..."

The leather didn't break, but the thin little metal bars it was wrapped around did. I sat up abruptly, fists clenched, and arms crossed over my chest. I gasped, and shook. The bandage ribboned down, the doctor holding the other end, but I closed my eyes and rocked for a moment.

I opened my eyes for a first look at my rescuers. Easy to tell who was who.

Sandy Hastings and Marko were the ones pointing handguns at me. He was tall and stocky, and she was taller. Dark suits. He was bursting out of his with dark skin and shaved head. She was built more like a swimmer, with dark hair just short of her shoulder. Both were very seriously considering putting me down before I got my legs free.

Doctor Pembleton looking bewildered to my side. No uniform, but all in blue and white, even down to the latex gloves. Blonde hair tied back tight. Glasses. Classic discover-she's-pretty-when-she-unpins-her-hair nerd girl.

Number three, I recognised. She was one of the female nurses from the Therapy Centre. I only saw her very early, back before segregation, when the staff went minimal and unisex to minimise the chaos. Everybody's eyes were wide, but hers were the widest. There was real terror there, and she was pressed back against the door. The sight of her brought me down enough to let out a slow breath.

"Let's... not talk about that right now, Marko." I said it calmly, and didn't make any moves as we tried to transition back from fight-or-flight to something a little more productive. "Everything goes better when I don't have to think about that *at all*."

I focussed on the nurse. Her obvious panic anchored me a little. "It's OK," I told her. "You've got nothing to worry about from me." I sat still, showing her. Letting the adrenaline settle. Her back never left the door. The silence stretched on, and even as it went into uncomfortable territory, her eyes stayed haunted. I was pretty sure I could put faces to the ghosts that were doing the haunting, because I saw them as well.

"For what it's worth, I was the one who pulled him off," I said.

Her brown eyes held my grey ones. It was a long time before she spoke: "Two of the... two people died in the brawl. Three were put in intensive care."

I nodded. "The first two to touch her. Would have finished the job, but I was one of the ones that went down. I've been on quadruple rations ever since."

"You killed them," she said. It wasn't quite an accusation. Or rather, it was; but it was more reflexive than vehement.

"Yes," I agreed, ignoring the Feds, "and if you'd been there with a gun, I'd hope you would have, as well."

She absorbed that without much of a flicker.

The question started coming out before I could squelch it. "Did the nurse...?"

The nurse flinched, and then seemed to sag a little. "Peggy died," she said with brave, glistening eyes.

I sagged, too, and we silently came to a temporary understanding. Since my hands were right there, I started on the ankle straps.

Suddenly there were a flurry of security and medical complaints.

To the latter, I assured Dr. Pembleton that if someone would bring me a startling amount of food, I promised to sit quietly where I was, still attached to all the beepers.

"You'll need to stay on the IV until the infection goes away," she said.

"Are you basing the infection diagnosis on my temperature?" I asked. When she nodded, I told her I'd had daily medicals since I'd been kidnapped, and that I have been running several degrees hot ever since the therapy began. I said that she'd have to disregard anything other than white blood cell counts, and then realised I should probably have let her come to that conclusion unforced. To her credit, she visibly overcame a conditioned resistance to going off procedure. She picked up the records of all the measurements the hospital had made since my arrival, and frowned as she reexamined them.

To Sandy and Marko, I gently explained that if someone would bring me a startling amount of food and nobody tried to kill anyone, I'd promise to sit quietly where I was, still attached to all the beepers.

I also gestured to the torn steel pins from the attachment points for the restraints. "Besides," I added, "these restraints are basically cosmetic in this situation. It's really a system of trust, not security. How about we just all act a little civilised?"

The nurse looked a bit confused, like I were a rabid dog suddenly suggesting we all have tea and biscuits. Honestly, it was a bit irritating, but I was trying very hard not to show that on my face or posture.

"We were flooded with hormones or whatever," I explained, "We weren't lobotomised."

A headache started to edge through the painkillers, so I lay back down and covered my eyes. "Although to be fair, the others did coincidentally seem like utter meatheads in the little time we spent together."

The headache started to get sharper. "Doctor Hastings," I said. "I'm really serious about the food. Please trust me - this is a repeat pattern from two weeks ago. I need a lot of calories very fast, and then as soon as you can, I need to be fed like two professional body builders with vitamin deficiencies." She twitched a little, put the bandage down, and left the room.

Sometime during the insistent pounding in my temples, Sandy holstered her weapon. Marko lowered his, but kept it in hand as he read from his phablet. I liked the fact that she was the dominant partner a little too much, but the stabbing pain helped keep that in check. I'd have to come up with some strategies, later. But first...

"So this is the part where you ask me a lot of questions," I said. "And fair enough. There's kidnapping and explosions and probably worse, and I'm a witness."

I gave a little pause, but she wasn't going to interrupt me when I was talking. Now that's a professional.

"You're on a clock, too. There's got to be more to this than what was in that building, and they've had a couple of days to respond. You're probably worried about their next moves."

I peered over at her, shading my eyes from the overly bright room lights, and arranging myself carefully so it hurt less. "Personally, I'm terrified, and that's particularly hard to manage in my current state." In the distance was the sound of Dr Pembleton going through some heavy doors. "And speaking of my current state, you can probably understand that I have a lot of burning questions of my own. Let's pool our information."

I expected reluctance here, and saw it coming on Sandy's face. "I'm sure it's not standard operating procedure to share information about an investigation with civilians. Or witnesses, or victims, or suspects. Or whatever you think I might be. But those people kidnapped me, along with many others, and it's been killing me having no idea what's going on for months on end. They did things to us that I don't understand. They treated us like a cross between wild animals and equipment. After things shook down, we were isolated and tested. They drugged us, and they gave us heaps of training. Most of the time they did it simultaneously."

Stabbing pain. Doors opening in the distance. "None of it really makes sense. Why me? Why those other meat-heads? I'm sure they took our whole cellblock, but where did the others go? When most of their focus was obviously physical, why did they put us through so much training?"

The nurse interrupted. "I didn't see anything like that," she said.

Sandy flashed a brief, irritated look. I felt sympathy. Of course, the nurse was the person most likely to know what I needed to know, and I wouldn't be talking so much if she weren't there to be prompted.

"What did you see?" I asked, trying to sound curious, but not pleased with myself. The hurt tone certainly came easily. "What did... what did they do to me?"

The nurse looked at Sandy and Marko, and then she heard Dr. Pembleton come back. The good doctor arrived with three tuna sandwiches in their wrappers, and I ate silently while waiting. Between number one and number two, I prompted: "Was it hormones? Steroids? They called it 'therapy', but I mainly remember injections."

The nurse looked slightly helpless as she shook her head slightly. "Nothing as straightforward as that. I don't really know any of the details, but I do know it was a kind of epigenetic gene therapy."

"Gene therapy?" I snorted. "What were they trying to cure? 'Not being an axe-wielding homicidal maniac?'"

No-one seemed to get the reference, but I didn't want to interrupt the nurse twice. She shrugged and continued: "I overheard bits and pieces. You know how cats that go into the wild get bigger? They go feral, and they don't just get large - they can become a kind of missing link between domestic cats and the big cats. It's not evolution, obviously, and it doesn't even take a generation. They just ... change."

"The DNA must already be there. All sorts of solutions for different environments. But how are they activated? Is it diet? Temperature? Activity changes? Some subtle combination? Anyway, I think the research team learned to fire similar switches in humans."

I frowned, and not just because I was out of sandwiches. "But why would humans have anything even remotely similar to... ?" It sounded like nonsense, but skepticism was hard to maintain against evidence. Even if the real process was quite different from that, I did seem to have an apparent myostatin deficiency. And much as my meagre understanding told me it was impossible, there was no doubt that I was significantly taller.

"Humans don't have the same switches as cats, but we did call you 'Ferals'." She had the decency at least to sound a little embarrassed at the term. "The testing we did showed you were getting faster, stronger, and gaining weight. There were also the behavioural changes."

She glared at me, daring me to deny it.

"Can't begin to tell you," I agreed. "The strongest emotions you ever felt at the peak of adolescence, turned up to a brain-melting torrent. I'm not a macho guy, but you can't sail against that wind. Takes an act of will just to steer."

Teeth were gritted with the memory. "It's not... I..."

I took a moment to find the words. Four faces watched me, silently. Listening. In the face of their patience, a part of me that had been shaking in the corner of my mind for months, silently absorbing trauma after trauma, tried to make himself heard.

"Your thoughts and feelings aren't just something important about you, they *are* you," I said. "When all that changes suddenly, it brings you face-to-face with... well, with death. I mean - what's left of me? Half my thoughts don't seem... I mean, did I die in there, and get reborn as a monster?"

No-one else could tell me the answer to that. Certainly not these puzzled, intent faces. I was talking, but it was really to myself. "The others sure acted like monsters, and it's hard to tell if that's just what this looks like from the outside."

A particularly bad memory flashed back. "Course, it seemed like everyone else there started off pretty monstrous, even before whatever-the-hell it was."

That was where Marko piped up. "That would fit with their profile. According to the subject files Ms. Andrews retrieved for us," he said, indicating the nurse, "the test subjects were largely socially isolated ex-prisoners with violent convictions."

Huh. Took me a few moments to resist denying that I belonged in that category. Sobering moments, all.

"Why?" I managed.

Sandy Hastings took a step forward. "We were hoping you could shed a little light on that. The isolated part makes sense, as they pulled off over hundreds of kidnappings by our estimates. Across multiple countries."

"Hundreds?" I asked. "I only ever saw a dozen or so."

Nurse Andrews' jaw clenched. "That's right, there were a lot of null results at first, and then just when they thought they had it sorted, they instituted a program that saw a majority of deaths. The nurses didn't see much of that, but I pieced it together when so many subjects came through in a month. That's when I approached the authorities. There were only twenty men that survived the treatment, and then there were the deaths from fighting."

That would have made it hard to get volunteers, certainly. And of course the violent crime connection was probably related to the odd training they gave us. I described the experience. "It was kinda military. Armed and unarmed combat. Other hardware."

"Military?" prompted Sandy.

"Well, we were by ourselves. So the training was not really to become a soldier. More like..."

I couldn't really picture the job with that training. Assassin? Terrorist? And were we just the experiments to see if 'Ferals' could be more than just muscular? Or were they planning to make us some kind of offer we couldn't refuse?

If we were eventually going 'into the field', as it were, then how were our creators supposed to keep control?

A nasty thought suddenly occurred. "Is there any chance they had some method of tracking us?" I asked, tensing up. Then I stopped. "No, scratch that. It's been days."

Dr. Pembleton retrieved a bio-hazard jar from the shelf. It held a small piece of mangled electronics covered in dried blood.

"From your upper chest," she explained.

I squinted in the lights. "That looks like a military transponder chip," I said.

"And how might you know that?" Sandy asked a little coldly.

Marko interjected from the far wall, gun still in hand. "Mr Arthurs was a defence engineer..."

And then, without warning, I felt another surge. My teeth clenched, and the urge to smash his smug face through the wall was almost overpowering. Through some tiny spark of the old me, I somehow didn't. That part of me knew these furnace-like feelings were unreasonable. Didn't make enough of a difference, though.

"Marko," I clipped, pinching my nose and covering my face. "Please don't argue or get stroppy, but I need you to get out of this room, right now. No questions asked." I covered my face and tried not to breathe too deeply.

Marko didn't move immediately; but fortunately for both of us, after a few dozen hammered heartbeats, he did go. Without saying anything. He stopped not too far down the corridor, but at least the door was closed. As his stench cleared from the air, I realised that the nurse must have waved him out. After a few moments she asked: "Are you going to be okay?"

Hah! Of course I wasn't. I was going to drown in this. After the attack on the female nurse, we had been segregated. I never saw another woman again until the last day.

And obviously the inmates were never in the same room as each other again. But by the time I was out of recovery, things had escalated, and they'd had to isolate us from all other men as well. Contact had been brief and armoured. We might as well have been rabid.

I'm told rabies is a virus that can make perfectly normal people afraid of water and want to bite people. Whatever had been done to us was a lot more complicated than a paralytic disease, and was probably supposed to leave us a lot more functional, but it somehow made us intolerant of other men. We weren't left with an urge to bite, specifically, but an urge to... well, dominate, I suppose.

When I was left quietly in my room, trying to make sense of those days, I could tell that I had changed. I was channeling the departed spirits of violent thugs and assholes.

What's the adult version of discovering there's no Santa Claus or god? Turns out I was only ever a brain chemical or two away from being everything I'd ever hated. It was a little like being earnest-and-loud drunk, and doing cringe-worthy things, half knowing how you're going to feel about it later.

Assuming there was ever going to be a later. Maybe I wasn't going to feel things properly ever again.

Having only women in the room, I felt like I could control myself. At least while I was still convalescent. And after that, well, I'd just have to work out a plan.

"Sure," I replied. "For now. Sorry about the drama."

The anger is bullshit, I told myself. Reasons to hate him kept springing up, rational and clean. Marko was peering at my file like some smug voyeur... No, *of course* he was looking at my file. The anger is bullshit. Without his smell in the room, the edge was going. The same breathing that worked in grief counselling was working here.

"Doctor," I said. She smelled a little antsy. Probably adrenaline from a couple of shocks. "Did you order the food? The sooner the better, I think."

She told me it should be here soon, and sure enough it was along within a couple of minutes. I loved her a little then, and if that sounds shallow, then you sing your love songs and present elaborate flower arrangements, and I'll keep saying it with food and care.

Sandy soon brought me back to the circumstances leading up to the explosion. The story was short, if eventful.

THE ROOMS we were kept in were pleasant enough, but there was no confusion about the fact that they were cells. The doors were electronically locked except when we were brought to testing and training under armed guard. There was no natural light, but when the door opened in the middle of my sleep cycle, I couldn't help feeling that the timing was strange. I woke immediately to the soft click, and padded to the corridor. No guards, which was a first.

The corridor was softly lit, and miracle of miracles, the interlocks were also unlocked. The possibility that this was some kind of test occurred, of course, but that seemed overly subtle considering all of my experiences in the building up to that point. The possibility that it was just a good old-fashioned screw-up, led me to try to exploit it all the way.

Everything was open. In the past I'd wandered along a carefully planned channel, but for the first time I could move at will through the building. Naturally, I preferred options I'd never taken in the past, and tried to keep a roughly consistent direction. When this all went to shit -

and no part of me doubted that it would - I wanted to be as far away from my cell as I could manage.

Seconds crept by, and I hurried. I was as quiet as I could be in bare feet. Bare everything, in fact, but I'd imagined standing in my room getting dressed while the building security realised their mistake and pressed the right button...

I found the lifts, and chose the stairs. I chose 'up,' because I'd never once seen natural light, so my hypothesis was that I was housed below ground level. Ending up on the roof was less terrifying than deliberately scurrying into the basement before the doors all locked.

When I first met another person, they were spread-eagled on the floor. Rounding a corner, I was confronted by something that was clearly a high security data centre. Dozens of rack-mounted storage units and servers, with a security interlock that was spectacularly insecure. The first of the two security guards was awkwardly propping the door open with his limp body. He looked dead, although I didn't wait to check. The door was protesting insistently at the obstruction despite its unlocked nature. The other guard was slumped, blocking the other door.

Through a plate glass interior window, I saw her.

She was large, armed, and saw me immediately. Short cut bear-brown hair framing a square face that started over six feet from the floor when she jerked upright. She was wearing the same kind of featureless light grey pants and shirt that I'd been wearing for months, with a guard's jacket over the top. And a guard's heavy sidearm, which she raised.

She didn't point it at me, though. She pointed urgently at something across the door, inside the data centre. It took me a second or two to follow the gesture, but when I did, I saw the explosives wired all over it. So much explosive! I'd had a good mate from university who let me onsite before some building demolitions once, so I'd seen the like before. Well, I'd seen the professional version. Back then it was all charges placed on opposite sides of supports, designed to shear them neatly, and similar fun plans for destruction. This was, I thought, more ordnance than I'd ever seen collected in a single room, and it obviously had been placed hurriedly.

Almost as though, I thought, someone had found a rather ridiculous stash of explosive, and had very, very hastily rigged charges with wires coming back to one point on the floor somewhere on her side of the glass. Making up for finesse and hours of calculations with a decision to just 'use it all.'

I couldn't see the detonator clearly from where I was, but her open palm was gesturing for me to back up. Probably so that I didn't blunder through that mess, and kill us both.

So we had a moment.

From her clothing, she may well have been one of my fellow inmates, although all the ones I'd seen were men. I found myself wondering if that were sexist of me. But anyway, by Occam's razor, my sudden freedom was most likely due to whatever the hell she'd just done here.

What she saw looking at me, I can only guess. Naked, wild. If she were a fellow inmate, the fact that she was storming through the building while I was merely exploiting a side-effect of her escape meant that she was certainly better informed than I had been. Was she aware of the existence of the men? If so, did she know about us? Was she letting us die with the building and our captors?

Was she seeing a killer? One of many mad dog rapists to be put down?

She heard something behind her, and turned and called out. I could barely hear her through the double glazed plate window say that she was coming. Then our eyes met, and I saw the worry in hers.

The explosives. Her plan, her escape, and probably her short-term survival all relied on some naked guy behind soundproof glass. If she knew about the treatments, then she also knew that the guy was probably insane. That must be particularly frustrating, since neither of us was going to get a second chance at this.

I backed up, and I saw her shoulders drop a little, and she let out her breath. She held up two fingers, and I dimly heard when she shouted 'two minutes'. Then she was sprinting away through an exit that I couldn't reach without going through whatever she'd jury rigged.

I was alone, and there was no way through here. Two minutes wasn't much time to get out. Unless I wanted to try to stop it. The stuff in the bags looked a bit like a blasting agent, because I thought I could make out both primary and secondary explosive elements on each one. The triggering mechanism was probably fairly easy to stop.

But did I want to? I didn't waste more than a second, but I searched my soul, and found that I did not. Let this building and all in it go to hell. Let the guards and sociopathic 'medical staff' on night duty have no time to register surprise as their jail cleansed itself. As for my fellow inmates, my last memory of them was when we were trying to kill each other over that nurse's screams. That was no misunderstanding. On either part. Let the slate be wiped clean.

I heard heavy steps in the passages behind me, then. Very heavy, belligerent. And the clock I couldn't see was still ticking. I took a new corridor, and ran.

Running attracted them, of course. The first half minute of that was fine - I didn't want them deciding to pull the plug on the detonators either. But then I really wanted to get out of the building alone. I started choosing my route for speed, but I'd have to try one of the side doors sooner or later.

Since it was night, I never ended up seeing natural light in that building, but my eventual choice of door led to a boardroom with external windows. City lights in all colours reflecting off copious quantities of polished wood. The night sky! Street noise. Would have been so happy with that under other circumstances. Unfortunately, my particular circumstances included imminent death. And then they included possibly the three people I hated the most in the whole world suddenly arriving to block my way back out of the room.

Two of them were the ones who had held her. The blank-eyed one with the scar grinned when he saw me. His name was Brett.

"Well, look what we have here," he said. All predator. They'd formed a kind of pack chasing me, and the others spread out.

I considered taunting him about that scar across his face. I'd done it with a table. But time was short, so I simply looked over his shoulder, and said: "Why'd you bring the guards, dipshit?"

His eyes flicked that way, and I tried to use a handy chair to re-open the wound. He was crazy fast, though, and it just sailed over his head and shattered on the door frame.

They were all fast. Fast doesn't cover it. Sudden. Before my head turned, I was flying towards the window.

Chapter 2

GUNSHOTS?

The third double helping of cod started to take its toll. I lay down, and just found myself drifting off. I was surprised there weren't any questions, but my best guess is that the good doctor pulled the other two out as she watched me drop. Shortest 'day' ever. Not that it matters:

Black,

... black,

... ... long (and troubled) dreams,

black.

MY EYES POPPED BACK OPEN, and my heart was hammering. Confused, I dragged reality from the rapidly draining plausibility of the dream. Images and feelings as it fragmented from a story to a unconnected collage: some kind of dispute, chase, gunshots. I was *not* racing through a city-sized spaceship in body-moulded armour. I was lying on a hospital bed in an empty room, half naked and coated in a thin sheen of sweat in the cool air. Just needed to calm the f-

Gunshots?

I lifted my woozy head, wondering if I'd heard that right. Could have been a-

No, that was a gunshot. I'd learned a disturbing amount about guns over the last few weeks, but mainly larger ones. That sounded more like something from a movie, so I was guessing a handgun. Or possibly two. And getting closer.

Let me admit that I assumed it was all about me. Ego, perhaps, but I had no illusions that I was suddenly free of whatever I'd escaped from. Fortunately, I hadn't been tied down again while I slept, so I was on my feet and assessing my supplies when SA Hastings burst in the room, gun in her left hand. I stood there, winding the rest of my sheet around my forearm.

"We have to move you," she clipped. "Marko's checking out the fire stairs." She waved me to the corridor.

"Nope," I replied, following her out there. Long, grey corridors. Old school drab.

"There's been an exchange of gunfire downstairs," she snapped back, pissed. "They're almost certainly coming for you, and so we're getting out of here now!" She tried to drag me to the left.

I had bare feet, so when I started walking the other way, she came with me. "I meant, not the fire stairs," I clarified. "Negligible chance they won't be covered."

She let go in time not to land on her face, but fell behind as I broke into a soft jog. I had a mental picture of armed goons charging up the stairs, and probably some in the lift? Those weren't exits so much as chances to join a gunfight armed with a sheet. I needed another exit. The idea of using the window exit crossed my mind again, but I didn't know how high I was, and I was pretty sure there was only so much of a beating I could handle.

Come to think of it, I felt remarkably good. Must have had a longer sleep than I thought.

I passed a fire extinguisher and its awesome friend, the little fire exit map. Suddenly I was oriented.

Sandy was still trying authority. "We have to get out! Now!" she demanded.

"Fire exits will be a fight, not flight," I countered. "We need to do something a little more unexpected."

Fight or flight? Or was there an option "C"? Suddenly I had an awful plan. As we reached the end of the corridor, I slid the manacle I'd been holding in my other hand back down the hall. It travelled past the door of the room where I'd been, and ended up resting at the corner of the T-junction several doors past on the other side. It was crude, but anything to suggest that we ran that way worked for me.

Meanwhile, I was concentrating on this way. Private room, private room, private room, nurse station (empty), toilets.

Toilets?

Nope, not stupid enough. Sandy looked like she was about to start shouting at me, and I put my forefinger to my lips. Praise be, she didn't. Lifts, private room, operating theatre, supply room.

Supply room?

Stupid enough, but probably locked. I tapped the door handle as I passed, and it moved. Stopping, and reiterating the shushing finger, I tried the handle properly. It opened, revealing a room the size of a small office, with floor to ceiling shelves stocked with linen. I grinned, and moved inside. Sandy's eyes went wide, and she shook her head.

"Argue inside," I said quietly, and pulled her in. Closing the door behind her, I moved behind one of the laundry stacks. Perfect. Couldn't see the door.

"This is insane! There is a *gunfight* downstairs, and you represent all the evidence we have on this whole thing." I appreciated that her volume was low, even if her tone was a little melodramatic.

"If they catch you, they will kill you! And this..." Sandy gestured at the glorified cupboard as she squeezed between shelves to get close to me, "...this is not a hiding place!" she hissed.

"I'm very pleased to hear you say that," I replied. "Because I'm counting on everyone else thinking that, too. I don't expect people to think I'd try hiding, and if they do, they'll assume I'd choose a hiding place."

Sandy looked like she'd punch me if she could. "This is bullshit," she replied.

Then, very distant, muffled sounds of gunshots. I could tell she was about to rush out there.

"I'm sorry," I said quietly. "Wrong or right, I chose to play hide-and-seek while they are playing chase-and-kill. This plan works best when they don't know we've switched games, and trying to mix games means you play both really badly. We're committed to staying here. Silently."

She bit her lip. "Marko."

He'd be forced to fight if he thought we were trapped. "Text him that we're out."

A few haunted seconds, and she nodded. She did so, and then we found our best hiding positions in the room and waited.

So. The waiting was so much worse than I expected. Even remembering it gives me painful cramps in my gut. I may have given the impression that I was convinced that it was a good plan to be standing still in a supply room, about a hundred metres or so from the room where I had been recovering. I think it came across that way to Sandy. In truth, what had felt like a flash of inspiration was rapidly spoiling. Over the span of seconds, my conviction morphed to horror, and I was kicking myself for my temporary idiocy.

The idea of changing the odds by changing the game made some kind of sense, but it was such a huge gamble. One we were locked into. It wasn't a plan that took advantage of my skills. It didn't even take advantage of my increased physical capabilities. If anything, the changes I'd undergone had made me almost uniquely maladapted to playing possum.

Everyone knows the 'fight or flight' reaction. It's powerful. I remember once when I was bullied by a stranger outside a burger joint in a strange town on a high school excursion. He punched me in the eye and walked off. I couldn't stop shaking until the middle of the next day, and kept coming up with violent revenge fantasies, or other ways I could have played the evening. Maybe it really was for the best. A black eye doesn't land you in hospital. Since the injections, however, I couldn't imagine being so restrained. My response to stress had become immediate and thunderous. Standing behind a wall of towels, I felt strong, fast, and committed to action. Movement was imperative.

Instead, I was trapped. Worse, I was holding myself there, quivering slightly despite a lunatic effort to be still and silent.

Tens of seconds. Many dozens of heartbeats. My hearing was good, but the building channelled footsteps so that I could barely tell which direction they were coming from. I could smell my fresh sweat. Sandy's too. I could just taste it.

She - Argh. Focussing on the fear worked to stop that line of thinking.

Down the corridor, several male voices, high intensity. Maybe seven? Then two sets of footsteps jogging down the corridor, opening each door. They spent about thirty heartbeats scanning the toilets, and I grinned at Sandy. She recoiled a little, so it might have come across more manic than I meant. The moment of truth came forty steps later, when the door opened.

What was I thinking? The place reeked of our fear. I could immediately smell the tang of a recently fired gun, and the two assholes. There was nothing between me and them but a rack of towels, and I suddenly knew I had to strike. Had to take the initiative. Fortunately, I was still waiting for the perfect moment when they closed the door again and continued their sweep.

Sandy and I shared a short 'how about that?' glance, and then her hand went to the pocket where she put her phone. A text, presumably. She pulled it out, and was about to tell me something when the sound of the two assholes started getting louder again as they ran past us.

"They're out, but the pickup teams don't have them," one said to the other. There was an accent there, but I couldn't place it.

When the sound of their boots clattered down the distant stairwell and were mostly lost, Sandy indicated her phone. "Marko's clear, but he's looking for us."

Her thumbs started flashing, and I tried to reduce the adrenaline fog. My breathing was still hard to control, and my heart hammering. I tried to repeat the mantra to myself: 'There's nothing to worry about. There are no immediate threats. There's nothing to worry about.'

I knew at some level that it was a fiction. Of course there

was plenty to worry about. But I needed rationality to do it - it was time to think things though properly, and not just panic and leap into danger. My body wasn't listening, though. It kept screaming at me that there was indeed something to worry about. Something immediate, urgent, and life-threatening.

And then my guts went cold as I realised that there was, in fact, something very urgent to worry about. "Don't - " I started, but at that exact moment Sandy looked up, having finished her text.

The one that I thought might have just killed me.

There wasn't time to think of anything good. A rushed signal to follow, I snatched her phone and sprang for the door. Sandy didn't give away our position with a shout, but her hiss was an elegant and efficient fusion of exasperation, irritation and confusion. I turned down the corridor away from the stairwell and sprinted. Running is actually quieter at full speed. Sandy behind me didn't have the advantage of either panic or bare feet, but she didn't have any breath to waste at that pace, either.

I didn't have spare time to figure out how turn the phone off properly, so I just crushed it in one hand as I rushed away from the pursuit. I came to a stop to peer around the corner of a T-junction, and Sandy pulled up. There was no-one left or right, so before she could talk I cut her off. "How," I asked, trying to picture the fire exits from the map and guess the most likely hole in this tightening net, "did they suddenly get so sure we were out?"

Her expression went through a couple of incompatible emotions, and settled on fear. It was kind of an angry fear.

"Maybe they just have his phone," I said, trying to be encouraging. "And they won't track us through yours, so we still have a chance to sell the idea that we really got out."

About that. What do they do when they don't find us in their outer net? Do they go wider, or do they come back? The roof would be a place to go, but also a place to look for how someone might have got away. Actually trying to escape now might be the wrong play. I was getting increasingly worried that my true optimal strategy might be to go back to that storage room again. My stomach cramped and I literally shook for a moment as I tried to guess how long it might take. There was gunfire, so a normal police response may well...

Gunfire?

Yes, gunfire. Somewhere far away. Street level? Then: an explosion. Probably also outside.

My first instinct was to run again. But it was just as wrong as the first time. So now there were two groups involved, and it sounded more like a war zone out there. That seemed to make rushing out an even worse idea than I just thought. And yet, the problem with being in the eye of the storm is that storms move.

"I've got to get to Marko," hissed Sandy.

Assuming he was still alive, I thought, *and not actually an inside man for the bad guys*. Though the tightness in her voice stopped me from verbalising those concerns.

I turned, planning to find some gentle way to... then I saw her face. Her jaw was clamped against an oncoming flood of grief, and her haunted, desperate eyes were only too familiar, somehow.

"Urgl," I replied, and then my spinning brain managed: "All right, let's get him."

About face, and off after the last set of goons.

I never said I was smart. I just used to test well, once upon a time.

Between stairs and the lift, we chose the stairs. Stairs

were faster, especially going down, and I think my hackles literally raised at the mere thought of standing still in a metal box with a single door.

The stairs were empty, though I could smell blood. Someone had been bleeding in the stairwell recently. It got stronger as we descended, so presumably that's where they still were. Perhaps two floors from the bottom, hell broke loose in the form of an explosion and sustained fire from multiple automatic weapons. Bullets ricocheted below us, and there were a few short screams. Sandy pulled up short behind me as I squeaked to a stop.

Then from below, the sustained fire ceased, replaced only by occasional crack from smaller weapons. Then heavy boots, racing. Many of them getting louder, and storming towards the stairwell. I spun, and seeing Sandy wide-eyed and blocking my way, I made a brief decision to sacrifice her dignity for a few extra seconds of safety. One arm just behind her knees, and one behind her middle back, I picked her up and sprinted up the stairs.

I felt a lot of internal pain, and knew I'd set my recovery back, but we were going up the stairs faster than I estimated she could run by herself. On Sandy's face, surprise was replaced by outrage, and then by shock as she made the same calculation. One or two floors before the top of the stairs, I pushed through the swing doors quietly with my back as I put her down, and raced off down the corridor. This level had a similar setup as the one we started on, so there was a mirror of the storage room from before. I pulled inside, and Sandy caught me.

It was to be hide-and-seek after all.

The heavy boots weren't far enough behind. I heard the doors to the stairs swing again, and then they were jogging down the hallway. I was guessing four of them as they passed.

Then they pulled up. I looked at my shoulder, where blood was seeping through the bandage. Did I leave any on the floor? I didn't think it was that bad. My nose was already flooded with the smell, but even under the dim green light from the exit sign, it didn't look like it would have given any visible signs.

Then the steps returned, obviously outside our door. Sandy's face cycled back to terror, and she gripped her sidearm tightly.

"Huh," came a deep female voice outside. "Hiding."

She said it with a kind of surprise. Then her voiced raised, clearly pitched for us: "We're covering the door with weapons, but we don't wish violence. Come out peacefully."

I looked over at Sandy, who was blinking in a slightly disconcerting way. The voice outside spoke again. "Please do it quickly. People are dying downstairs, and we need to get out of here."

Maybe it was the way the phrase 'get out of here' resonated with the spirit of the moment, but somehow my inner debate short circuited, and I stepped forward. Maybe it was the 'please'. That shit works at the oddest of times. Resting my hand briefly on Sandy's weapon hand, I whispered: "Both hands high, and obviously off that. That's the only way we don't get shot now."

My own hands went up then as I came to the door, and I raised my own voice. I was still a little winded from the sprint. "Coming out, no threat offered," I said, and nudged the door handle with my elbow as I took my own advice and raised my hands in front of me.

The door swung open, and I saw them. Four, as I guessed. All armed, as they said. Military gear, including the fatigues. All in full helmets that covered most of their faces, but clearly all women. Tall.

My nose involuntarily flared as I regarded them, and two of them were doing the same. I stepped out. Eyes flickered between me and Sandy. As I moved aside to give her room to emerge as well, the four soldiers kept a few strides distance, and despite the presence of Sandy's holstered pistol, all four guns stayed trained on me. Part of me thought that was unfair, and parts of me were pleased, for several reasons.

Sandy's hands were high, and her body language was unthreatening. "Who the absolute fuck are you?" she snapped. "And what the fuck is going on? What have you done with my partner?" Reasonable questions, and the last one was even genuinely urgent.

Two of the guns swung to her for a moment, and then settled back on me. I could barely tell the soldiers apart except by height and scent, and the four scents were all mixed up, so the only things I knew about the one that spoke was that it was the one that spoke before, and she was the shortest.

"We are the ones shutting this program down. And you are..." There was a brief moment of consideration. "...some kind of federal agent?"

Sandy nodded. The shortest of the amazons tilted her head. "...And if you're hiding around with the last subject rather than delivering him downstairs, then you're presumably even a clean one."

The helmet turned to me. "Hello again. This one wasn't part of the kidnap raid?"

I shook my head, confused. "Again? What? No, Sandy is one of the few people who haven't kidnapped me recently."

"Then she can walk away." The amazon leader

addressed Sandy again. "Gun down, now. Plus your holdout. Then I'd advise hiding again until your backup arrives. I'd estimate two or three minutes should do it. But wait until the shooting is well over before revealing yourself."

Sandy stood, a little stunned. The orders were reiterated, abruptly, and two guns targeted her again. She did a text-book-looking removal of her gun, and she placed it carefully on the floor. Smoothly, she reached behind her back, and did the same with something smaller. The guns twitched in the direction of the supply room door.

"My partner?" she asked, as she backed inside.

The amazon slid some handcuffs over to me. I picked them up with the same care that Sandy had disarmed, and snapped them on my wrists. I'd never handled any before, but it wasn't complicated.

"If your partner went downstairs, their situation is stable. We took out the active resistance, so if they weren't involved with that, they were either down before we got there, or stable." Sandy's face went a little blank, and the amazon hardened. "We will shoot you if you follow. Nod if you understand that."

Ten heartbeats later, call it about three seconds, Sandy nodded. One amazon swept up her guns, and we were off. I was kept in the middle, and there was no talking as we went for the roof.

Outside, the sky was a mottled grey, and I could hear sirens distant in the city streets. We emerged from a utilitarian door, and ran over to the edge. Two of the amazons pulled long, brown ropes from the packs on their backs, and secured them to the edge of the building with a grapple that popped open.

I wondered how they were going to descend on that, when I noticed that their armour included harness loops, to which they were clipping carabiners and friction devices. *Where's mine*, I wondered. Putting on a harness was going to take the minutes they claimed they had. While I was distracted, there was a lancing pain in my neck, along with a distant 'Pfhut'. While my right hand flicked up to my neck, there was another pfhut and pain in my right buttock.

I pulled them out. Orange and black, plastic fletching, needle. Tranquilliser darts.

Behind me, one of the amazons was holstering her dart gun. The other one was covering me with her assault rifle. A couple of seconds went by, and I became very light-headed. Woozy. The one who holstered her rifle freed her hands, and flexed. It looked like she was ready to catch me.

One amazon rappelled down the building into the alley below. As the seconds ticked by, the sirens got closer. I didn't get any woozier. The four remaining up top eyed each other, waiting for the shoe to drop. Or, more precisely, me. The pause started to get a little uncomfortable.

I giggled. "So. The plan was me over your shoulder?"

"Yes," she said after a few moments. Kinda embarrassed, but clearly very stressed. The one pointing the gun at me was starting to look a little twitchy.

"OK," I said, and took a slow step forward towards the empty handed one. She was ready to catch me, but pulled back a little. I looked at my cuffed, raised hands. "I might be able to hold on, but the balance might be bad, and we don't know if this stuff is suddenly going to do its job. Don't want to fall off...." I wobbled a little, and recovered. "I think I should go over your shoulder."

Dart Lady looked over at her boss, who shrugged. "Do it," she said, as the sirens got nearer.

It was an awkward little dance as she approached, and I tried to help by going up on my tiptoes. After a little shuffle, she got her shoulder right in my bladder, and one arm went around my hips. I was lifted into the air. As I went upside down, blood rushed to my head, and I chuckled again.

She was the largest of the four, but she must have been even stronger than I guessed, because she climbed on and abseiled down the building fast and smooth, with only a few grunts to betray any real effort. When we hit the ground, I lifted my head, and she put me on my feet.

The van barely fit in the alley. It was unmarked, white, and quite small. Before things could get awkward again, I staggered towards it. "In here?" I asked, and then burped. Stupid question, because the engine was already running, and the amazon that dropped first was holding the back doors open. She seemed a little disconcerted at my mobility, but I tried a smile. "Thanks," I said, and stepped in.

Manners. Like momma always said, always kind, and sometimes magic.

Chapter 3

MANNERS

The ride away was odd. The sirens never got close, and I had no idea how far we were going. Or why. Or with whom. I looked around for clues, but they all stayed alert, helmeted, and tense. I reviewed what I knew.

One. I escaped that place. That prison, or whatever it really was... Bad, I decided. It was bad, and I'm glad it exploded.

Two. I somehow landed in hospital, with federal agents on the scene. Maybe the hospital notified the authorities as they patched me up, or maybe they were around anyway. The Feds did seem fairly clueless, although they did have at least one other witness in the form of one of the ex-nurses from the kidnapping-evil-experimentation prison.

Three. Some people came into the hospital, guns blazing. My best guess was that these were the original kidnappers, or their associates. Whoever they were, they were clearly capable and willing to murder a security detail to get me back. Or perhaps to get me dead.

Four. A third group arrived, heavily militarised, but decidedly *not* the Feds. They also came in guns blazing, and took out some or all of the re-kidnapping force, and then took me away. In the circumstances, away was good, but it was hard to feel safe when I was being tranquillised and constantly threatened by assault rifles. Who were these people? What did they want? Why did she say hello *again*? What did they mean when they called me the 'last subject'?

I felt a wave of paranoia, which I tried not to show. Although as they say, it's not paranoia if everyone really *is* out to get you. But I imagine the feelings are pretty identical with or without reasonable justification. Was I safe? Even just a bit? Should I be trying to overpower these four while I have a semblance of a chance? Or is going with them the safest option? It was impossible to read their expressions under those helmets, but the general body language was edgy to say the least. The van smelled of stale and fresh sweat, sharp and adrenaline-touched.

I glanced over at the tall one who carried me down the building. She turned her helmet in my direction quizzically. And with that tilt of the head, suddenly the whole thing just struck me as hilarious. I failed to suppress the guffaw that hissed out of my clamped jaw, and my sides shook.

"What... the... hell?" I managed to gasp out. "I mean... this day.... Come *on*!" I couldn't sit upright, and just sagged a little in my seat. The way the goggled heads swung to each other in pairs only made it worse. Tears leaked out, and I laughed in silent heaves, gasping for air.

"Trank him again?" one asked.

"Could easily be lethal," the tall one responded. "It's unbelievable that he's conscious with two doses in him. He should be right on the edge of cardiac paralysis."

I gasped for air.

"Why is he laughing then? Is that some kind of allergic reaction?" the leader asked.

"No," I panted. "It's working. I'm super-relaxed right now. Considering…" More giggles, but I struggled to pull myself together. Strangely, the more I tried to be serious, the more absurd everything seemed. I felt a tearing sensation in my shoulder.

"It's just…" I pointed in the general direction of their faces, and then gestured to my own. "You have no idea how ridiculous those things make you look."

There was a trickle of something down my back, and I listed a little to my right. I think the tall one snorted a little. Then my laughing fit ended with a wave of nausea, and then I finally gave her a chance to catch me as I fell. She wasn't so prepared this time, and I think I got to the floor.

AWAKE: bed. Smells of fresh sheets. Distant murmuring.

Asleep: nothing, blessed nothing.

Awake: bed. Smells of fresh sheets and blood and worry and wet earth. Sound of rain. I think someone's…

Asleep: tense dreams. I think. They boil and churn away, and then I'm

Awake: Eyes are scratchy and dry. Throat is sore.

The room was small, white. The window wood-framed, with heavy white curtains open, and gauzy ones, closed. Sensing my arrival, she roused and stood up from an old armchair in the corner as I stirred. No mask or helmet, I saw black curls just short of a shoulder bobbing as she peered down. It was the tall one - I knew her scent already, but I found myself squinting against the light of the little table lamp, so I didn't see much.

"Water?" I croaked. It had been prepared, and one firm hand came behind my shoulder to help me up while the other held the cup. It was agony adjusting my head to take the offering. A sharp artificial taste - some shop-bought lemonade that'd been left out so long that it was flat and lifeless. I struggled to get as much past my ragged throat as I could. Despite the pain, that turned out to be all of it.

She lowered me down. There was a surge of relief at being able to lie back, close my eyes, regroup. But as I lay there, panting, each pant became slower and heavier, and I finally relaxed a little. Then away I went.

MY SLEEP WAS SHORTER the next time, and I woke more resolutely. Everything still hurt, and I was more connected to the pain than before. It felt like I had a fever. Or maybe that I'd been battered and stabbed. Both, probably. I looked around, my eyes still scratchy. This was not a medical facility. From the size, furnishings and decor, the room was a guest bedroom. One of my hosts sat, drowsy, over in the large, ageworn armchair in the corner. Close-cropped red hair haloing an angular, pixie face. A table next to her, with a lamp illuminating a book, and a pistol.

Sounds outside, someone saying:

"I'm not saying we should kill him, I was just saying that we'd be better off if he *didn't* recover..."

I turned my head to look at the door, and whatever they had been about to say next was drowned out by the warden in the room calling out "He's awake!"

The conversation aborted, and four of them came in. They were still in their fatigues - I could tell they weren't fresh - and the room was suddenly very full. At the back came the tall one, holding a cup of coffee in one hand, and a pistol in the other. The redhead that had been keeping guard, or charitably, looking after me, also picked up hers from the table. The other three had weapons, but they were holstered.

The shortest one I recognised twice. Most recently, she was the one who had led the group at the hospital, who instructed me to come out of the storage room. And now that her helmet was off, I could see the spiky brown hair of the woman who had locked eyes with me through a double plate glass window, and then left me in a building about to explode.

We had another, longer moment. I wasn't naked this time. But the hospital robes and sheets weren't really adding much to my dignity. Nor the bandages. But for the first time in what had to be several days, there suddenly wasn't any rush. She stood with authority, her light green eyes curious and thoughtful.

I kept quiet. There were plenty of clues here, but it was hard to feel particularly insightful under the circumstances. No longer adrenaline-swept, I found that I had little motivation to seize the initiative. My heartbeat was pounding in my temples, and I felt uninterested in seizing much more than some painkillers.

"So," she said at last. "Would you like to start by confirming your name?"

It was the way she said it, more than anything. "Huh. You're a cop," I replied.

The others, who'd largely been looking at me, all turned to her at once. Kinda fast.

A look of surprise flicked over her face, and one eyebrow raised a little, appraisingly. "What makes you say that?" she asked.

I shrugged, very gently. "Just a guess," I replied. Then,

after a brief consideration of the forces required and the consequent costs, I offered a hand. "Patrick Arthurs."

She smiled briefly, and shook: "Alannah Warner. Nice to meet you."

Alannah's handshake was firm, and she looked me in the eye. Her confidence helped me relax, and for the first time since I could remember, I felt like I might be in good hands. Once more, ladies and gentlemen, the power of manners. I even managed to hold back the grimace as I discovered that my right arm wasn't healed to the point where it was up to the task of the shaking part.

Then, Thor give me strength, it was handshake introductions all round. The redheaded guard was Natalie, the black woman with the English accent was Brooke, the one with a faint kiwi accent was Lourdes, and my tall porter was Georgia Frankland. Luckily, since my shoulder was killing me by that point, she just waved from the back. She said to call her 'George'.

"Lovely to meet you all too," I said. "Thanks for getting me out of the hospital. And for looking after me since." I indicated the new bandages. Then I scratched a little at the places where the tranquilliser darts had got me, and smiled.

Alannah just shrugged. "Please don't feel bad about the tranquillisers. We got access to the subject data on the male branch of the program a long time before we made our play to get out of there. I'm sure you wouldn't begrudge us our safety."

I didn't, but I just raised my eyebrows. Even if it were smart, it was still a little rude. It was quiet for a little while, and then George, looking down over Alannah's shoulder, cleared her throat. "She means 'sorry'. Don't you Al? Now, how about we swap stories? You go first."

I chuckled a little, regretted it quickly, and tried to stop.

"Apology accepted. Fine." And then as I was marshalling my thoughts, my stomach rumbled. Really loudly.

"Kirsten's cooking dinner. I'll fetch a snack," said Brooke, and she slipped outside. I watched her tight black curls vanish from the doorway. Moments later she reappeared with a plate of soft, buttery, homemade chocolate chip cookies. "You," I announced to Brooke sincerely, around a mouthful of delicious biscuity goodness, "are my current favourite captor/rescuer. But don't let it go to your head - I'm pretty shallow and fickle."

Soon after, I began my tale of escape. Before I got past waking up to the sound of the door unlocking, Alannah stopped me and asked me to start earlier. "Tell me about when you first came to Project Lycan," she said.

"*Project Lycan*?" I replied, "that's a bit on the nose."

I sighed again, and slipped my fifth cookie off the plate. "They fetched me from prison," I said. "One night we were just - "

"Prison?" said Alannah. Her voice was definitely colder suddenly.

"I *knew* you were a cop," I replied. "Yes, from prison. We were taken to the warden, cuffed, and transferred. No-one was expecting a transfer, but we weren't given options, or information, so it was really just trading one jail for another. Except the second one involved hospital beds, scientists and they just made up the rules as they went..."

I was struck, suddenly, by the realisation that the 'transfer' from my original prison had clearly been all set up by the warden and his staff. Maybe they pretended we were still there. Maybe they'd staged a fake breakout. In hindsight, everything that happened to me since the 'transfer' was highly illegal, and at some level, we must have been sold to it. What kind of prison could get away with that?

Still, I did hate the second place more.

Project Lycan, huh?

"So what did you do?" asked Alannah. Her voice was heavy with impending judgement.

I held her gaze a moment, while considering telling her to mind her own business. Then, just as I opened my mouth to tell her to fuck off, I heard myself say, coldly: "I killed the man who had just raped my wife to death." I shuddered.

Silence. The pounding in my head was suddenly less oppressive. Lourdes and George looked shocked. Natalie looked fierce. Alannah and Brooke looked blank. I don't remember doing it, but soon I wasn't looking at their faces any more. I was curled into a ball. There on the single bed that didn't quite fit me.

Someone drew their breath. "Not now," I said. "Nothing now."

They didn't. They left. Even Natalie. And for the first time in weeks, I cried. Tears clogging my nose, and several parts of my shaking body soon weeping blood, too.

FOOD BROUGHT ME BACK. The grief consumed me, but my body simply reached its limits.

I read once about a treatment for phobias that used that idea. It went something like this. Let's say you're cripplingly afraid of birds, and you hear about someone who is renowned for curing people of phobias in a single session. So you go there and chat, and find out that the session takes all day. Well that's OK, you think, if it lets you go outside once again. A day isn't much if it might allow you to reclaim your life. So you commit to the treatment.

The first thing the practitioner does is put a feather on a

table across the room. Your chest squeezes, your heart pounds, and the urge to flee rises within you. But the feather doesn't move - it's just over there. And you hold steady, the fear pounding through you. After a while, you get weary. This level of panic just isn't sustainable. But there you are, and the feather's over there. Soon after, the panic symptoms diminish, just because you're tired.

And they move the feather closer. Fear floods you anew. Repeat. Then the feather is next to you. Then you touch it, or it's near your face. By the end, you're just begging to go to sleep as you're patting a fat hen and feeding it bran.

It's probably nonsense. I've never checked. But just as my soul required time to wail, my body required things as well. I'd never met Kirsten, but after half an hour or so, I *did* know what she was cooking. It was some kind of beef-based oven roast. Which had come out. My mouth watered, but I dried my eyes. Searching for tissues, I saw there were some over by some medical supplies set out on a little dresser. I made myself as presentable as possible, and staggered from the guest room.

The door opened to a hallway, and the hallway to the dining room and kitchen. It was an old, weatherboard farmhouse, rambling, with a lot of rooms, but none too spacious. All six of the women were there, Kirsten the only one I didn't recognise. I read concern on many faces. Alannah's seemed reserved, but not exactly cold any more. Lourdes had a laptop out, and I could half see my face on one of the windows.

Anger, sadness: they weren't over. I couldn't really imagine what that might be like. But life goes on, and they were partway through serving, so I simply joined them at the table. It was the kitchen of a large family, or possibly some semi-commercial operation, because one tray held a significant portion of the cow. There were also two more trays full of roast vegetables. A lot more potatoes, carrot and beetroot than I'd care to peel. Plus garlic and other extras. Not much was said as the seven of us showed our respects. I tried to be last to reach for things, but after everyone had their thirds, I relaxed a little. By the time I was starting to feel uncomfortably full, there were offers of tea and beer, and the conversation slowly started up again.

"So, tell me about Themyscira," I said, sitting back and sipping on my peppermint brew. A few puzzled looks, and a nonplussed snort from George, so I clarified.

"You obviously all know a lot more about what's been going on than me. So tell me your story. Where are you all from? The same as me? If so, were you kidnapped as well? Or were you volunteers? What was that place?"

Quiet for a few moments, as everyone looked at everyone else. I half expected Alannah to take up the story, but it was Natalie who broke the deadlock.

"There might have been volunteers once," she began tightly, "but from what we read in the records, the fatality rate was huge. We were all kidnapped, as was anyone brought in during the last year."

"But how do you..." I started, and then stopped. "Sorry, just start somewhere near the beginning. Consider me totally clueless."

I sipped again, and we all made ourselves comfortable. Natalie collected her thoughts briefly, and then asked: "What do you know about the process they used on us?"

I let out a slow breath, and emitted thoughts in little bursts as they came to me. "Well, I know roughly what it did to me: muscle growth, huge metabolism increase." I gestured at my body: "Everything growth, really. I grew significantly taller... Massive hormone changes that melted my brain. Think it killed most of the guys I was brought in with... Made the two others psychotic. Aggressive, deranged. Me too, I suppose... Nurses called us 'Ferals' apparently."

I tried to remember what I heard in the hospital. "It was some kind of gene therapy? Switching on dormant genetic code. Don't know the proper language. Or even if that makes sense."

Natalie nodded. "You're a bit right. We've got copies of all the research notes, and although none of us are experts enough to understand them, it's clear that whatever it is has huge implications for health and medicine. And more. The initial discovery was made by a man named Karl Wüster. He worked for a company called Bowline. There's not much on them online, but reading between the lines, it seems they developed specialised equipment for the military, including things like stimulant-based performance enhancers for elite forces. Karl Wüster had a fancy title in the company that makes it sound like he was involved in that area of research."

I nodded encouragingly as I thought. I had no idea that military forces used such things, although thinking about it, I had to admit it wasn't a farfetched idea. Anything banned in the Olympics is probably worth having in a life or death situation.

"His logbook doesn't give us the full tale, but it seems like he was thinking quite outside the box when he triggered an absolutely massive performance increase in a test subject. Essentially by accident. Reverse engineering it, he traced it to some change in genetic expression. Then he tried to repeat it, and killed someone. Gave them a sudden, massive and rapidly lethal auto-immune problem. He spent a year trying to analyse it in other species, and it didn't lead anywhere."

"As far as we can make out, the issue with doing tests in other species was that he was essentially triggering effects dormant in human DNA. Traits and adaptions that haven't been bred out of the source code, as you might say, but are typically inactive. Maybe parts of them are switched on sometimes, or maybe it's just like the appendix - destined to disappear, but not causing any selection pressure while quiescent."

"Anyway, Bowline pulled Wüster from his previous work, and started up Project Lycan. Massive funding flowed in, and he was teamed with a computational biologist named Adam Gannt." Natalie's face looked intense suddenly, and I felt temporarily unsafe. "Plus a huge supply of human test subjects. Unwilling ones. From the research notes, we just have a list of names, not their origins. But all the survivors," she said, indicating everyone in the room, "were kidnapped. Others, when we've searched for them online, have been listed as missing. We've found a few obituaries."

Huge supply? What are the chances a company could possibly get away with something like that? What kind of people would try? "What was the fatality rate in Project Lycan?" I asked. "Did they think they'd sorted out the problems when they started?"

Lourdes, who'd stopped reading about me on her laptop, and had been skimming something else, spoke up: "It reads like they almost did. They'd pulled so much data on their initial success that they thought they could trigger the same result. And they sort of came close - even the first trials were exhibiting huge boosts in speed, stamina, you name it... And then, one by one there'd be some major complication. Heart attacks, aneurysms, cancer... It was a disaster, but the logbooks read like they were written by a classic mad scientist. We read the reports and see a bunch of dead victims, but they saw a bunch of nearly living super-soldiers."

Lourdes continued as Natalie refreshed her beer. "Then they had a success. And another. And in the space of a month, Adam Gannt's huge machine learning algorithm just learned to replicate it. They'd sequence the victim's genome, and the machine would create some kind of targeted epigenetic cocktail. And it could almost guarantee success."

Her fingers flashed across the keyboard, and then she was scrolling through a spreadsheet. "For example," Lourdes continued, "you had a... 93% chance of surviving the process."

"Of course, well more than half of those survivors died after a few weeks," she added, somewhat alarmingly. "But the machine learning model even began to make pretty robust predictions about who that would be. Wüster and Gannt were getting to the point that they could see themselves being able to do this predictably. Possibly for enormous sums of money. They'd have to refuse to treat maybe 70-80% of their applicants, but the rest could take pretty good odds of getting superpowers."

"Superpowers," I said dully, not really able to take in the scale of the monstrosity she was describing. The room seemed to darken as my reduced blood supply left my brain. My fingers tingled, and I wondered whether this was just my own post-treatment heart attack.

"I may not have officially died back in that building," I said, as I slipped off my chair and laid down gingerly on my back, "but they did basically kill me."

No-one seemed to know what to do with that, so after a moment there was a group clean-up. I stayed on my back, waiting for my system to settle, and the sense of impending doom to leave. George and Brooke came over to check up on me, but I brushed them off. George's frown came with a bit of a glare. I wasn't all right, I knew, but I wanted fuss less than I wanted to just lie there.

And the doom didn't fade. I just sort of slipped into it, and

terrors I
couldn't see
chased fragments of me,
round, and through, the night.

Chapter 4

CONVALESCENCE

I woke in the guest bed again, Alannah my guard. The dreams were nothing but sweat now, tangled in sheets. It was hard to separate the false fears from more reasonable ones. I turned to see Alannah alert, hand near her gun. My heart lurched a little. That felt a little like shame.

Yes.

Alannah indicated the pills and water by my bedside. "Take those," she ordered.

I did.

"What were they?" I asked. There had been a lot of them.

"Vitamins, antibiotics, sedatives," she answered, a hint of challenge in her tone.

Still shame.

"I'm sorry," I said.

An eyebrow lifted slightly. "What for?" she inquired.

Not a bad question. What was I sorry for? "For causing trouble," I said. "It can't be easy looking after..."

"Yes," she snapped. "What exactly *are* we looking after?"

What, not who. Even though I basically agreed, I found myself getting a little aggravated.

"It's me, for now," I snapped. "I think it's more the injuries than the sedatives, though." I still felt torn, and battered, and like hiding in my cave, in the darkness, while the world stayed away.

Alannah's hand didn't reach for the gun, but for some reason, as I watched her face and posture, I thought about it a lot. She was really scared, and not just for herself. Holding herself ready and prepared to do something the others maybe wouldn't. If it were necessary.

Was it necessary? I really didn't want to die, not even this last little bit of me.

She wasn't going to execute me in panic. I felt that much. But however carefully considered her decision, I could tell all the options were on the table. "*What's* more the injuries than the sedatives? What happens when you get well?"

A fey mood crept up. The truth shall set ye free. Whatever 'free' might look like. I sighed. "I go half way to insane," I said. "More or less. Everything is fuck or fight. Everyone is male or female. If I'm alone, it's like swimming in the maelstrom. Around anyone else, it sort of takes a direction. From maelstrom to waterfall. I can barely think at all most of the time."

She took a few moments to think about that. "We have very... *clinical* descriptions of subject behaviour. And the incident that caused them to start isolating you," she said.

I nodded. "I heard it too late to stop it. They weren't just," I choked a little. "...they were *fighting* over it. One of them was laughing, but the fight was serious. Doing real damage to each other. When I came in, I..." My chest was hurting, my gut started cramping. I started to quiver. "I just don't think I've ever been that angry, possibly even when - "

The quivering became shuddering, and I was trying to rock it away. I wanted to explode. I wanted to be dead. I didn't want her to shoot me.

Alannah, distant, sharper. "They were attacking her and fighting, and you joined in."

"I. Did. Not. *Join*. Them." I bit out, as shudders became full body spasms. "I fucking killed two of them, and I broke a lot of the other two. Then we were tear-gassed just as they were taking me down."

"You killed them," she said, muffled by my arms.

"Only two," I corrected. "From then on we were always isolated. Moved by people with guns and armour." I glanced at Alannah's pistol, cradled in her left hand. "The only time I ever saw them again was just after I saw you."

The shuddering just wouldn't stop. It was like I was freezing to death, except I was sweaty.

"You killed them," she repeated, like she was processing it. I wondered what was recorded about that incident. There were cameras everywhere, but they wouldn't have seen much more than violence. We were all isolated after that, but otherwise, I wasn't treated particularly differently.

"Yes, I killed them," I said. Some of whatever it was I was feeling turning into anger. I looked up, and she was clearly struggling with something. "What would you have done? You see a victim, and four blood-crazed psychopaths smashing on each other. Go."

Alannah didn't answer quickly. I waited.

There was a creak of the floorboards outside. Some of this had probably been pretty loud. "Suppose you knew with certainty that shouting at them and threatening them wouldn't do anything. You can watch it happen, or you can shoot."

"You didn't have a gun."

"Of course I didn't."

"Why didn't they just kill you?"

The simple answer was that in those first two or three seconds, there were two very different fights going on. They were going hard, but it was still just dominance play to them. They wanted to see the look on the others' faces. Wanted them to know who was the alpha. I couldn't care less what they thought. I didn't want them to feel pain. I felt as little about them as I felt about a rabid dog. When I launched off that door frame, it wasn't about justice or retribution. I was just trying to end the threat. Thought I could save her.

But I didn't have the words for all that. I remembered being thrown across the room, and feeling both arms break as I hit the wall.

"Oh, they would have," I replied. "They certainly would have."

The pauses between the shuddering bursts lengthened, and then lengthened again. I breathed deeply and deliberately, and they slowly stopped all together.

"Alannah," I said. "Many of them were psychopaths well before they got caught. Most of them were assholes. And yes, I'm dangerous. And yes, I don't trust myself. And when I tell you I need space, I mean it."

I gestured to my body. "I hate what they did. I hate all of this. I've killed three people in my life now. Each time I did it has etched itself on my soul. Burnt some part of me that I can't see healing. It's not OK, and I strongly doubt it ever will be. But what I don't have..."

It was a delicate explanation, and I took a moment to make it clearly. "What I don't have is the slightest doubt. Wind time back to those moments again, I would still kill them. It wasn't exactly self defence, but I might have saved that nurse… Anyway, there's a line, you know? Some people just need killing. I know that's not how society works, and that attitude is why I got that sentence and went to that prison in the first place. But I wasn't like them. I'm not them, Alannah. I'm just not."

I sort of ran out of words. She had asked a few questions, but mostly she'd just been standing there, measuring me. It was how we met, I suppose. Mysteries with few clues, and plenty riding on guessing right.

"I'll get you some breakfast," she said. Then she left the room. In the distance, I heard a cow bellowing.

I lay back down and pondered the ceiling.

"I just don't think I'm me anymore, either."

BREAKFAST, brunch, lunch, second lunch, afternoon tea, and first dinner were brought, rather mechanically, by one or more of my rescuers. They quietly checked my bandages, but didn't stay. I thanked them, and healed. Slept and slept, until it stopped working. By the evening I was just lying there with my eyes closed, hoping for something like oblivion.

Second dinner came late, brought by Natalie. "Got a book or anything?" I asked.

"Sure," she said. "There's a shelf in the lounge. What are you after?"

No invitation to come out and browse.

"Fiction," I said. "Escapist. Or just bring me three random ones."

She nodded, and did. Two mystery novels and soaring epic fantasy.

I read the first mystery in the night, and the other one

before breakfast. The soaring epic fantasy was much heavier on the epic than the fantasy, and felt a bit too much like work. But I stuck at it with a strange kind of determination. Sometimes, you've just got to find out how it ends.

At second lunch, I asked for replacements. Brooke scanned the backs. "Didn't like 'em?"

"They weren't great," I replied. "But better than staring at the wall."

There was a sort of awkward pause. I added: "I notice I haven't had a guard since Alannah and I had that little confab."

"We weren't guarding you before," she said a little defensively, "we were watching you to make sure you were OK."

My hands came up in front of me. "Thanks for that part of it, but obviously it was more than that. Don't worry, I'm not offended. We don't know each other, and what little we do know is hardly reassuring." I saw Brooke's nose flaring, and I wondered if her sense of smell had been amplified as much as mine. If so, there were a lot of things we couldn't hide from each other. "What I don't understand, is why that conversation with Alannah didn't make your security tighter. I'm pretty sure she started close to freaked out, and I'd bet my last dollar that's how she ended."

Brooke just checked my shoulder bandage, and left it unchanged. "You'd be bankrupt then," she said. "Alannah was the one who convinced us you'd be right in here on your own."

Then she went and fetched me some replacement books, and left me to think.

∼

THINKING DIDN'T WORK. So I tried reading again. The

choices were yet another mystery, and two romances with steamy covers. I immediately hated the smarmy hero-looking types on there, with their stupid shirts, so I focussed on finding out what happened to the bachelor and the jewels.

Reading didn't work, either. Whatever will had sustained me to read for the previous day had run quite thin. One might even say ragged, as it got to the point where I forced myself through a paragraph five times in a row, each time taking absolutely nothing in. The book hit the table, and I looked around. I felt a strong inhibition to roaming the house uninvited, but judged that a trip to the toilet was kosher.

To my surprise, only Brooke and Kirsten were still around - the presence of the others had faded significantly. Kirsten was cooking again, and I smiled at her as I passed the kitchen. I couldn't see where Brooke was, but I suspected she was somewhere on the other side of the dining area. Somewhere I'd never been. I suppose I hesitated in the doorway, debating.

"How are you feeling?" asked Kirsten, and I was struck by her accent - a stereotypical drawl from southern US. She was blonde and blue-eyed, too, which somehow seemed to fit the image. Although maybe her hair would have been longer if she was going to go on the movie poster.

"Much better, thanks," I replied. Then I blinked as I realised it was true. "Although I don't think I can manage another nap or book for a while."

She smirked, and wiped a bit of flour off her nose. It left some on her cheek. I peered over the counter between us, and saw her kneading a huge, monster pile of dough.

"Where did you rise that?" I asked. She tipped her head at something on the ground in the kitchen. I approached, and saw the two huge metal tubs resting under the sink. "Is there anything I can do to help?"

She wrinkled her nose as I came close. "Shower before coming into the kitchen, I think," she said.

It was probably just strict food hygiene. That's what I told myself.

Kirsten directed me to towels, and then I went to make myself presentable. The shower had old tiles, and was almost too small to turn around in, so I stood in front of the bathroom vanity to try to peel off the bandages. Gingerly, I picked at the edges, and peeled them off. They weren't too messy, and each one had been changed several times. In the mirror, I could see stitches, angry welts and tears. Bruises all over as well, now flared yellow, purple, brown and blue. Past their most horrific looking stage, but colourful.

The shower water came out scalding. By the time I got it comfortable, it was almost on full cold. The jets of water made me wince, and I tried to get clean without breaking any scabs. New painful places on my body kept announcing themselves when I moved, especially when I stretched. The soap stung my back where I seemed to have a light burn.

But peeling off my bandages, I'd caught a whiff or two. A lot of my recent history was still on my body, and it felt amazing to carefully wash it off. It took me at least half an hour, but by the time I was clean, I felt my mood buoy.

I stepped out of the shower, and grabbed the towel. It was that moment that I wondered how I was going to get new bandages on. Or clothes. An embarrassed minute in the bathroom, and I emerged with the towel wrapped around my waist. It felt like a tight miniskirt.

Kirsten was bent over the oven when I came in, pulling out some loaves.

"That's better," she said as she pulled out a large tray.

Then she turned around and saw me, standing sheepishly, with a tiny trickle of blood running down my side from one of the wounds that I'd accidentally unsealed. "Woah!" she said. "Give me a minute, honey."

I stood there while she transferred the loaves to racks to cool, and swept in another lot of uncooked dough. She poured a little extra water into a tray inside the oven, flicked the timer for another twenty minutes, and straightened. "Ok, let's have a look."

She came close, and turned me around. I almost lost the towel as I switched hands, but she examined my back and sucked in a breath between her teeth. "Imma get Brooke," she said. "You head to your room."

The tone she used was a little concerning. I twisted to see, and then desisted when it twinged. I headed back to my room, and when I opened the door, it smelled funky. I opened the window wide, and looked at the sheets coated with my grime, blood and sweat. Brooke and Kirsten came in, and Brooke pulled the bandage supplies from a drawer, and told me to lie face down on the bed. I did so, and then over the next few minutes she and Kirsten tortured me kindly with tissues, antiseptic creams and gauze.

I rolled over and swung my feet onto the floor. "Are there any spare sheets?" I asked. "And I reckon I could manage these if you point me towards the laundry."

Apparently there weren't any sheets, but I wasn't going to need a bed in hours, so the sheets went into the machine while I went to the couch in the lounge. The bookshelf was there, as was an old free-to-air television. Looking across the titles of the former, I could see I'd done reasonably well in my 'random' sampling. There were mysteries on two shelves, sweeping epic fantasy (by which I mean a single, particular sweeping epic fantasy) on half of another, and then just steamy books with puffy shirt men on the cover.

My legs started failing me, and I had a big yawn, which was a bit of a surprise, but as the entertainment options were limited, I managed to snare the polite-but-shy Kirsten into a conversation. It was punctuated by occasional timers, and a couple of rather majestic snacks, but for the first time in a very, very long time, I started to relax. And several things became clearer as she told me her story.

KIRSTEN HAD BEEN half way through a year of a round-the-world holiday when she was taken. She wasn't the first, and she'd spent many months in the Project Lycan building before the plan to escape hatched, and a few more weeks before it had come to fruition.

Her first thought after the big escape was to immediately contact her parents and brother back home. The others, particularly Alannah, had instead persuaded her to wait.

"Alannah does seem more cautious," I noted.

"Oh, you don't understand," she said, stressing the last syllable. "This isn't about what kinda person Al is, it's about Bowline. Al was doing some kind of undercover work." Kirsten stopped and thought for a moment, and it looked for a second like a caricature: crease between the eyes, hand on the chin, staring into the distance, the whole bit. "Ah've never really understood exactly what her job was, but somehow she came across major ties between Bowline and organised crime. It went to court, and for a few days she was put into Witness Protection."

Kirsten poked her finger at me as she emphasised her next point. "That's where she was taken from! Witness. Pro.

Tection! What does that say about Bowline, huh? We're out, but where does that leave us? Do we go back and trust our safety to the cops? The feds? Do I go to the embassy?" Kirsten petered out, shaking her head.

Witness protection. I didn't know much about it, but obviously its whole existence was predicated on keeping people out of reach of organised crime. What did that say about Bowline, that they could kidnap people out of that level of security as easily as they could take a whole section of a maximum security prison?

"I thought they were connected to the military," I thought out loud.

Kirsten nodded. "Yep, that's what Al said. Selling high end equipment and stuff that doesn't make it to the bulk of the troops, but is worth spending on a few. According to Al, they split themselves across multiple agencies, and used operational security to keep everything compartmentalised. And things that get used in clandestine operations make at least as much sense in the organised crime world. And so..."

And so, indeed.

I had been in Project Lycan for a little longer than Kirsten, I felt. A lot of that was a blur, but the remnants of my inner clock told me it was something like a year.

"So what was it like for you after you were kidnapped?" I asked. Hoping thinking about it wouldn't freak Kirsten out. Talking about trauma was supposed to be good, wasn't it? For myself, I felt that without other stories, I'd never really know mine. It felt like my life was a piece of rope that had been cut, and I couldn't quite make out all the frayed strands.

Knowing, I felt, was a lot less creepy than not knowing.

Before she could answer, Kirsten went to do something in the kitchen. My body protested when I went to get up, and my extremities felt a little numb, so I waited politely. After a few minutes, she came back with a beer, and settled into an armchair, feet tucked under her in a kneeling position.

"What was it like for me, honey?" she asked. "Terrifying. I was just scared witless. They kept me in those rooms, and drugged me, and tested me. Thought they was sex traffickers. Thought I was being prepared for some boudoir somewhere." She took a large swig. "All the drugs, I could tell they were doing things to my head. I always felt fuzzy, off balance. And then," she shook her head to clear it, and gestured at her body, including her very feminine curves, "then, I started growing. Couldn't believe it. Thought it were all about sex then, too. Making me into their perfect little fetish. Made me so angry, I would sometimes scream and hit the walls in the room..."

She continued, clenching her fist, and getting very animated. I made appreciative grunts and little echoes, and her story came out with gusto. But my attention started to wander. I'd finally realised that something was seriously wrong.

Perhaps not for Patrick Arthurs. He would have heard this story and been horrified. He would have been angry and upset. He would have tried to be gallant and soothing, which he would probably have done badly for some reason. He would have planned to spring into action to right the wrongs. I didn't feel that. I didn't feel anything.

Perhaps it was the shared horror. Perhaps Patrick Arthurs had been burned out of this shell by experiences exactly like the ones Kirsten was describing. I didn't think I was being prepared for involuntary sex work. I had no idea what was happening at all. In fact, Kirsten probably wasn't being prepared for anything of the kind either, because as she detailed the intrusions, indignities and violations that were visited upon her daily, it all sounded perfectly familiar. Perhaps a traumatised Patrick Arthurs would have been triggered by the conversation, and found himself overwhelmed by the weight of memories that had taken his psyche and smashed it to rubble.

I didn't feel that either. I didn't feel anything.

Kirsten was expressing an anger that sounded like a sane response to the barbarous treatment she had received. She described her anger at the time, and the way she kept it in check with the aid of fear, upbringing, and side effects of the drugs they kept giving her.

That perfectly justifiable anger sounded like a shadow of the anger that had effectively killed Patrick Arthurs. The all-consuming rage and urge to violence that hijacked his every waking thought. As the treatments had progressed, Patrick had become stronger, faster, sharper. Somewhere along the way, he realised that it was more than that, and that he wasn't really the same person at all. Someone else slipped into the driver's seat. Someone who took offence at everything, who snapped and barked, and fought. At least when dealing with men. Someone who, when dealing with women, had such an overblown sexual response that it wiped out all thought. Someone who, when listening to a beautiful, slightly exotic lady tucked into a chair opposite him, would be unable to focus on a single word of conversation. Someone who, when guided by a lady to consider her increased female sexual characteristics, would have been, in any sensible definition of the term, insane with lust.

I didn't feel that either. I didn't feel anything.

For example, I couldn't feel my legs.

I MANAGED TO SAY SOMETHING, but I'm not sure what. The numbness came over my vision, and it was a sensation of concentric circles flowing away from me. And then peace.

IT WAS REAL PEACE. Something I never expected. No expectations, no feelings, no thoughts. Virtually no sensations. Trapped in the moment when you just begin to fall.

It was ripped away rather violently. A pounding on my chest, and I coughed. My eyes opened again, and there was nothing but confusion. Hands were on my sternum, shoving rhythmically. It hurt. Many figures. The hands belonged to George. George was a person I'd met recently. Ah yes. Alannah. Brooke. Both close. Brooke with a needle. The others behind. Kirsten crying and shaking, looking angry, upset, scared.

I still couldn't feel much, but I feebly resisted the CPR. A loud recorded message announced "**Stop CPR. Do not touch patient. Analysing.**" It subsequently declared the whole circus over. There was relief visible on all the faces. That was nice.

I used to think of them as Amazons. A bubble of clarity formed, framing the scene above me. They were actually Valkyries, come to drag my soul from my broken body on the battlefield. Pity my soul was broken too, but it was still really very decent of them to try.

Chapter 5

HER BIG SISTERS

For what may have been the first time in days, I didn't pass out from the trauma. I was lying on my back on the floor, large pads attaching me to a defibrillator, and a generally busy cloud of women being concerned above me. The numbness hadn't passed, but apparently my heart wasn't doing anything worrying any more, and I slowly assembled the idea that I wasn't in danger of immediately dying. The sheets from my bed weren't dry yet, so I was just given a couple of pillows where I lay.

One pleasant thing about the numbness was that it also made it hard to panic. I sometimes forget how much energy that takes. So by the time my brain started working properly, I felt like I could approach things in a fairly analytic manner. What does all-body paralysis imply? First thought: neck trauma. I'd had a lot of it. Outright nerve damage would have manifested more or less immediately, though, so maybe this was more of an impingement? A broken spar of bone or something like that?

Conclusion: I was going to need some kind of X-ray. Addendum: I had no hope of getting any kind of X-ray.

Perhaps an anonymous A&E visit in a distant city? Could the Valkyries drive me there in the van? Probably not, their van was almost certainly known to the authorities by this point. On the other hand, they had to have gone somewhere just now, did they have access to another car?

George lifted me a little to slide a seat cushion under my ass. "Thanks," I said. "For all this, just now."

"No worries," she replied. After sliding it in, she did the same for my ankles, getting me briefly off the floor. "How's that?" she asked.

"Fine," I said. "Although I'm sure I'd be in a lot more pain if I wasn't so heavily sedated."

George winced. "Sorry," she said.

I blinked, and considered my statement. "No, pain is bad."

George scratched her cheek. "Yesss," she drawled, "but it seems that we just came within a gnat's whisker of sedating you to death."

Oh? Ah. "Not some sort of spinal injury then," I checked.

"No. Just a nearly lethal combination of paralytic and depressant."

I considered that for a moment.

"Well, that's good news."

Her eyebrows raised.

"I imagine it's easier to have less paralytic and depressants in my system than it is to get neck surgery or repair my spinal cord," I explained.

"There is that," she said. "In fact, we have no choice but to fix that problem right up."

"No choice?"

"Yeah, the stuff we left the compound with is gone, and we've just discovered it can't be replaced without help from the medical establishment," George added.

Alannah came over from the far side of the lounge, and put her phone back in her pocket.

"And not without raising a lot of red flags. While we obviously didn't know what we were doing with the drugs we had, that matters less now that we're out of them, and we can't get more. You," she pronounced, "are about to go off your meds."

I looked up. The feeling that was seeping back into my body started specialising in a very bad feeling building in my gut. "OK," I said, "but just in case you're hoping a lack of medication will make me normal again, I'm not sure it will work that way. I suppose that the mood changes *did* coincide with being force-fed pills and fluids basically every day for the last year. There were a lot of needles involved as well, with injecting things and taking blood. It might make sense that the crazy stuff that happened to my head was drug-induced, but I think if anything, it was the other way around. I'd wake up hot and crazy, and then some pills or an injection would bring me down a little."

A less sinister thought jumped up, and I grabbed it. "Maybe I was addicted to something, and the morning madness was part of the withdrawal symptoms?"

Alannah shook her head. "No, we have a fairly clear idea of what's happening. We just don't know how to fix it."

"So what's happening?" I asked, in a tone that stayed well short of shrill.

Alannah sat down. "So most of this we've pieced together from the lab notes, inventories and the like. There's a lot of gaps, but the general timeline is pretty clear." She took a deep breath in, and let it go. "What they wanted was to develop a process that provided permanent, dramatic increases in strength, speed, stamina, and healing. They almost got it in Project Lycan. Everything but the stamina, really, and even that is only limited by the ridiculous calorie load our changed metabolisms require. The point was to be able to boost people, without the fuss of providing drugs, and to a much greater extent. Can you imagine what you could sell that for on any market? You could name your price. Worth an absolute fortune."

"But," she said, "there were two problems." She held up one finger. "One, an embarrassing fraction of the subjects died. Either on administering the process, or a little while afterwards. Wüster and Gannt had high hopes of improving that. Their system was delivering treatments assigned by a computer that took as its input the gene sequence of the subject, along with a lot of epigenetic data. This couldn't be done under any ethical rules in the world, but the computer just kept trying things that humans wouldn't. It had no understanding at all, but some processes are just too complicated to codify, and that's where machine learning shines. People died, and the machine got more data."

"A few hundred more trials, and they could probably have offered their treatment to approximately half the population with some kind of acceptable risk. Except for problem two."

Alannah ticked off the second problem with her fingers. "Every single subject went batshit crazy. Hyperviolent."

She held me with those light green eyes. I wondered if she was expecting a reflexive denial. Sometimes when people say something awful about you, the automatic reaction is to fight, even if you know it's true. But the challenge in her eyes wasn't unkind. It felt more like a death sentence: a doctor telling the patient the bad news. Sidebar: what a shitty job that must be. One more reason I chose not to go that way when I was a teenager. So what *does* a patient say that might make the giving of such news easier?

"Yarp," I said.

George, bless her once again, snorted.

Alannah took it in, and moved on. It may have been my imagination, but she did look a little less burdened.

"So anyway, this is terrible news if you're making a product to sell. People might accept one time dangers when undergoing the treatment, but not 100% chance of complete personality change."

"No, they would not," I affirmed.

"Their main problem was, there was no optimisation they could do. Every single successful treatment had been coupled with a change in personality. It was just part of the package. They had no real understanding of what they were doing, or how it worked, so there didn't seem like much they could do on that end of things."

Brooke pulled out a large, heavy case of empty vials. "So they tried to control it after the fact," she said. "It wasn't that long before they showed that the personality change wasn't so much a subtle rewiring as a flood of hormones and neurotransmitters. So the theory went, maybe the body could be souped up by the treatments, and then the brain chemistry could be stabilised by drugs."

A lot of the last couple of hundred days suddenly reassembled itself into something resembling sense. "Bang-bang control," I agreed.

Brooke's blank look was shared by the others. "I'm half sure that meant something."

"It's an engineering term. When you want to do optimal control, and you look for the best solution without considering any kind of cost to the control process itself, you end up with crazy answers."

The looks stayed blank. "Ok, so you want to balance a pencil on its point, and of course you don't balance it perfectly, so it starts to tip. You could try making a minor correction, but you want it to get back to balanced as quickly as possible. You have a big hammer, so you smash it as hard as you can back in the direction of vertical. Then when it gets there, you smash it again to stop it."

I modelled the process with my hands. "Bang. Bang. Bang-bang control."

The faces stayed blank, but I persisted. "So they want our bodies hyped up and our brain chemistry normal, so they smash us with these treatments, and then flood us with drugs to try to stabilise the brain. Bang-bang control. It's technically optimal, but usually massively impractical."

Still nothing, but I'd known within that my explanation was doomed. Never explain yourself, that's the lesson. "Sorry. Go on," I added.

Brooke did. "I've read your file, it's a lot like everybody else's. You were brought in a bit before they came up with this plan, back when they still had hope that they could fix the problem through some change to the epigenetic process. But it was all too complex and interconnected to have any real hope. The death of the nurse Peggy Adams led to the full isolation of the subjects, and there were some pretty panicked emails from that time. Then the drug regime was designed. Nothing ever really worked properly, but they kept changing the formula while attempting to train the surviving male subjects. Looking for something where they could at least concentrate and focus."

"What did they put us on?" I asked. Then my mind caught up with a little stress on a word in Brooke's explanation. "What you do mean, 'male' subjects? What about you?"

"Turns out," Brooke said wryly, "that all of the trials to that point were on male subjects. Some kind of assumption about the target market, I suppose. Someone made a comment - I'm not sure who it was, the lab notes don't take time out to attribute ideas that weren't Wüster's - noting that the crazy aggression was stereotypical male bullshit. Only turned up to maximum volume."

"Until the speakers blow," I confirmed.

"So they decided to kidnap female subjects and try the process on them. Most of them died, but the six of us survived."

I looked at them. Brooke, taking a gap year that turned into two. Kirsten, the caterer's assistant who was travelling for a holiday. Both barely out of secondary school. George, Natalie and Lourdes, who I didn't know much about. Alannah, the cop nabbed out of witness protection, where she was about to testify against the very company that nabbed her.

"I would have thought it was risky kidnapping Alannah given the circumstances. When people are taken from witness protection, there's a very obvious potential motive," I said.

Alannah shrugged. "Maybe, but it was still a lot safer than leaving me in there. This way they could even use me once they got me," she said. She said it kinda dispassionately, but I had a feeling that I wouldn't want to be wearing a Bowline uniform with her in a dark alley.

"So does the Project Lycan process affect females in the same way as males?" I asked.

"Yes and no," said Alannah. "We have nearly all the same physical changes: size increase, strength, etc. Except that they're not as dramatic. Our metabolisms aren't quite as jacked, and as a bonus, we have far greater stamina than male subjects. We *do* have elevated hormone levels, including testosterone, as well heightened aggression. But all of that is turned down, too. It seems we can function comparatively well."

"So did they test that by giving you training as well?" I asked. "I think they gave us combat training because it was easy to focus on. If you stayed properly sane, they could have branched out."

"Yes," smiled Alannah. "First combat training, and then other kinds of tasks. Then teamwork. They were so happy."

I remembered Alannah's face across the huge pile of jury-rigged explosives. "They never really understood, did they?" I speculated. "They were happy with your results, and maybe you were co-operative, so they let their guard down. And they never really grokked how fundamentally angry you were. They never really saw themselves."

A pleased, but slightly sinister expression came over Alannah's face. "No. They didn't."

Natalie's face was positively gleeful. "As we got to know each other, we started to figure out what was going on. The research assistants thought we were being so helpful, but really we were just figuring out our limits, and learning our environment. Then, when Lourdes volunteered to do data entry for some of the tests, they went for it."

Lourdes smiled shyly. "All their computers were on the same intranet," she said, as if from that, everything that followed was perfectly obvious.

"Comp sci major?" I asked.

"Actually no, but I was a system admin for a small company for eight years," she corrected.

She didn't look old enough, but then I looked younger than I had as well. "Huh," I said. "I can't tell you how happy I am they got lax at the end. And even happier that it was their own inherent sexism that really smacked them down."

"Sorry for nearly killing you in there," said Alannah.

I thought of the other inmates, and shuddered. "Not at all, I quite understand," I said. "It was nice to have this little bit before the end, and I'm glad the rest got destroyed."

I thought about that. "Or did it? What's to stop the bigwigs just starting over?"

"Not much," replied Lourdes. "We have the only surviving copy of the research data, unless someone disobeyed operational protocols. But given what Wüster and Gannt know, the whole thing could probably be repeated given time and money. Plus, of course, several hundred expendable test subjects."

I thought about that. "Even given what little I know about these people, I'd still bet that they'd disobey operational protocols any time it felt more convenient for them. So they probably have copies of the research data. Which, to look on the bright side, means that they wouldn't have to kill quite so many people to start up again."

Alannah started pacing. "Except they never had any success with the drug-based treatments, so they've got a product that basically only works on women that want to be athletes or fighters, and don't mind a permanent personality shift."

"What's that like?" I asked.

"It's fine," dismissed Alannah, in a tone that made me suspect that it wasn't. "But we've got to find a way to stop them kidnapping more people. And then killing the majority of them."

Natalie interjected as she rummaged through a backpack. "Not to forget, we also have to stop them from killing *us*. Since we pulled Conan here from the hospital, they'll know we got out of the Project Lycan building. There will be heavily armed people looking for us from both sides of the law. Underworld goons from the world of organised crime, plus federal and state agents and officers, some of whom will be dirty, and some of whom will be duped. Also the in-house ops people from Bowline, whichever side of the law they count as."

"Unlawful," replied Alannah, before frowning. "Although, depending on who knows what, that might actually vary from individual to individual."

"Bowline has in-house military personnel?" I queried.

"Remember what they sell," said Natalie. "Top end gear for military operations doesn't appear full-formed in a lab. And it doesn't provide its own military-grade security. Anyway, we're more or less out of the money we took with us, we'll likely be shot if we're caught by the wrong people, and arrested if we're caught by the others." She sniffed, and started rummaging through the bag again. "And then killed slyly."

Alannah's face went hard. "Even if it is more dangerous than running, we still have to stop them," she declared.

"Little would please me more than seeing Bowline stopped and brought to justice," agreed Natalie, without looking up. "Apart, that is, from not being shot. That ranks even higher."

Alannah was about to argue the point a little hotly, but Brooke jumped up. "Tea!" she announced, with a hint of desperation. "Let's get everyone sitting down at the table, and we'll have some tea."

The frowns showed that Brooke's particularly British incantation to ward off conflict didn't have enough mystic force to settle things down. Fortunately, Kirsten jumped up with her. "And fresh bread rolls," she added. "With cheese and honey from the farm. Come get them while they're warm."

I was still lying on the floor, so I had to stay still to avoid the flurry of legs. George glanced down as she passed. "Stay there, I'll bring you one."

"Two?" I said hopefully, and she accidentally tripped on my buttock as she stepped over. Didn't break her stride, so I just rubbed my sore ass and shut up.

The good news was that I could feel the bruise. It reminded me to ask, but I forgot again as George came back with two warm cheesy rolls.

I REMEMBER hot cheese rolls from the canteen at school. That's an old memory. They'd be wrapped in foil, and heated in a little device, and the cheese would get melty. My second favourite thing about them was that I could afford them most days, especially if I scraped under the vending machines with my ruler in the morning on my way to school. My favourite thing was simply the taste and texture. Cheese and bread is a combination that has been touched by the greatest of the gods. The memory of a half-day old overtoasted bun still gives me a warm glow. By comparison, these fresh-baked rolls were mind-meltingly majestic. Plus, the cheese was sharp, and voluminous.

What I'm trying to say was that I forgot what I was going to ask again, until mine was gone, and George's was gone too. I eat really fast - I'm not proud, it's just a fact - so I spend a lot of time watching people eat. I think she saw me watching, and made a bit of a show of enjoying her second one. It was a bit captivating. When she licked her fingers, and leaned back in the chair, nursing a complacent little smile, I shook myself out of it.

"I'm starting to feel things again," I said, realising it was true in all ways, "so do we try to replicate the cocktail you gave me earlier, while skipping the near-lethal dose part?"

Brooke pointed over to the empty vial case she'd displayed earlier. "We're out. And when we did our research, we realise why they brought in a specialist to try this. Half the things that work build tolerances really quickly, most of the rest do damage if used for any time. About half of each are addictive, and the whole lot of them have side effects. The tranquillisers we shot you with didn't work, but though we didn't quite put you out, it turns out we did nearly stop your heart."

Brooke's matter-of-fact tone and cultured english accent contrasted with Natalie's more abrupt: "Which matters squat, because most of those ingredients are impossible to buy over the counter anyway. Even if we *did* know what the hell we were doing."

My head started to hurt. Yay, feeling.

"So," I asked, "speaking of buying things over a counter, did someone say we have no money?"

Natalie jiggled her boots as a nervous twitch. "Diddly squat."

"I suppose I can't access my money either. I imagine I'm officially an escaped convict who's been at large for months. Have they pinned stuff specifically on me?"

Lourdes, who had gravitated back to her laptop again, shook her head. "Nope, you're dead."

Dead? I suppose I was, at that. My ghost had a bit of unfinished business, though.

"That will make it hard to get funds," I agreed. "Although won't it make it hard to put out things like APBs as well?"

"Nope," said Alannah. "All they need is a story and a description."

"Well you've got the hardware for a life of crime," I suggested lightheartedly, indicating the pistols many of them had handy, and the assault rifle butt visible in the back hallway.

"More like a single attempt," suggested Alannah. "It was a miracle we managed to get the van out into the country without it being tracked. Only managed it because it was a cloudy day and we turned off the highway to travel on fire trails."

So she'd half considered it. Not an encouraging thought, for some reason.

"So what is the plan, then?" I asked, looking around the room.

No answer.

"We've got nothing," Natalie shrugged. "Basically, as far as we can tell, we're fucked."

"What was the original plan for the escape?" I asked, figuring there had to be something from there that could be adapted.

"We got out!" Natalie answered, irritated. "We co-operated until they let their guard down. We took the armoury, copied what we thought we might need, stuffed duffels with all the gear we could, rigged the place to explode, and then unlocked everything so we could skedaddle. Then we saw you being taken away in an ambulance, and figured we'd better tie up that loose end on our way out. Took a couple of days to find a van and contact my mum's step-sister. Then we grabbed you and got out. Clean getaway, so suck on that for a plan!"

I held up my hands in appeasement. "Such an amazing plan that it worked on shitty info. Well done."

My hands indicated the vials. "You even thought to bring drugs in case you needed to sedate a feral."

Brooke looked surprised. "Oh we mostly tried to take our drugs, but there was practically nothing on site."

"Your drugs? I thought..."

Natalie bounced up and closed the lid with a snap. "Our drugs were why they thought we were safely being so co-operative. They were definitely addictive. So there's going to be some withdrawals soon. When you go beast, we're going to go pretty bitchy."

There were about four thousand ways to phrase what I wanted to say, and I was pretty sure I was going to trigger an emotional land mine. "If they got you hooked on something designed for the purpose, the withdrawals are going to be..."

I paused, and considered if this were even wise. Suspecting not, I struggled forward anyway. "I mean, even if it was just opiates, they're famous for breaking down willpower when push comes to shove. How -?"

"Oh, write that down, fold it, and use it to get fucked," snarled Natalie. "You fucking question our *willpower*? After we just fucking *told* you what we went though? And how we smiled at those fuckers for months?"

"I - "

"All six of us! We were fucking superheroes! You're looking at Natalie-motherfucking-Romanov and her big sisters."

"It's -"

"And you hear about the fact that we're going to have to go through withdrawal symptoms, and you're suddenly worried that we're going to crack? You will show us some fucking *respect*, you ungrateful sack of -"

I jumped up. Rather than looming angrily over me, Natalie was suddenly pointing her sharp finger up at my face. My sudden movement had primed her for battle, and I didn't care that she had a pistol handy. I felt strong. All of the seated Valkyries leapt to their feet. It was on! George was very slightly taller than me, but considerably lighter, I judged. Although looking at her...

I stopped. My body probably wasn't in great shape yet, but the crap my brain had been swimming in for the last day was flushing its way out of my system, fast. "Shit," I said, as I became aware that my breathing was making me flushed.

Eye contact was difficult, not to mention embarrassing, so I tried closing my eyes. That just focused my attention on what I was smelling. "Oh, shit," I clarified. "I've gotta go."

I staggered through the laundry to the side door, pulling a couple of scratchy blankets from the linen cupboard as I went. Natalie grabbed my arm before I reached the doorhandles. "You are not-"

Turning to her, I held her fierce eyes. It was a dangerous, delicate moment. She wasn't heavy enough to stop me, even if she could easily kill me. More importantly, what I needed was peace, which can only be given, not taken. I was briefly balanced, and I desperately didn't want to tip over. She was angry, but the part of me that understood why also knew that I didn't have time to argue. "I'm going to the barn now," I said. "I have to leave, and I have to leave immediately." She looked mutinous, but I didn't give her a moment to speak. "If you come out too, whatever the hell else you do..."

I looked down the corridor, where everyone was bunched, armed and confused. "Stay. Downwind."

It was either a sudden insight, or else the mention of the barn as an acceptable option, but Natalie's grip didn't tighten as I pulled to the doorhandle and stepped outside. No-one followed, but they watched. The wind was in fact considerable, and I made a dramatic exit into it, to the sound of Natalie's continuing tirade.

Chapter 6

COWS DON'T JUDGE

There were several barns, and my feet got muddy and cold before I made it across the paddock to the big one. The wind was loud, a constant pressure, and the barn itself was little more than three and a half corrugated iron walls, and a roof. The spotty rain drifted in a little, and later, when it fell harder, some of it dripped down in one corner, running from a tear between two of the iron sheets. A muddy little pool there spattered, but that corner was slightly downhill, so the rest of the floor would have been dry enough, if it weren't for the enormous quantity of cowshit.

The cows had already wandered in, taking shelter after a long day of eating. They were large and inoffensive, once you got over the stink. I could see some rough wooden steps up to a half-full hayloft, so I made for it. After moving a couple of bales around, I had a well insulated little nook. A gentle murmur of cows below, and the rain beating out a white noise tattoo on the tin roof above. I heard George's voice below.

"Your antibiotics!" she called. "And some water."

I had a flash of frustration - I'd only *just* said I needed space. But my brain was still mine, and it told me that if I was part way through an antibiotic course, I needed to finish it. Still, I hopped up rather peevishly. When I came down the steps, I saw George in the distance. She was already half way back to the house, stomping across the paddock in huge gumboots and a rain jacket that barely made her waist. She was carrying a twee little umbrella with bright coloured dots. All probably borrowed.

I looked around for the antibiotics she mentioned, and saw there was a little picnic basket there by the doorway. One of the heifers was taking an interest, so I squeezed between the others quickly. Inside, on a folded tartan tea towel, was a sealed jar holding a set of pills, along with some handwritten instructions (*three times daily,* it scrawled). The cow's huge head snuffled, and watched curiously as I peered in under the cloth. There was a huge water bottle, a large piece of dark chocolate, and one more bread and cheese roll. I decided I'd better save the roll for later, and so I didn't eat it until I was back up in the hay loft, just before I got back into my blanket-lined cranny. I wriggled until I had a kind of solid hammock.

I'd felt my head clear a little almost as soon as I left the house. Though the grey skies and insistent rain outside was somehow comforting, there was definitely a nagging sensation in my head. The sense of importance, of urgency, was growing. I could feel my mind sliding towards fight and flight. Sliding towards an all-too-familiar state. It was going to grow until it had all the implacable energy of a panic attack, only instead of inviting paralysis, it would be inciting action.

First thing, I reminded myself, *you don't fight this by staying calm.* Resolving to stay calm under the coming hurricane of feelings was impossible. Like putting all your fireworks in a huge box, lighting them at the same time, and then resolving to catch them as they came out. *No,* I thought, *what I have to do is point myself in a constructive direction.*

With that imperative to action, my only real option was to act. A bit of planning beforehand, while that was a thing I could do, and I thought I might be able to launch myself at something appropriate. Or at least not inappropriate. Or at least neutral.

Shattering Bowline into an inactive pulp struck me as a decent use of my time. The people at the top of that company were clearly rampant, fully resourced psychopaths that needed to be stopped. Thing was, as strategies go, 'hulk smash' is fine when fighting large monsters, but rather useless in attacking corporate structures, or pitting oneself against distributed, equipped, forewarned, badass military targets. That was a more of a political operation, requiring allies to be found and cultivated for a coordinated legal process.

I wasn't really fit for anything that required me to be near another person. Men incensed me, and I couldn't bear having the 'Feral' reaction around women. The thought of presenting some kind of threat to the six (seven? ...where was Natalie's aunt?) women in the main house was sickening.

What were the parameters of that reaction? How near did they have to be to cause problems? The only situations I'd experienced this effect had been in very close proximity. If I didn't have to smell people, I suspected the reaction would be much closer to manageable. Still, that ruled out essentially all city life, and the vast majority of farm life. I needed a task fit for a hermit. A lifestyle that could be obtained by an officially dead man, who was nevertheless being simultaneously hunted by the mob and the Man.

I thought about just going bush. Walking out of the farmland, and into something a bit wilder. Of embracing the primal aspect of my situation and simply roving and hunting. The main problem with that plan, as far as I could see it, is that just because I had a huge impulse to assume I was the biggest and baddest thing out there, and that I could hunt successfully, there was no reason to really believe it. Lions have to be taught how to pull down prey, and even in my delusions, I didn't put myself in that category. It would be easy to imagine going bush, and then getting very, very cold after getting caught in a storm. Then a chest infection. Or finding that it's hard to kill what you can't find.

Imagine the lifestyle in more detail. Catching a rabbit in the morning with cunning or speed. Then you have a rabbit in your hand. Do you know how to gut it? Do you carry a knife to gut it? (Flintknapping? I don't think so.) Once you have a skinned, gutted rabbit in your hand, do you eat it raw? Do you know how to make fire? Did you take a flint and steel? Is it getting worn out? Is that wood and bark dry enough? To top it all off, that's your new body's idea of an appetiser. With your brave new metabolism, you'll want to find several more of them to get to lunch.

Maybe that was a clue as to why this 'feature set' is deprecated in the phenotype of modern homo sapiens.

So my absolute best available option was something like heavy work farmhand. Will work for food and board. Specifically, lots of food, but a remote little shack would do for board. That would give me the ability to sponge a little off civilisation, without ever really interacting with another human.

None of the viable possibilities sounded remotely attractive. All of them sounding empty and unbearably lonely. Which, I reflected was nothing new, as I'd felt so lonely since... *No. No, no, nope, nopey nope. Look at the cows.* The cows had started settling again, since the excitement when the humans came through.

I watched the cows for some time, naming them and learning/inventing their stories and their ways, until they settled on the ground and fell asleep. Somewhere in that process, so did I, dry in my hay hammock, and washing my brain in the white noise of the hammering rain.

SOMETIME IN THE NIGHT, the rain stopped, and a thick, white fog came in. The cows left early, except for Wilma and Louise, who just lay there amicably.

I woke with a pounding heart and a raging erection that wouldn't go away. Physically, I felt better, but I couldn't trust my altered instincts in the slightest. Instincts that tended to get one thrown through windows of exploding buildings. So I looked as best I could at my injuries. It was unfortunate that the worst one was behind me, but I felt it out carefully with stretching. I was slow, but this time it didn't reopen. Major progress.

In the fog, I could barely make out the outline of the house. I wondered if anyone was up. I wondered what the time was. Why wasn't anyone up yet? Why was I expecting to see them when I already told them I couldn't? I wondered what the time was. If I listened carefully, would I be able to hear anyone? The time, what was it?

The thoughts just kept looping around my brain. I was bouncing out of my skin, and I wasn't even up to full speed yet. *I'm not going to go insane over a few months. I'm actually going to go insane today,* I thought. I couldn't think of anything to do while in the barn, or at least nothing that was appropriate in front of Wilma and Louise.

There were other farm buildings. I investigated. Bare feet on the icy mud quickly became so cold they were itchy, but urgency kept me going. I discovered a woodshed, stashed full of logs. At a quick guess, there were maybe twenty cubic metres of wood in there. At more than a tonne per cubic metre. There were also spare gumboots, and a block splitter. Heaven!

Woodchopping has always been one of my favourite chores. It contains brute force destruction, which is always fun, but also rewards the acquisition of skill. Landing the blade where you aim is hard, and splitting the blocks with a few well placed blows requires you to read the wood grain carefully. I briefly considered keeping the job in reserve for the coming few days, when I might *really* need it, but life being short and unpredictable, I set up one of the larger pieces to use as a chopping block. I told myself that it's only possible to keep sane tomorrow if you stay sane today.

Later, George came with another basket. She even approached from downwind, which meant she had to come the long way around. I appreciated the effort, although in the end it didn't save any embarrassment. I had to place the axe handle strategically, which I tried to do casually.

"How are you doing?" she asked. She didn't sound afraid of me, but she was obviously somewhat apprehensive.

"This is good," I said, indicating the growing pile of split wood ready for the hearth.

She didn't reply, and after a while I addressed the heart of her question: "It's happening as expected. Think I'm healing well, but I'm going to need isolation. Can't imagine that would be easy under normal circumstances. With all this going on..."

"We were up arguing and planning half the night," she said. "Talked out every plan we could invent. Everything from throwing ourselves and our story at the media, to trying to assassinate the bastards ourselves."

"And?"

"And on inspection, every plan was deeply, deeply, stupid. We'd likely end up dead at the end of every single one."

"Yeah," I drawled.

George sighed and looked down at the basket she was carrying. "Should I just put this here?"

"Thanks," I said, and she did. It was a heavy basket, which was very interesting.

"Which plan was your favourite?" I asked.

George looked a little dubious, and then: "Acknowledging that there were no viable options from anyone..."

There was a long pause while she waited for a response.

"Yes, go on."

"Therefore you are not allowed to trash my plan," she insisted.

"Fair enough," I agreed.

"OK," she said. "I wanted to find some drug dealer kingpin or some other mobster, go in guns blazing, take their cash, and then run away and assume new identities." She looked at me, hands on hips.

"You did not," I said.

"Yes I did, I wanted us to be a cross between masked vigilantes, thugs, and Robin Hood."

I giggled. "Any takers?"

"Nope. They thought I was taking the piss."

"They do all seem pretty clued-in for a bunch of randos," I said.

"Yeah," she agreed. "Did you have any bright ideas?"

"Not really," I said. "I've got the same constraints as you six in that I'm recognisable, hunted and bankrupt. Plus also, I basically have to stay away from all human contact and purpose." I came over a little black for a moment, and I think George spotted it. My voice wavered just a little. "So all I need is a life of hermit-level manual labour until I can't use that to distract myself any more and I go play in traffic."

"You mean," she corrected, "then you sign up for my masked super-antihero project."

"Only if I get to be 'Robbin' Pat' and I can call you 'Little George'", I replied.

She smiled a little, and gave a flick of a wave. "See you this arvo," she said, then she turned and left.

A grin twitched on my face, and then I started to fidget as an urge to cry welled up suddenly. In solitude, I managed to let a little out quietly, and reduced a few more tonnes of logs to convenient firewood.

Later, when I was ready for a moment to sit, I found breakfast, morning tea and first lunch all in the basket. As I chewed through the hand-thick slices of black salami, I wondered how the Valkyries were going to work out their differences. Would they even all have to choose the same option? Some of the crazier plans could potentially mix-and-match. For example, one or more could go to the press, or a trustworthy branch of law enforcement, while the others ran and hid in case it all went horribly wrong. I supposed that in the worst case scenario it would be possible to hide more or less indefinitely.

The sandwiches ran out as I contemplated that outcome. Staying that far under the radar would only be possible if they were completely out of the system. I supposed that there are plenty of homeless people in the world, and I knew that many of them ate regularly. Not that I'd met one that seemed happy. Hell of a life to choose.

I grunted to myself in the chill air, and a small plume of white puffed in front of my face. Going off the grid might not seem pleasant, but I agreed with George's summary: anyone going to the press or the law would most likely end up dead. Though at least it *did* come with the promise of at least causing some damage to Bowline's operations.

Not that I cared in the least about the fate of an abstract corporate entity. Personally, I wanted trouble to land on the people responsible. People who, as I stood in the mud in a paddock somewhere, I couldn't even pick out of a crowd. Placing the basket back down reluctantly, I thought briefly about what I might be able to prove in a hostile court, and became increasingly depressed.

Even if I couldn't think of a non-extreme option for me, maybe the others had compromise options in between homelessness and justice. Could the Valkyries live on the fringes of their old lives? For example, we were all living off the good nature of Natalie's aunt. Maybe some of the others had similar connections they could use. Hide on the edge of their old networks until the heat was off. How long might that be? Definitely many years. Possibly a decade? I didn't know. I wouldn't bet my life on it, and certainly not anyone else's life.

But maybe the others didn't see the odds the same way. Not that I had to consider that option myself. Exile was the only option I had. Apart from Not Exile, which felt like one of those options that made sense, but I wasn't sure I could ever bring myself to taking the long walk off the short plank. I supposed I would find out, over time.

The conversation with George had gone better than I'd expected. The physical distance and open air helped a lot. Maybe I could make myself appear fit for human contact over videoconference or chat. If I had a legal identity, maybe there were jobs I could do. Getting a legal identity would require justice, though. Or, if the genie grants three wishes, a large cash supply and a black market that by some luck wasn't connected to the parts of the underworld that wanted me dead or recaptured.

Was there a way to make justice stick? It would presumably need more direct evidence than putative written laboratory notes by the defendants. That would require... getting it? Getting close to the relevant people somehow? And if they were all in jail, and their misdeeds part of public record, what would stop someone stepping into that power vacuum, and seeing the survivors as a resource?

With that thought, and a full stomach, I restarted my transformation into Patrick Forestbane. The splitter landed more and more where I tried to put it, and I was starting to judge the strength of the blows more accurately. Cows came. The first cow wandered over to see what I was doing, and the others just followed the first, I think. After a while, I had a ring of heads facing me, maybe twenty metres distant, all watching idly as they chewed damp grass. Most of them wandered off again over the course of the next few hours, but there was always one or two keeping me company.

As the day was getting late, Alannah came to visit. She stayed well back, and replaced the picnic basket with a large Tupperware box.

"Any decision yet?" I asked.

"Would you testify in court?" she asked.

I laughed. "Unless I were dead, or kidnapped again, sure." I tried to picture the scene, if we somehow made it to the courtroom. In front of the Bowline lawyers, who would presumably know everything incriminating about my past, and how sensitive I'd be to rage. "Although I probably wouldn't be the world's most credible witness. Maybe I could take some of them with me, though. Is that the plan?"

Alannah looked surprised, and then thoughtful. And then frustrated. "No it wasn't. You're right, we can't use you for that. We can't think of how you fit in to any of our plans, really."

"Excuse me for not being the convenient kind of victim," I said, hackles rising a little. Telling myself that her frustration was just mirroring my own helped me shake off those kinds of thoughts. Post-Patrick being who he was, though, it wasn't long before I needed to place the axe handle strategically again. It was humiliating, which was infuriating, which was childish and embarrassing, which made me want to blame Alannah and the others, which was almost exactly wrong. My head hurt.

I sat down to massage my temples, which also made my discretion much easier to manage.

"Sorry, I didn't mean it like that," Alannah reassured me, "we don't know what to do with ourselves, either. To answer your original question, no we haven't come to any kind of decision yet. In fact, we might be about to agree to disagree."

I raised my head, and couldn't keep my voice credulous. "What on earth does that mean? Everyone wants to try something different?"

"Not quite everyone, but yeah. Kirsten and Brooke want to go to their embassies, and contact their families. They've probably got the best chance of not being infiltrated or corruptible by Bowline, but I strongly doubt that diplomatic sanctions will protect them sufficiently from Bowline's operations or their apolitical connections. Kirsten feels differently, because, well, you know how strange Americans can be when it comes to their government and military stuff."

I waved my hand. "They still get all that indoctrination stuff at school. You can't fight your childhood."

"Brooke doesn't have the same excuse, but I think she just doesn't really believe that Bowline would *dare* cross that line."

I thought about it for a second. The British High Consulate didn't post any threat I could imagine for Bowline. At least, not one that they hadn't risked a hundred times over already. "I'm not sure they're susceptible to *social* constraints at this point," I suggested.

"Exactly!" she agreed. "But she wants to risk it anyway."

I tried to think of the implications. "OK, so if Kirsten and Brooke go in, and the worst happens... Oh, Bowline will know everything about us to this point. They'll know about Natalie's aunt. We'll have to move at the same time."

"We will," agreed Alannah. "Although it probably won't come down on Natalie's aunt. Natalie lied to her thoroughly, and we're all here under false pretences. We couldn't stay indefinitely anyway. So if we go rapidly and steal some stuff when we do, she'll be pissed, but probably not used against us."

"You just said 'probably' twice," I pointed out.

"It's that kind of a world this week," said Alannah.

Fair enough, I thought. "So what do the rest of you want to do?" I asked.

"I'd rather go public and turn those fuckers in," said Alannah, "only I can't think how to do it in any way that sticks. Certainly not quickly. Most importantly, the only way I see it sticking is with real evidence, including our own eyewitness accounts. And I agree with you and George - we'd never live to deliver it. There's a reason I haven't just called my work contacts. Someone I've been trusting is crooked, and I don't know who. So anything we attempt legally is really just interference while we try to find some way to live."

I nearly pointed out that staying away from her old network forever would be a shitty life, trading away contact, visibility and connections to anyone you've ever known in return for a continuing heartbeat. But I heard myself just before my mouth got past the first 'sh'. "Sh..ould be possible to stay under the radar. If you commit to it. But it's time to stop planning in front of Kirsten and Brooke," I said.

Alannah's mouth hardened. "True. Anyway, the rest of us think we'd rather fight. One way or another. In order for us to win, I think it's necessary that Paul Adams and Bowline lose. We just can't agree what our best strategy looks like."

"Potentially stupid question: who's Paul Adams?" Maybe they'd told me about him over a meal, and I'd blanked on the name.

"Bowline CEO. It's a surprisingly small company, considering. And the whole thing is his. He was the guy I was trying to put into jail, back when, well, you know. He's a sandy-haired, blue-eyed, square-jawed, smiling, rich, popular, powerful and successful, utterly soulless vessel."

"Eight out of nine ain't bad," I suggested.

I got her - she snorted. My head hurt worse.

"I'd still like to see him reap a little of what he's sown."

"Really?" I asked. "Because he's effectively had a lot of people killed for personal gain. What's a fair price for that?"

Alannah didn't answer, but looking into her eyes for a moment, I thought I caught a glimpse of a momentous internal debate. I wondered if it would still suit her if she ever got a chance to return to law enforcement. She was definitely angry that this Paul Adams had put her in this position.

Personally, the only reluctance I felt towards a violent solution was largely artificial. A position I took just in case I ever regrew some kind of innocence. Also, I felt that bringing those kinds of plans to the table might scare the locals. Even the old part of me didn't, in all honesty, miss the feeling that civilised society required compromises in its justice system. But I did miss it for Alannah's sake.

"So," I asked, "is Paul Adams afraid of you? Is he worried by your freedom and existence?"

The question caught her a little by surprise. Alannah swallowed her immediate scoff, and then said: "I think so. We're a hell of a loose end."

"That means he has vulnerabilities. That means he'll be doing some very dangerous things trying to protect himself. That means your best option is to do the thing he'll dislike the most. Whatever causes him troubles without offering an option to respond."

"Like what?" she asked. Not unreasonably.

"Let me think about it?" I said.

"Sure," she said distractedly. "And we'll do the same."

Left with lunch, logs and my thoughts, I ate, chopped and chewed on them, respectively.

Becoming someone else is insidious. Most of the atoms we start with are gone after a while, but we still think of ourselves as the same person. We imagine that the body changes, but the spirit stays the same. Thing is, the spirit changes too. I've known friends and family change in important ways over the years, and presumably I have too.

Under all those changes, it always felt like me, however. Mama's little boy, now a man.

Now a monster. By the afternoon, my headache and I had swapped places. My body was on fire. I felt physically amazing, and ready to move mountains by screaming at them. Even in the midst of it, I knew this sensation of strength was delusional, though I did finish the wood rather abruptly. A haze of desperation fell over the task, and the feeling never cleared, I simply ran out of task. I stacked the last of the firewood in the shed, and fetched the splitter and the chopping block. The splitter hung uselessly in my hand as I breathed deeply, dripping with sweat. I drank the last of the water, ate the last of the food, and paced like a caged animal. Specifically, a predator. My mind kept trying to latch onto something to serve as the Hunt. I seethed at my position, and found that I hadn't thought about strategies for hurting Bowline and avoiding consequences at all. The patience required to organise my thoughts had fled, and I cursed and paced until the Valkyries came.

They came with the rain. George, Alannah, Natalie and Lourdes came marching across the paddocks in mismatched gear. Alannah and Lourdes were wearing borrowed rain jackets that looked uncomfortably short, and George and Natalie, who were taller, were using the umbrellas. I was patrolling the woodshed, stinking it out with my sweaty body as I saw them. Nothing to do with their physical presence, even the simple sight of them approaching caused me to shudder with gut-clenching spasms. I'd tried to prepare for it, but how does one prepare to be overwhelmed? A dozen finely-differentiated shades of embarrassment warred for my attention, and I shoved them away. I hated what I'd become. I hated what I'd lost. The anger came far too easily as well.

During my days at Project Lycan, I'd felt that shame and that anger. Much of it was directed at my captors, but there was a substantial portion that focussed on myself. I knew how poisonous the self-loathing could be, and this time I did have a strategy in mind. I was not going to resist the anger. I was not going to try reassuring myself of my own value. That I still had purpose. For one thing, I do not believe the Buddha himself could swim against emotional currents that strong. For another, it may well be untrue. Maybe my value to the world had been effectively nullified.

My plan, such as it was, was to do the very least Buddhist thing I could imagine. I was going to focus on whose *fault* this all was. Direct the anger where it belonged. Away, and on the people who actually made the choices that led here. As I saw that spotted umbrella bobbing in the greying rain, I found this approach to be quite effective. Actually, the anger was better for keeping control.

They got closer, and I realised the woodshed was far too small. Especially this full of wood - splitting the logs had inevitably made them take up a little more space. The prospect of talking to them this close felt decidedly unsafe, not to mention the fact that I hadn't had a shower. On the other hand, I could hardly ask them to stand in the rain. Especially not with the meagre wet-weather gear they'd assembled.

Nothing for it. I pulled off my gumboots, and put them right at the edge of the space. My shirt was still dry, and not too funky, since I'd pulled it off as I warmed up. I left it in the corner to put on afterwards, and strode out into the rain.

The water was cold, and I shivered as it drenched my skin. I gave the women a wide berth, and gestured for them to head into the woodshed. Once inside, they shook off their umbrellas, and took off their dripping jackets. I prowled and paced in the gathering dusk outside.

"Didn't get much of a chance to think," I said. Having just spent hours by myself, this seemed absurd. Or sad. I fought through those thoughts, and noticed my teeth were not just gritted, they were bared. All four faces were watching me, noting the changes from earlier. I didn't see judgement, just anger. Same as mine, I supposed.

I could deal with anger, I hoped.

"Let us tell you where we landed then," said Alannah.

"Did you tell him what Brooke and Kirsten are planning?" asked Natalie. She was obviously taking it personally, and the thought that came into my mind from her posture was 'untamed'. I'd stepped a little closer before I turned my head up to the sky, and let it wash my face. My hair was sticky, and the point here, I thought, the *point*, is that we were trying to figure out how to survive, and that Brooke and Kirsten might be about to *die*.

"Yes," said Alannah and I together. The rain on the woodshed roof was loud, but my hearing was a lot sharper than I remembered.

"Think they're wrong," I said. "Hope not."

"Right," said Natalie, "except there's just no way they'll be safe. And we have no right to stop them. So we've decided to use them as bait."

Alannah interjected. "That's one of the things we're going to do. I thought about what you said: doing the things he least wants us to do. He'll be expecting legal attacks and possibly physical attacks. He'll be planning to discredit us, kill us, kidnap us or threaten us. He'll be hiding everything against investigation, and pulling in favours to make sure it has blind spots. He'll be beefing up security. He'll be hoping we underestimate his reach... like I'd do that again! Anyway, he wants us to put ourselves somewhere vulnerable without revealing too much that he can't cover up."

Natalie took over again with a kind of relish. "So we're not going to give them a target at all. We're not coming forward, we're not giving testimony, and we're not going to try to support any kind of due process against Bowline. We're just going to do a complete data dump of almost everything we have, and everything Alannah had stashed for the trial. Redacting only the parts that might help people recreate their research. We're going to give it to everyone, at all levels, simultaneously. Police, federal agencies, media, bloggers. Maybe nothing will come of it, but maybe someone or some group will step up. Mostly reveals like that just drown in process and apathy, and the public react how they're told, but sometimes these things hit a kind of tipping point. You never know."

"The fun part," Natalie continued, "is that we'll do this anonymously and disappear. That will look like our strategy. Kirsten and Brooke will present to their embassy and high commission respectively. Bowline will almost certainly go for them, and we will get our hands on whomever does that. Then we see if that can be exploited. Physically, we'll do to them exactly what they expect to do to us."

I wanted to do it. It was insane. "We can't win a war against these people," I said. "They are experts with world-class technology."

Alannah shook her head. "We don't have the ability to outgun them. But we're not planning on fighting. We're also not going to make demands, rush to any particular timetable, show our faces or even ever talk to them. They'll be under siege from the outside world, and our existence will be entirely abstract. They are the ones with houses and offices and political constraints. They're the ones with something left to lose."

I frowned at that, and stopped pacing for a moment. "You have something to lose, believe me," I said.

Lourdes spoke up: "That's only half true. If we slink away, we really do have nothing. If we put our heads up, we believe they'll be promptly chopped off. So if we're right, then breaking Bowline utterly is actually the only option we have."

Natalie went to say something, and then apparently thought the better of it. Alannah looked at George.

"George?" I asked, "What's your view?"

She spoke steadily. "The data dump stuff is an easy choice. Lourdes can handle the technical aspects given access to a library or a café, and between them, she and Alannah can plan the distribution pattern. Keeping our heads down is obvious. I want more than homelessness and barrel fires out of the next however many years, however. I want justice, and for that, we'll need some resources. I like the idea of taking them from the people who we expect to come for Kirsten and Brooke. But," she said, and she said it kinda quietly, "I think we're going to have a much better chance with you on board."

"Huh," I said. Then I gestured to my position out in the rain. "This is about as on board as I can manage. Don't get me wrong, I'm not worried about the risk. Just don't think I can make decisions around other people."

"Thought you might say that," she said, "which is why I've been thinking that we should go visit Penny Whitman."

Chapter 7

PENNY FOR YOUR THOUGHTS

I didn't bother asking, I just waited.

"Penny Whitman," said George, "is the consultant they brought in to develop the customised drug concoctions to try to make the male subjects effective."

"Who, as I recall," I said carefully, "was also designing addictive combinations to help condition and control you."

Lourdes interjected. "There are very few lab notes of Whitman's, she kept her thinking and planning very close to the chest. But just reading what there is, it seems like she pulled back in the last month or two. Before that, the drug cocktails were being adapted every few days. Then the notes just say something about a 'long-term test', and the regime doesn't change. Best-case interpretation, the timing suggests she may have gotten cold feet."

I was not filled with a sudden urge to trust her. "Employees that maybe perhaps had coldish feet are not therefore our friends and allies," I replied.

Alannah knew more. "Penny Whitman may have been contracted by Bowline, but she certainly isn't one of theirs. In fact, she's one of the most famous sellers of drugs in the entire world. Despite that, she's got a perfectly clean record. She's never had the slightest run-in with the legal system."

That struck me as odd: "How can she be so hard to catch if she's so visible?"

"That's a complicated story, and I'd have to check the details with people I can't contact right now," Alannah said, "but essentially, she has a unique angle that leaves her virtually immune to charges of possession. She owns a small pharmaceuticals company, and she rarely actually manufactures illegal substances. Certainly not in any quantity. Her deal is that she crafts unique drug regimes for each client, adapting according to their needs. She combines drugs to produce specific effects, cycles them to avoid dependencies and tolerances, and charges like a personal guru. As I understand it, her client list is quite narrow, and if you have any interest at all in what she charges per client, then you can't afford it, and probably never will."

"I wonder if Paul Adams was a client before he brought her in to deal with us," I said out loud.

"Maybe. She was never contracted officially by Bowline, but they did suddenly give her company an absolutely astoundingly large subcontract to research an improvement to one of Bowline's own stimulants. Given those things haven't changed in decades, it was almost certainly a way to pay Whitman for something else."

"While writing it off on tax," added Lourdes.

"Well, her involvement certainly makes sense from Bowline's point of view. Sounds like she was perfect for the job," I said. "Pity it didn't work."

"I've got an odd feeling about that," said Lourdes. "From the way the tests changed just as there was a reported uptick in task focus. I think maybe she had ideas she never used."

I shook my head. "Those things you had me on might

have kept me mellow, but I think being blown up had as much to do with that," I said. "The stuff they had me on in Project Lycan made it a little easier to learn things, but I was still strictly isolated the whole time. It's hard enough standing out here in the rain right now. Don't think there was a drug that ever would have let me help out on your other crazy plans."

It was a bit of a stretch to say that I was 'standing' in the rain. I'd worn noticeable muddy gouges in a little line of the green paddock as I paced and jogged on the spot.

"Plus," I added, "an 'odd feeling' is hardly enough of a basis to trust our lives to revealing our presence to a Bowline contractor!"

"Good point!" said Natalie triumphantly. It sounded like she'd been against that part of the plan. "Shockingly dangerous idea, and I don't think we should go anywhere near there."

Alannah sounded like she was repeating an argument they'd been looping on for some time: "We're planning a combination of espionage and break-in theft. The point isn't to do any trusting. We're just betting on her having something useful in her own notes, and we need to restock on the things we know we need anyway."

Before Natalie could continue her side, I tried to bring in my concerns: "I wouldn't have thought pharmaceutical supplies or manufacturers would be too lightly defended. Seems like an obvious target for all sorts of attacks. From wanna-be drug lords to actual drug lords. Not to mention the fact that if she's got her own illegal angle, then there'll be extra layers of vigilance. What have you got that everybody else doesn't?"

Alannah smiled, and I was minded of those older faerie stories where you find that the 'fey' had a rather bloodthirstier reputation than modern versions of pixies and nymphs. "We've got no constraints. We don't need bulk materials, we don't need our visit to be undetected, and we don't need to follow any laws. We can smash through obstacles using military force, and only worry about obtaining personal quantities of drugs. We can totally avoid the main stores."

Natalie scoffed. "Still too much that can go wrong. Don't see it's worth the risk."

Lourdes sounded dark. "That's because your withdrawals haven't started yet."

Alannah added. "In terms of risk management, it gives us a better chance of having Patrick available for the guaranteed military-level opponents we'll meet when trying to protect Kirsten and Brooke."

THE CONVERSATION WOUND on without approaching a firm resolution. The prospect of accessing a drug that would let me tag along was very attractive, but I had to agree with Natalie about the unreasonable risks to everyone involved. Apparently, dealing with their own short term dependency issues was also a major goal of that plan, but it was hard for me to judge the importance of that element. I'd read about the intensity of withdrawals from some of the more well-known addictive drugs, so it was concerning to imagine what might be experienced by someone going cold turkey from a mixture specifically designed to reinforce regular compliance.

Morally and intellectually, every other option also seemed fraught with its own dangers. If I'd been of a normal mindset, I might have refused everything point blank.

Instead, my whole being quivered with the call to action, to disregard consequence, and leap into the fray. This made it incredibly difficult to sustain multi-sentence arguments or comments, and most of my effort was spent on self-control.

Deep inside that, maybe my old self was thinking about the gloomy predictions I had made the previous day. Before my easily predictable descent into the storm. Those simple, logical arguments described the way my future had to unfold if I did the wise thing and stayed away from mad plans, and other obvious dangers. If my old self was still in there, then that defeated, grieving spirit had probably given up. Perhaps it was better to leap in and earn a quick death?

Regardless, I didn't voice any sustained resistance to their plans. Once I'd made my observations, I was happy to leave the decision-making to those with both the capacity, and a sane investment in the potential outcomes.

There was shouting, and it wasn't mine. The four of them seemed determined to reach a consensus decision, however. I got the sense that they weren't going to split off into even smaller groups.

After an amount of time I could neither measure nor guess, the rain ebbed to a drizzle, and the drizzle went away. Paradoxically, I felt damper and more miserable after the rain stopped. Perhaps it was the mud, or the quiet. Or perhaps the anticlimax of the ending of the rainstorm. I don't think the debaters in the woodshed felt it at all. As the sky grew dark and starless, and the moon shone weakly through a thick cloud, I excused myself and went for a light run before retiring.

"Decide what you like, I'm prepared to try anything that stands a chance of helping. Just remember I'm serious when I talk about my limitations. I can't do people without trouble."

With that, I saluted them and ran off into the night. Away from the house lights, my eyes adjusted very slowly, but adjusted a long way. I saw well enough to find my way to the top of the nearby hills and a little beyond. There I saluted the cloud-burred moon, and let some of my inner demons weep and cry out, far from where Wilma and Louise would shame them.

MORNING BROKE, and to balance that out, I felt healed. Physically, at least. I slipped out of my hay-walled bivouac into a thick mist. It was cold, after dawn, and the cows were inside, all still lying down. Those were all the clues I had regarding the time, when there was a commotion down at the farmhouse.

There was an eerie echo of the feeling I had when I woke to find the doors open back in the Project Lycan compound, which was odd, given that almost no aspect of the situation seemed comparable. Maybe it was just the parallel sense that I should be ready for action. There were muffled shouts of instructions, and doors slamming. I approached warily, and George loomed out of the white in front of me. I flinched a little, and backed up until she was just a ghostly silhouette.

"Brooke and Kirsten got nervous about something they half-overheard, and they've already gone," she explained, sounding much closer. "Left us the van, so depending on how far they go on foot, they might be some time. They left a note saying they'd be very careful not to reveal themselves on the way."

"Why did they feel nervous?" I asked. "Did they feel

threatened by something?" It came out much more coherent than I felt.

"It seems they think we're about to do something stupid, get caught, and bring the crazy down on all of us," she replied. "So they're slipping into what they see as protection before this place becomes compromised. Pretty much the exact thing we have to do now, for exactly the same reasons."

"I see," I said. The sounds made a little more sense.

"So you're loading the van?"

George's silhouette nodded. "Most of the stuff we left Lycan with was loaded already, so we'll be off in a few minutes. If any of us make any kind of mistake, this place will indeed become a trap. We're all going to have to go now."

I nodded, presumably visible as a ghost in the mist to her.

"*You're* going to have to leave too," she added. Then, almost shyly, "and we were thinking you might decide to come with us."

I couldn't. But I couldn't stay. So I'd have to leave by foot, just like the other two. Could I maybe ask for a map before I did? I still didn't have ideas for where I'd go or what I'd do, but I'd start with away. I opened my mouth to tell her, and said: "How? How would I...?"

"I was thinking you could drive, and we could be in the back. We daren't use phones in case we trigger the communications monitors, but we have short range comms gear in the packs. So we'd be separate, and you wouldn't have to do anything but be up the front by yourself. But you could come..."

The little hopeful tone. She wasn't pleading, but this was clearly what George wanted. As stupid as it was to head cityward in a van, I found myself weak in the moment. I'd lost everything that ever mattered to me, but the thought of turning and running off into the hills made me feel hollow.

"OK," I said. "Call me when you're ready."

And then I did turn and run off. Only it was to retrieve the blankets, smooth the hay back, and do one-armed chin-ups until my head cleared a little.

THE CALL CAME VERY QUICKLY, although sense of time has never been a strength of mine. Certainly, my head had *not* achieved anything resembling clarity. "Ready!" shouted George, and she banged on the van door. By the time I jogged back, the back of the van was closed, and the front door was open. On the seat was a cap with a long peak, some sunglasses, and small device that looked a little like an earpiece. I put it in, and a small chime sounded.

"Hello driver," said Lourdes, her accent a thick parody of English royalty. "Please take us to the library carpark as indicated by the satellite navigation device." I glanced at the dash, and the route was already loaded.

"Can you hear me as well?" I asked, in a normal voice.

"Yes," came four voices at once.

It was a little like having them in my head. Under my breath, I muttered: "What about when we just mumble crazily to ourselves?"

"Yes," came four voices at once.

"Doesn't that get a bit much after a while?"

"Yes," came four voices at once.

Then Natalie added: "I've learned to just face how crazy they all are. You shouldn't feel especially judged, just because you're a man, and you came late to the party."

"I shouldn't?" I asked dubiously.

"Yeah," said Lourdes. "That will just make you really self-conscious, and it won't help you in the slightest."

I started the van, but couldn't find the handbrake. After the engine had been idling for half a minute, Alannah's voice in my head said "it's the button on the dash marked 'P'."

"Thanks," I said, and realised that despite their sarcasm, Lourdes and Natalie were literally right. It was best to put it out of my mind, to whatever extent that might be possible.

"Damn straight," said Lourdes.

Did I say something out loud? I was sure I hadn't, but the possibility kept me distracted for at least half the drive.

The country roads were winding and empty, and I found them pleasantly mesmerising, much like the chopping the day before. Panic and urgency came up in waves, but it felt good to be on the move. To be acting rather than holding myself passive. After an hour we reached the highway, and I faced my first real challenge. Traffic. I had my cruise control set to two kilometres per hour over the speed limit, and every time someone passed, I felt a wave of road rage sweep over me. I imagined their smug assumptions about how slow and pathetic I was, about how I might have time to potter along, but *their* trip was important, and *their* time was valuable.

Road rage had never been a particular bugbear of my previous life. I'd experienced anger and frustration like anyone else, but my parents and instructors had modelled good habits, discussing their emotions as well as the technical aspects of driving. So it took something particularly egregious to upset me, and even then I had plenty of practice in calming back down. I'd seen spectacular examples of road-induced insanity, though. I'd seen people speed in front of tailgaters and slam on their brakes. I'd seen drivers flash their high beams on right at passing cars, and speed angrily past people that caused them the inconvenience of having to drop out of cruise control.

This time, every car I encountered felt like the last straw. Assailed by virtually unstoppable urges to mimic all of that madness, I hissed in frustration. Several times it was only my fierce desire to keep out of the attention of any police that forced me to stay in my lane. I must have been muttering a lot. Once, Alannah tried to calm me verbally, but I snapped back. Then, focussing as hard as I could, I took a deep breath, and asked her to let me manage it in my own way, in silence. She complied, but it was still difficult.

The towns were the worst. Down at the ludicrously slow speeds, with cars in front of me making arbitrary and dangerous decisions, my control wore thin. After a couple of them, the return to the highway was comparatively pleasant. In a small way, I felt I was actually improving with practice, although I was also becoming quite weary. After inquiring about snacks, I learned that what I'd assumed was a toolbox was actually my morning tea and first lunch. After that, things went noticeably more smoothly.

A couple of hours later, we passed through our fourth medium-sized town. This was the one with the library marked on the GPS, and I managed to park the large van in the designated carpark. There was a sound at the back of the van, and someone jumped out. Lourdes approached in the side mirror. She was also wearing an oversized cap and large sunglasses, and had a backpack over one shoulder. She also seemed to have something in her cheeks, as they puffed out a little more than normal.

"Is that..." I asked.

She touched something in her ear under her cap, and

then I heard her. "Just a little tweak to mess with facial recognition," she said. "I'm all prepped up now, but give me about half an hour to upload - there's still a lot of data. I'm hoping it won't be possible to track where these mails come from, but just in case, this is a burner site - we're not using this again. Plus, I'm going to be sitting in the library, but using the free wifi from the coffee shop. If they do track, I hope that gets them all sorts of confused."

The comment about facial recognition made me pull the cap down a little lower, and then I remembered the sandwich I'd been afraid to eat one-handed. That took my attention for a little longer. With the windows up I didn't smell the town or the people, but I saw the occasional stranger passing by. It felt like they were all looking at me, judging me. My heart seemed to skip when anyone made even brief eye contact. Each felt like an urgent challenge, and it took great willpower to keep myself from visibly reacting. It was maddening and frenzy-making, and yet simultaneously it was also utterly draining. It would have been a lot more tolerable if the exhaustion had mellowed the hysteria in any way, but instead I just kept feeling like I was being stretched closer to breaking point.

"How you holding up?" asked George in my ear.

"You've been awfully quiet the last couple of hours," I said. Which was true, but quite unfair, given the way I'd spoken to Alannah.

"We've been chatting on another channel," she said. "Didn't want to disturb you."

I felt a little odd about that. Was it possible to want to be left alone while still feeling excluded? Evidently so.

"It's hard," I said. "Need to get out and get away soon."

"We can't rent a hotel anyway," replied George. "They nearly all want credit card impressions, and we don't have enough cash. We're going to be stretched just keeping ourselves in food and petrol for much longer. So the plan is to camp by a river tonight."

"That sounds good," I agreed. Then, as my manners kicked in belatedly, "and how about you? Cramped back there?"

"You have no idea," she said. "But we've gotta stay out of sight as much as possible. Looking forward to stretching my legs as well."

My legs were the least of my worries, but I didn't want to complain. At least I could see.

A lady with two screaming kids who were whining loudly about not getting to have ice creams struggled past, her country clothes and styles reminding me of my childhood. Lourdes in my ear: "OK, all done. Let me get back in, and we'll head out of town via the petrol station. Put some distance between us and the delivery point, in case all that palaver was not as clever as I think it was."

Two minutes later she slipped into the van, and we moved out. We made an odd loop before the petrol station so it looked like we were travelling the other way to the cameras. None of us had any idea if the footage would ever be seen, but once again, better safe than sorry.

Three hours later, I pulled off the freeway. Forty minutes after that the road was dirt. Fifteen minutes after that, we pulled up in a campsite that was a stone's throw from a river. I jumped out, and found that my legs were stiffer than I thought. I raced down to the water to check it out. There was a campsite, but we didn't have tents. There were bivouac kits, however, sort of glorified sleeping bags that could go straight on the ground. The plan was to find somewhere under shelter to set them up, so that they could be packed away dry.

The river itself was more of a creek, with multiple little waterways winding across a boulder-filled, rocky stream bed, with gently rising eucalyptus-filled bushland on either bank. There was a waterfall a little downstream, and the carpark above was well positioned for picnic goers who wished to splash in the myriad little freshwater pools.

Leaping over the water on the rocks was pleasant. In a childish exploration mode, I located some boulders that made a viable lean-to, and some scooped out rocks on the side of the river. The water clearly went a lot higher sometimes. I relayed this back to the others, and they instructed me to return the earpiece for charging, and pick up my bivvy and dinner.

They were left on a wide, flat rocky area, well away from where Natalie was setting up their own bivvies. The food box had considerable heft, and I realised that I was starving. Again, it was odd being treated like a slightly wild creature, somewhere between a pet and a threat. Even if it were at my own request.

I grabbed the box and bag, and went to my little cave upriver. Being cooped up in the van had left me very edgy, and suppressing my reaction in the town had left me deeply agitated. I thought I was going to have to work off a little restless energy, but I found that in the quiet of the light eucalyptus forest, and the gentle murmuring of the water itself, my eyes grew unexpectedly heavy. I lay down for a moment, and then woke, cold, in the dark. I ate again, and slipped into the bivvy bag. I was heavy, the night was light, and the water carried my dreams away downstream.

Chapter 8

CASH AND TROUBLE

I woke after dawn, after what felt like a very long, very important sleep. Straining my ears, I couldn't hear anything from the other camp, but we'd deliberately picked a distance where that would be hard. Packing up, I thought I smelled something. I couldn't quite identify it, but my hind-brain felt strongly that it would like to try eating it. I followed the compulsion downstream, skipping over the water. As I moved from rock to rock, I found myself trying to do it quickly, but silently. In a minute, I was a hunter, stalking his prey. Padding quietly on the smooth rocky expanses, I felt the huge drive thundering through my head once more. The new 'normal' madness. So why was it tinged with nostalgia?

Intellectually, I knew that being a hunter was just a game. My gut did not. It came to me then. This sense of ill-defined importance had a strong flavour of the childhood games from the school playground. Or compelling escapist fantasies I would create as a child when left to my own devices. They would sometimes get quite elaborate, as I slipped past the trees of another world.

Creeping along the river, self-awareness was no defence against the instinct that it was important to arrive unseen. Maybe these hammering drives were a new kind of immaturity? The movie trailer voiceover rang in my head: Puberty 2: Puberty from Hell. Revenge of Puberty: The first one was just *practice*!

Peering around the corner, I spied three of the Valkyries staring at a huge pot that was heating on a compact camp burner. The smell was coming from that, and at this range I could tell it contained oats. That was the slightly nutty smell of porridge. With honey and cinnamon, no less.

My eyes saw movement far further downstream, near the bottom of the waterfall. I thought I saw a little flicker of naked flesh. I pulled my head back. Lourdes was obviously using the river as a convenient method of getting clean. I took a deep breath. The porridge was going to taste delicious. Now that the info and accusations on Bowline had been leaked to the media, the public and law enforcement agencies, what were we going to do today? There was a small list of options, and they wanted to do them all. Which made sense to do next? Why weren't any of these questions stopping me from thinking about a one second flash of possibly naked flesh a hundred metres away? How could I possibly get myself into a presentable state to go have breakfast?

Looking down at the bivvy kit and food box in my hands, I sighed. Arranging them carefully once more, I came round the corner.

"That smells great," I called out. "Could smell that right upstream!"

A gentle breeze was coming right down the valley, in fact. My stomach grumbled.

Alannah and George looked up as Natalie kept stirring,

and then switched off the burner. I fancied that they were waiting to see how close I would come. *Probably not*, I thought again. *They're probably thinking about their own troubles.*

"I, ah, need to go have a quick cleanup," I said. "Leave me some brekkie here with the empty bowls? And I'll wash up."

Turning, I placed the bivvy bag and food box in sight, and then slipped away upstream/downwind again. This time I went further, until I found my own little pool that was deep enough to submerge in. After stripping, I went to the edge and put my foot in. The water felt painfully icy. Unable to make myself go deeper, I was stuck standing ankle deep for at least a minute, a chilly breeze giving me goosebumps all over my body. After that minute, I slowly became aware of the fact that my feet themselves felt OK, and the main cold sensation was the small ring around each ankle that marked the water line. Figuring that it might therefore be better in than out, I resolved to jump in.

Insanity induced by epigenetic treatments might have explained that piece of stupidity. Unfortunately, the decision to jump in did seem more or less in character from before Project Lycan, so it may have been something more fundamentally wrong with my brain. The shock from the freezing water paralysed me in a way that George's tranquilliser darts never did. I couldn't move, I couldn't breathe. Every muscle in my body tried to flinch away from the cold at once, and I became rigid. If the pool had been deeper, maybe I would have sunk. As it was, it was all I could do to hold my nose above water by standing on tiptoes. After several attempts to reboot functionality, I managed to get my arms and legs working on an escape plan. The side of the rock turned out to be a lot more slippery where it had been touching water, so I needed to part wade and part swim over to a different spot to get out.

Possibly cleaner, and definitely wiser, I staggered back to my clothes, and did jumping jacks in the breeze to dry off and warm up. The traditional 'cold shower' had indeed helped straighten out my head and distract me from socially unacceptable thoughts. After a few minutes, I deemed myself as dry as I was going to get, and wrestled back into my single set of borrowed clothes.

Slinking back to the campsite, I found a large tupperware bowl of porridge waiting, and it was even still slightly warm in the middle. There was also a thermos with some hot tea, and it really hit the spot. Wary, I still kept my distance, but enjoyed feeling a sense of campground camaraderie, however remotely, as I washed the dishes in the river water, dried, stacked, and packed them. I carried my small amount of gear up to the van, and gave the others some room to do the same by stretching over on the far side of the car park. When everyone was in, I rejoined the van, pulled myself into the driver's cabin, and put the earpiece back in my ear and the cap and glasses back on my head.

"Good morning," said George.

"Hi," I said. "So what's on the menu today?"

"Drive as we chat?" asked Alannah.

Either they were in a hurry, or they wanted my hands full because they thought I was going to be upset with the plan. It was, naturally, both.

Pulling out of the carpark, I sent a mental goodbye to the river. Then it was up the hill through the forest on the fire trail.

"So, we have to make some timing assumptions," Alannah started. "As soon as Kirsten and Brooke are discovered, the clock starts ticking. How long does it take them to assemble a strike? We're guessing about a day. If that's right, then we'd better be ready by tomorrow night, or maybe even by tonight. We also have no idea which one to go to first. So we don't know how to even be on the scene, and if we're not, our best guess is that our friends will die. That's some of the bad news."

I grunted, and Alannah continued. "More of the bad news: We're all pretty sure you're not going to be very functional until we get supplies from Penny Whitman's place. Even that is a bit of a long shot, so going there first is probably a mistake. Until then, we might be able to use you as a getaway driver?"

The last was definitely something she wasn't sure about, but I couldn't tell whether there was question in her mind about my capacity or my willingness. "Sure," I answered to both.

"Even more bad news: we're getting desperate for cash. We need a lot of it to operate off the radar, and we can't access any funds legally."

"Now," Alannah went on, and despite her careful choice of tone, I felt that she was working around to the part she thought I wasn't going to like, "there aren't many places that even have large amounts of cash - most transactions are cashless these days. So you might think that it's bank-robbing time or else we're sunk. However, did you know that even though less and less people are using it, there's a actually lot more cash in circulation than there ever was?"

"I did not," I answered.

"Well, there is. And the accepted reason is that there's a huge cash buildup in the black market. In organised crime. One of the long-term options governments have for controlling organised crime is to move the entire economy to a cashless one. Watch for where the outcry comes from, and you'll see who owns who."

"So," I said, trying to catch up, "you want to hit some mafia boss? Or drug lord? I'd be happy to take their money, but I can't see how we'd stand a snowflake's chance in hell. If we could even find them." I thought for a second. "Could you find them?"

"A couple of them," Alannah admitted, "but I agree that hitting one of those guys on their own turf would be suicide. But it got me to thinking - the whole black market is cash-based, right? So it stands to reason that a lot of the off-the-books sales and connections that Bowline has will be based on cash transactions. That could be why there was a fair chunk of change back at Project Lycan, but even if they have efficient laundering operations, they must still have literally many, many millions in notes somewhere."

The others were being conspicuously quiet. I had a feeling they knew where this was leading. "So do you know where those many, many millions might be held?"

"Not really, no. Although I could make some guesses. Plus I imagine they have unbelievable security there. Wouldn't dream of going for it."

I struggled with a smartarse response for a while, but finally resigned myself to being the straight man. "I'm hearing that you think there's a lot of cash being passed around, and you have some idea of where some relatively undefended fraction of it might be," I thought out loud.

"Probably not undefended, but something we could imagine getting to," Alannah replied. "I am prepared to bet that the bigwigs in this game have lots of cash personally that they aren't going to be depositing in banks and declaring."

"What, Wüster, Gannt and Adams?" I asked.

"Probably less Wüster and Gannt," she replied. "I was thinking the people more directly connected to the money side of things. Definitely Adams, but as an official billionaire, his security, in terms of personal security and property, is probably unbreakable. I was thinking of his right hand man, his head military advisor, Marc Hordones. He's a notorious womaniser, but he's not married. Lives alone in a huge mansion overlooking the harbour. There will be solid security there, but personal house kind of level, not troops. We're thinking burgle the place, and that both solves one of our main logistical problems, and strikes a minor blow for karma."

"That still sounds insane," I said. It did, didn't it? To be completely honest, I couldn't really tell any more. It sounded to me like an excellent, forward-momentum plan. One that our enemies would never suspect, and one that came with the probability of exciting action followed by success. And since I was insane, in precisely that sort of direction, that probably meant that the plan was also insane. And since I didn't want anyone else to know I was insane, that meant I had to disagree with the plan. My head was hurting again.

Natalie heard something of my true thoughts in my voice, though.

"He's up for it," she laughed, sounding relieved.

"I didn't say that," I protested.

"You don't have to," she said. "You just have to say 'That still sounds insane', with a tone of appreciation and delight."

Busted. Bloodlust aside, I still had valid worries, however. "He certainly deserves to get robbed, but I worry about his security. There will definitely be guns on the premises. Maybe I can..." I started.

"No," said Alannah. I tried to go on, but she cut me off. "There will be guns, and probably other security guards. If you go in there, they'll be hurt, or you'll be hurt. The only person I don't have a problem with getting shot in this operation is Marc Hordones himself. He has kidnapped and killed, as well as sold weapons to crime lords, assassins and worse. The others may well be assholes too, but they might also just be hired hands."

My fierce, violent desire to countermand that injunction was proof that Alannah was right. After an internal struggle, I managed to keep my mouth shut. I might have gurgled a little, because it was a long time before anyone said anything. At least on my channel.

I had to look at the earpiece more next time, and figure out how to change channels.

Finally, it was Alannah who spoke up. "How are you doing?" she ventured.

"It's hard," I said. We reached the bitumen. "Right?" I asked. "Follow the signs to Sydney?"

"Yeah," she sighed.

THE TRIP to Sydney was pretty mindless as far as I was concerned. In the back, they were probably preparing weapons and discussing plans. In the front, I blanked out on a long, long stretch of dead straight highway in a van set on cruise control. Pity the van wasn't self-navigating. Although it was probably for the best that I had my attention forced on a task. It kept the creature quiet. The one that always prowled restlessly along my spine, growling and sniffing the air.

Once I'd had time to think about it, I believed I could

put a face to Marc Hordones. He was certainly the top dog of all the hounds in the building. If I was correct, he was the one who supervised our training. And the conditioning that came with it, too. Even after the isolation, I'd sometimes see him through a window, hear his voice over a speaker. More often, he'd be giving instructions to some other assholes.

He was tall, handsome, confident, and knew more about weapons and gadgets than I'll ever know. Smiled a lot. When he was telling us something directly, he was genuinely enthusiastic. Blokey. Quick with a wink and a laugh. I hated him so much. Well, the beast hated him. The enmity was kept quiet, but the beast hated him long before I saw him laugh at a fellow inmate. A perennially clumsy guy, who fucked up a detonator insertion, and lost two fingers and an eye. After that, it wasn't just the beast - I hated Marc Hordones with my whole heart. Thing was, I was afraid of him, too.

Once we got there, it was mid-afternoon. Lourdes, after a burst of wifi as we parked outside a café, directed me towards the north shore, where she'd plotted a route to the street address of Marc Hordones. There was a park diagonally across from his house, and the plan was to put the van on the other side of that. Without a decent cash supply, there wasn't an option to buy clothes and trick their way in, so their choices were the limited selection of the clothes they wore in Project Lycan, the combat suits they pilfered, and the few sets of ill-fitting clothes liberated from Natalie's aunt's wardrobe.

"If you're going to go in combat fatigues, hadn't it better be at night?" I suggested. "Last thing you need is to attract a hefty police blockade to stop you from getting back out."

"That's true," said Natalie, "but we might have to get to the embassy tonight. We discussed this for ages."

I looked at the clock, and the heavily overcast sky. "We're nearly at midwinter here, if you wait just a little past five, it'll be *fairly* dark, but you'll miss the workers arriving home. That should give us a few hours to get ourselves organised, and still make it to the embassy."

There was more discussion, but in the end they agreed. Balancing the various theoretical risks was aggravating, especially given the plethora of unknown factors in play. Upon a slate-grey early dusk, I pulled up on the far side of the park. It was a small affair, but had a newly-built complex playground in the middle. Now, though, it looked cold and empty. Many of the houses had their lights on.

"Go time," I said. "Stay on this channel."

They flitted out of the van in full combat gear, including assault rifles and gadgets. Their heads fully covered by those helmets. They moved like professionals, silent, smooth and quick. When they were gone, my mind couldn't helping gnawing on the obvious point that they weren't in the least professional. I knew perfectly well that they'd been trained about as much as your average action movie star. I knew that this was *important*, that it meant I should *act*. I knew I had to stay the hell in the van.

I was out of sight, so for me, the whole thing played out on audio.

Natalie: Watch out for the sensor light at the front and the side, there.

Lourdes: There's a light on up top. Better scout around, see if we can spot anyone inside.

[Puffing sounds.]

Alannah: Two of them. Guards with monitors. They should have seen us, but they're talking. Shit - it's Hordones!

Natalie: Where?

[Silence for several seconds]

Natalie: Inside?

[More silence]

Alannah: Talking with the guards. I can get close to the window, but I don't know if I'll be able to hear. Gonna turn you guys down. Definitely won't be able to talk. Look for a way in round the back.

[Clicking sound, silence]

Lourdes: Spotted two cameras. They're on the side and back doors. I reckon we'll have better luck with a smaller window.

Natalie: If they're moving around inside, the alarm won't be on. But they'll probably hear a window. Try the other side from Al.

George: The upstairs bedroom window is open.

Lourdes: How do you know it's a bedroom?

George: Well, the bed is a giveaway. And the ensuite.

Lourdes: ... you up there?

George: Yep. Up the bricks. Went round the sensor.

Lourdes: OK, move carefully. At least three of them downstairs, probably armed. Go silent like Al, and turn us down so you can hear. Unless you're in trouble.

George: Will do.

[Clicking sound.]

Natalie: Found a window, but they're all double glazed. I think it'll make a helluva noise. I reckon we should go up like George.

Lourdes: 'Kay.

[Half a minute of silence]

Natalie: How the fuck did she get up there?

Lourdes: Sure that's it?

Natalie: Yeah, look at that.

Lourdes: She said she climbed the bricks. But you'd have to...

[Grunting.]

Lourdes: Wow. I am fucking spider-woman.

Natalie: Shit. Okay, here goes.

[Puffing.]

Lourdes: Good work.

Natalie: You too. We'll have to go quiet when we go in.

Lourdes: Yep. Since we're all quiet, I'll leave my volume up.

[Scratching sound. Silence.]

SILENCE. Nothing. I opened the window so I could hear at a distance if there were gunshots or anything.

There weren't. Just the occasional huff of breath. Crazily, given I was the safest person of the entire group, I felt like I was going to die. Holding myself ready in the van was as difficult as keeping a match lit in a storm. My head pounded, I could feel my pulse hammering away throughout my body. My chest was tight, and I felt dizzy. Nauseous.

After about a minute, there was another clicking sound, and I started hearing more rustling and scraping sounds, as well as some carefully exhaled breath. It sounded like someone had turned up the gain on their microphone up to its maximum. Then I heard the voice of Marc Hordones. He *was* the same guy I knew from the testing and training sessions. I could picture him standing there, dark brown hair cut short, framing a half-smile. Utterly assured as always.

Marc Hordones: ...so he said she turned up at the US embassy?

Unknown man: Yes sir, two hours ago. Walked right past our informant, and got swept upstairs.

Marc: Okay, okay. That's a problem. Is it?

[Sounds of pacing]

Marc: Maybe. Yes. But not now. Right, here's what I want you to...

[Phone rings. The ringtone is a series of crunching guitar power chords.]

Marc: Whoop. It's Mr Adams... Hello sir.

[Sound of a man talking very loudly on the phone, but too indistinct to make out]

Marc: Yes sir... Yes. Yes. Yes, I... No sir. No...

[Shuffling sound, like one of the girls finding a new position. The sound from the phone is quieter.]

Marc (more firmly): No, this could be good.

[Definite shouting at the other end.]

Marc: I'm not saying it isn't a shit show, sir. I'm just saying if we can manage this right, it could be a huge opportunity, too. Since all this stuff went public, we've had huge, huge interest in certain markets. I've had three contacts in the last hour. Expressions of interest so, ah, formidable that I had to pick up even in the midst... Yes sir. No, we can't let it go now.

Lourdes: OK, I've got into the garage. There are three cars in here, but I bet I know which is Hordones'. Al, do you have that tracker we took?

Marc: Yes, I know we're going to be under the microscope. The whole operation is going to have to get very tight. No matter how much we stall, we've got to expect warrants absolutely everywhere. Everywhere on the books, that is... Yes, I know. Yes sir, I think we can. It'll be a tight fit, but we'll only take staff who are completely sound. With us all the way... Yes...

Alannah: Fuck me, I do have that tracker. Coming round to the side window. Can you open it from the inside?

Lourdes: The little one? Yeah.

Marc: The hard part is going to be cleaning the rest. All our premises have to be pristine. No cash, no records, no illegal gear. Should be pretty straightforward - we built it that way all along. The irony is, with the Lycan building down so thoroughly... I've been over the site, it's no problem. All the equipment makes sense given our dual official research lines, and all the computer records were slagged.

Marc (aside to someone not on the phone): Clear the safe, sweep the panic room for contraband, get my laptop. Put it all in the car.

[Heavy steps, and some quick puffing as the listener moves again. The sound of Marc on the phone is fainter again.]

Marc: No, that's the thing. Gannt tells me he kept a backup... Yes, I've already spoken to him about that... Yes, I know, but it's bloody brilliant for us. We'll need to pull Wüster and Gannt away, but we can start almost where we left off, except with the kind of demand that will accept almost any... Yeah, the black site basically has... Yep, hardest thing will be getting supplies...

[The listener gets closer again, and the volume goes up.]

Lourdes: Okay, I'm out. The thing with the safe sounds too good to be true. Are we going for it while they're loading? Or do we follow them out?

Alannah: Follow them out! We need to know everything we can about this move, and we can take them in transit any time. Time to reduce our footprint!

Lourdes: 'Kay.

Marc: Yeah, a hundred or so, apparently... Women and men. Thinks he's got some ideas, but it might be expensive.

While we're staying under the radar, I was hoping you might be able to buy them off the Russians?

Natalie: I'm out.

Alannah: Careful with sound, I heard you landing, Nat.

Marc: Wüster still wants her, but I reckon we don't... No, fuck Whitman. Her shit didn't work, and I got a weird vibe before the end. Got a couple of eyes on her. Certainly don't want her involved once we go dark...

Lourdes: I'm out. George, the side door facing the park, through the laundry, latches as you go. It's quiet, and easy to reach from the stairs.

Marc: Just one. The chick at the US embassy. What do we do there?

Unknown man: The safe is clear, sir. I have your laptop as well. John's doing the panic room.

Marc: She's a witness, and I imagine she's talking, but the full story's already out there. We're already at the point where our rep is more or less shot, so it's about protection of assets and staying clear. So does she have any evidence, that's the question I... Really? That's good news... Right! So all they've got is eyewitness stuff. We've got time there. Worst case, we use the emergency backup on... Yeah, but I presume PR are spinning these people as terrorists? Yeah, that always sticks...

Alannah: Careful, George. I hope you've got somewhere good. We've got charges on the garage door if we need to come in fast, so just say the word.

Marc: Yes sir. My house will be clear once I make it out there, and Wüster, Gannt and the other core team members are already on their way. Mark and Mika have a full cleaning protocol for your houses, and they'll be clean in two hours. From then, if things get too hot, we can always go completely dark by just not coming back. If we pull this off, the money will be astronomical either way... Yes sir, I'll get there tonight, see you in seven hours. Yes sir.

[Beeping sound, and the sound of someone walking into the distance. Doors slamming.]

George (whispering): I'll need a couple of minutes to get clear. Might have to time it with them reaching the garage.

MY GUT CLENCHED, hard. She sounded trapped. I could cause a distraction. For example, I could distract those assholes by snapping their necks. Remember how one blow to the neck does the trick? Nausea. The steering wheel started making some strange sounds, and I let go of it.

The sound of a car starting in that direction? No, a car driving past on the other side of the park.

Alannah: They're in the garage. Doors opening. Everyone clear of lines of sight. Watch for sensor lights as well as cameras.

Lourdes: George, time it well. There were sensors in the house, so it will be alarmed when they go. There's typically a few seconds of grace, but I wouldn't push it.

George (whispering): The other guy's still downstairs. Can't go safely without eyes on him.

Alannah: All the guns and cash are in the guards' cars. Marc is driving clean, even out to the black site. Hang on... the other guard has just arrived. Go, George!

[Shuffling sounds. George's microphone was still at maximum gain as she slipped through the house.]

Natalie: So all the money is in the cars we *can't* track?

Lourdes: Maybe, but I did put charges on all of them.

Alannah: First car exiting. Second one starting.

I could see lights, and felt glad we'd left the van

completely out of sight. I glimpsed the car as it went past - a huge and black SUV. I wanted to chase it. I felt sick.

The second car looked dark as well, but it might have been blue. It raced off after the first.

Alannah: Third guy is going, door going down.

George: I'm out.

I let out a breath I didn't realise I'd been holding.

Alannah: Don't get sloppy, but everyone needs to get back to the van. Whatever happens next, we need to keep in range of those guys. The tracker is supposed to be used across a town, not a country. It will do a few dozen kilometres, I understand. Patrick, fire it up once the other car is clear.

WITH SOMETHING TO DO, my heart actually slowed. The third car blazed off into the twilight, and almost before I even got the van lights on, the four of them arrived, panting. George had got her microphone back to normal settings, and they were obviously chatting on another channel, because I could hear their voices through the van rather than in my ear.

"Directions!" I called out.

"Forward," said Lourdes' voice in my ear. "I'm looking it up. OK, left at the intersection, and then out towards the Pacific Highway."

I complied, and had to fight myself to stay at the speed limit. Or at least at a speed that stood a good chance of driving past a police car. Marc's car headed onto the motorway, heading north. He'd said the black site was five hours away, which put it out in the country somewhere. Marc was happier to speed than I was, so he slowly got further and further away. There wasn't a lot of danger of losing them absolutely, but it was frustrating not being able to see if the three cars were together. Were we chasing the boss and giving up on the cash? Were we still after cash, or had the intel we gained on the regrown Project Lycan changed the plans? What about Kirsten? How long did she have?

Two hours later, we were no closer to answering any of those questions. I added my own.

"Do we have any more food?" I asked. A gentle buzzing and lightheaded feeling was the first sign of low blood sugar, but the current one was a raging appetite.

"We're pretty low," Natalie replied. "I'll fix you something, but we're going to need to take out those cars if we want to replenish."

"We all know what you reckon, Nat," said Alannah, exasperated. "And you also know the counterargument: we need to know where that new base is, and we're not going to get two chances to surprise them there."

"I know that," Natalie replied, starting the loop again, "but without food and petrol, it's going to be a..."

"Thanks for the snack, Natalie," I said, trying to interrupt. "I'm sorry I'm so needy, but that's how the bad guys made me."

"What do you think, Patrick?" asked Alannah. "You've been awfully quiet since we left Sydney."

There were good reasons for that. First, I kept missing chunks of the conversation, as they switched between broadcast, and old fashioned shouting at each other. It hadn't been particularly acrimonious, but tensions were raised along with the stakes. Anyway, it felt like intruding to throw in comments under those circumstances. Second, I didn't have any good suggestions. There were clearly good points on both sides.

"I think you're both right," I said. "We can't hit the base without getting stuff first. We can't, I'm sorry Alannah. I don't know if your new metabolism is anything like mine, but you won't have a driver in a day. You'll just have the delirious remains of one. They tried out normal rations on me three times. Not even Wüster bothered doing it again. You won't be immune either. If you've got only half my metabolic needs, then skipping a few meals will still render you error prone and dangerous."

Before it sounded like I was all good with the other plan, I kept going. "It's also obvious that we can't hit any of those cars and then have any chance of success at infiltrating their new site. It would be so easy to defend against us if they are forewarned, particularly in a specially designed bolthole. We have one chance to finish the job you Valkyries started."

I blinked. Was that a microsleep? I fought against it, and a surge of adrenaline followed cheerfully.

"All of which means," I said, thinking out loud, "that we're going to have to downgrade our ambitions, and get a little cash another way. Or else obtain food and petrol directly."

"How on earth would we get petrol?" demanded Alannah.

"Bet one of these farms we're passing would have a whole tank," I mused. "A lot of them will have tractors and such. They're usually filled from drums rather than driven to a petrol station..." I peered through the darkness. A few minutes later, I killed the lights, and pulled up a side road. Near a likely looking cluster of sheds, I jumped out, and slipped up to the fence. A dog barked in the distance, but I found what I was looking for first try. Well, third shed, but first farm. A tractor, a forty-four gallon drum, and a siphon. Looking around, I saw that there was no way we were going to secretly get the van in here, so I picked up the drum. Luckily, it was only half-full, so I didn't strain anything hefting it back. Popping it up on a fence post, and wicking the siphon, we soon had a full tank. Feeling a little bad, I put the drum back. On the way back to the road, I asked the others to mark the place on a map. I wanted to pay when I had the means.

Plus, all going well, we might need to revisit on the return trip.

Alannah was annoyed with me. I had enough of a guilty conscience that it bothered me.

"Want to rob a supermarket for the food?" she asked, snappishly.

Lourdes perked up. "Supermarkets toss huge amounts of edible food," she said. "Some of my bohemian mates ate nothing else for weeks. They try to keep people away, and you have to be prepared to dig a little, but 'best before' doesn't suddenly make things inedible."

"That's disgusting," said Natalie.

"We'd need a large supermarket," sighed Alannah. Resigned, rather than pissed. Why was she specifically pissed off at me? Seemed unfair.

"If we keep going this way, we'll pass a large town in about 80 kilometres," said Lourdes. "Looks like a good chance from the map, but from there I have no idea which direction we'll go. A lot of the major roads around here kind of pass through it, see?"

Whatever she was showing them on the map obviously made sense, as there were affirming grunts. "Oh well, it's better than starving. What do you think, Nat? Gives us a clean shot at the black site."

Natalie made a general noise of agreement, although it never made it all the way to a word. She wasn't keen on the idea of eating expired food. But she clearly agreed that it was better than being shot.

We were really hammering through the dark, trying to catch up to the tracker on Marc's car, but even so, the 80 kilometres took a lot more than half an hour. It was long enough to get extremely hungry. Again, again. Many of the changes to my body that Project Lycan had made over the last year were really very good, but they also came with real problems. Before we got to town we were within a couple of kilometres from the tracker, but it bypassed the town to the south, and headed out west. There was a brief panic about catching him, but I simply couldn't wait.

"If we're quick, we'll catch up to them again before too long," I said. "It's not like we're trying to catch them before they get there anyway. In fact, that would be a bit of a disaster. We need to come in quietly, not blaze up behind them at the gate." I took a little drink of water from my bottle. "Assuming there's a gate."

I didn't get the impression that the others were quite as needy as me, but there wasn't too much grumbling as we arrived in town. The main supermarket was indeed quite big, as it was serving a community that was quite large for a country town. It was closed after eight o'clock, because it was a *country* town, after all.

This was good news. A quick scale of the tall fences that shielded the trash bins from dogs and bohemian flatmates gave us access to a large amount of awful refuse. True to Lourdes' word, there were a lot of gems hidden in that dirt. We stayed clear of eggs, but there was a large amount of packet bread and processed food still in its packets. There were even plentiful boxes to carry it away, so within ten minutes, the van was filled with viable food, though of a rather random composition.

Munching on a loaf of stale, uncooked fruit toast, I drew us out of town at a comfortable, legal speed. Though still doing its now-familiar thumping, my heart was lighter. It wasn't that I was free of the oppressive feelings of doom and drama, it was just that they... were a little less important for a moment. More stale, uncooked fruit toast followed the last.

Chapter 9

TWO HEADS GROW BACK

We never caught the car. They only seemed to go faster as they got further from civilisation and major roads. We had to be careful not to use high beam, which limited how fast we could take unfamiliar roads. Also, we knew where Marc's car was, but we didn't know what roads he'd taken. Back when there were fewer choices this was less of a problem. By the time we had to decide to turn off main roads and go on dirt roads, it got harder to be sure we were doing the right thing. We nearly balked when we came to a chained gate.

"We're just going onto someone's farm now," said Alannah, as she peered into the darkness.

Lourdes was peering at her map in the light of her phone's screen, and then trying to see landmarks in the hills around us, weakly lit by a half-hidden moon. "They're well on the far side of that hill," she said, pointing to the one in front of us. "There's no road on this map anywhere in the area. It has to be this one." She looked critically at the old wooden fence posts and the decidedly well-worn steel frame of a gate hooked across the road.

"It's a big road for a farm," I observed, though dubious about whether it was a useful observation. This was definitely a long-established gate and road. I half agreed with Alannah's assessment.

Natalie poked her head out of the van. "The tracker's really stopped! I know they've paused a few times, but it's been nearly ten minutes now," she said.

"Same place?" asked Lourdes, looking up. "Two kilometres that way?" she pointed again over the hill.

"Yep. Not a budge since we stopped."

"All right, let's leave the lights off, and go through the gate," Alannah decided. I almost suggested walking from this point, but the hybrid van was pretty quiet, so we could probably get a lot closer while staying undetected.

We slipped through the gate, and locked it again behind us. Then we followed the road through the dark. A wan moon diffused through a wispy cloud, and the handful of trees by the road waved in a restless wind. The road wound around the hill, and then turned what was clearly the wrong direction as it reached a more substantial copse at the corner of a field.

"Maybe this is wrong after all," Alannah reflected.

"They're still stationary," said Natalie, "about a kilometre and a half over the hill. Maybe we should go on foot now anyway."

That became the plan. Everyone piled out of the van. I did as well, and gave myself a fair bit of room, instinctively pulling away upwind. I bounced on the balls of my feet, trying to loosen up a little. I didn't have the hardware, so I had to stay well at the back, but that worked out fine, because the way the wind was blowing would make...

"Patrick," said Alannah carefully. I looked up at her, and saw that they were all looking at me. "It's still not a good idea for you to come. Everything we said before applies now. This starts as a recon mission, and then when we've got our best shot planned, we're going to go in hot. You're the one that told us you can't operate near people. Especially not in a high-stakes potential combat situation. Right?"

They were all waiting for an answer. Looking at me like it was a delicate moment. Like they had to handle me carefully. I bounced. Mentally, I tried to assemble my reassurances. Spent a few seconds with my eyes closed, trying to visualise staying controlled, at the back of the pack. Not even I believed it. Visions of the fights back at Project Lycan kept inserting themselves into my imagined scene.

Jaw and fists clenched, I nodded. Trembling, I backed off. It wasn't a good time, socially speaking, to scream and rage. It possibly wasn't even safe.

The four of them did a quick equipment rundown while I clung to a tree. Three of them went over the fence, but before she went, Lourdes called out softly to me: "Patrick, can I show you something in the van?"

She wasn't asking my permission, she was really asking if she could. As in, she knew there was a possibility that she might not be able to. Or I might not be able to.

"Yes," I said with a strangled voice, and walked over to the sliding door. It was difficult to figure out how to walk. I just wanted to run everywhere, but controlling my gait to make it casual seemed fake. Unclenching my fists made me wonder what to do with my hands. Maybe that's how movie extras feel when they're in the background of some scene. Lourdes had the luxury of jogging over, smelling slightly of fear and excitement.

"In here," she said, stepping in. Following, I took one step forward before my eyes watered. The four of them had been cooped up in there for basically a day, door closed the entire time. Defending their honour, it wasn't a *bad* smell - not in the slightest - but there sure was a hell of a *lot* of it. I leaped back, got some distance, and took a few deep breaths. My body had reacted predictably, and I found myself humiliated once again.

Fortunately, it was too much. "Fuck... knuckles!" I gasped, and then giggled. Lourdes was looking out of the van, framed by the door. Her dark eyes were wide, and her expression a little unreadable.

"My eyes are up here," I gasped, stifling a chortle. With a little flash of alarm, she met my gaze.

"You gonna be OK?" she asked.

I kept taking deep breaths. "Give me a sec," I said, then took a really big breath, and held it in. Jumping back in, she pointed to a blocky device. My engineering experience told me the enclosure was bigger than it needed to be, probably a prototype. There was a little electronic map on the interface, with various coloured glowing points.

"These are the trackers," she explained, pointing. "Those four are here in the van, and that one is the one I got on Hordones' car. If you hit the menu, here, then you can see how to send it passive. You also see this tab... Where you can see the armed detonators. They're on all three cars. There's a timer, or you can just direct detonate with this. OK? There's no confirmation process, so careful when this panel is open."

My breath ran out, so I rushed out again, beet red. Lourdes followed me, "That's all. Thought we might need you to fire them if things get really tight."

I just nodded, and tried to walk it off.

"Right," said Alannah. "Time to go. Earpieces on Patrick's code, and whisper."

"Good luck," I offered, as Lourdes leapt the fence, and they jogged off into the darkness.

I CHUCKLED QUIETLY TO MYSELF. It was good to know that was still possible. That there was some kind of mental fuse that would blow before my brain simply fried. I was still overwhelmed, however, and a strange combination of mentally exhausted and physically wired for action. I tried pacing quietly around as my night vision kept improving.

In the distance, I saw what looked like headlights. But they were not on the road we left. I raced over to the map in the van, and as far as I could tell, there was no road where those headlights were coming from.

"Can everyone hear me?" I asked the darkness.

"Yes," came several responses.

"Miss us already?" asked Lourdes.

"I see headlights to the northeast. Not on a road," I said.

"Which way is... no, I've got it," said Alannah.

"I'll try infra-red," said George. "Nah, can't see anything. Although... yes, there's something to the left, see?"

The headlights went out of sight, behind the trees, and then the hill. I could hear the engine very, very faintly in the distance. I scuffed the dirt, and then opened the rear van door to air the thing out a little. It was back to waiting again. Waiting, cloaked and trapped in the grey light from a cloud-spread moon. Waiting, and listening.

ALANNAH: Buildings, embedded in lots of trees, new road up

to them, and with no exterior lights. And that's about where Marc's car stopped. Looks like we've got our place.

Natalie: Is that a heat plume?

[Rustling]

Lourdes: Heating wouldn't do that. No need for a vent. Unless it was a combustion fire, which would be crazy.

Natalie: So what's that, then?

Lourdes: I'd guess that'd be air-conditioning.

Natalie: This time of year?

Lourdes: Best guess, tag that as the server room. The one we blew up would have needed commercial-grade aircon. Looks like they planned this well in advance.

Alannah: There's the new car, watch where it goes in.

Natalie: That's a pretty serious looking fence back there.

George: Outward-facing razor-wire.

Alannah: Remote-controlled garage door. If only we had one of those receiver gizmos.

Lourdes: Can't win 'em all. But if they're parking inside, then that hangar would be where the heaviest hardware would be, right? And the other buildings must be for research, lodgings... mess hall? Still seems like a lot of area for that.

Alannah: Remember the scope of the research. They'd need indoor rifle ranges, serious machining capacity, electronics, pharmaceutical labs. And room for hundreds of human slaves.

Natalie (dead voice): Probably not hundreds at the same time. But maybe a few dozen.

[Long silence]

Natalie: We go down there?

Alannah: We do. While we have surprise and they're still getting organised. This is our chance to take 'em out. However, we know how much they're playing for keeps here. We go in wholeheartedly, or not. Last chance to back out.

[Silence]

~

LOTS OF SILENCE. My breath was starting to become visible in the night air. I needed to do something, so while I was alone, I tried going back in the van. It wasn't very messy, just extremely cramped. There were eight seats, and possibly two more folded down under the very large amount of equipment. Ammunition boxes, solid black packing crates, maps and electronics in piles on the spare seats.

Concentrating, I could make out their individual scents. In that spirit of inquiry that requires absolutely no-one to be watching, I leaned in to the seats to see if I could guess where each person had been sitting. In a minute, I had it narrowed down to a couple of options. Maybe they switched a bit. Thinking about what it must have been like, I realised that the two back ones must have been used as a makeshift bed. They could have taken it in turns. It was still alien to me that I could tell the difference.

There were still a lot of explosives here. Demolition blocks of a few sizes, with plenty of spare detonation cord clips, and some fancy detonators. I reckoned I could figure out how to use it given a couple of attempts. Not that it would be possible to get a second attempt, depending on your exact choice of mistake.

There were also another two assault rifles. Wondering whether I could remember what to do with them, I tried loading and unloading one. Yes, it wasn't too complicated. Probably harder to clean than to use, I chose not to try to strip it down. Not the right time. Distractions thinning, I went to the maps, and tried to figure out why Bowline chose this area. Just as I was about to break radio silence from sheer tension, their voices came back.

NATALIE: That's the last building. They've got cameras on all the corners, and we'll have to presume they're being watched. But we've got a decent guess what's in each part of the building. There's a lot of area there, though. It's not obvious that we can take it all out at once, unless you can think of something I can't. So we need to choose our target. To fire up Lycan again, what they need the most is their data, right? So we want Wüster, Gannt and that data centre to go up together.

Alannah: I'd rather take more, but if that's all we get, then at least the human trafficking can be stopped. And we can broadcast this location publicly, see if we can get someone to check it out while there's still some evidence here. We'll be wiping out the most damning stuff, but even the existence of this place will hurt them.

Lourdes: So why aren't we just walking away and publishing?

Alannah: Because even if they're finally burned legally, they'll probably still be able to slip away and start again. Project Lycan alone could make billionaires out of all of them. And if they start it up again, that means doing more experiments.

Natalie: This isn't the time to go soft. They've killed a lot of people, they're planning on doing it again, and it's all so... clinical! So creepy. Sick! I'll never understand what's going on in their heads.

Alannah: After a while, you stop asking that question

about certain kinds of people, and you just work on stopping them. In some ways, not being able to do this the proper way is liberating. I've seen a lot of people walk away from charges that should have put them in a cell for life. And I've seen most of them cause havoc afterwards, too. Smiling. I'm here to make sure Paul Adams is not going to be one them. Agreed?

Natalie: Oh, yes.

George: Agreed.

Lourdes: No, you're right. Don't worry, I want these fuckers stopped. Just don't want to die in the attempt. Let's go. Data centre?

[Rustling]

Natalie: So how do we get past the cameras? It's already really dark down there, so we can't really kill the lights. We could kill a camera?

Alannah: They'd have to be IR, surely.

Lourdes: Yeah, we'll have to kill a camera. Or drape the right kind of blankets over us and move slowly.

Natalie: Is that why you brought those?

Lourdes: Yep. Well, that, and it's a faster way to deal with fence wire than cutting. Wasn't really worrying about being cold. Now, don't wrap tightly, and there will be some image still, and that means that the movement sensors will detect something. We'll want to move fairly slowly to stay under the threshold.

Alannah: How slowly?

Lourdes: Probably depends on how close you are to vegetation that moves in the wind. They'll have to have set higher tolerances there. Think the speed of waving leaves. It helps us a lot that they've buried this place in trees. A clearing with easy sight lines would have been basically impossible.

Alannah: Maybe they did that so it's harder to spot from above?

Lourdes: Presumably. Maybe from the road as well. Secret base is secretive.

Alannah: OK, well, there's only one door. Let's go for it.

Natalie: It's going to be locked.

Alannah: We've seen three people going in and out. None of them stopped to unlock it. I didn't see a card reader or anything like that.

Natalie: How does an ultra-secret base work like that?

Alannah: Very small team. Card access systems only tend to come in over a certain size. You can keep your pessimism, though. There'll still be locks on specific areas inside.

George: I have a different suggestion.

Alannah: Which is?

George: I reckon we go via the garage. That's got money, and is the natural internal access point. I reckon that most people will be asleep in here over the next few hours. If we manage to take out the ones staffing security, then we could systematically go through this place. Wipe out the whole thing.

Natalie: Bloodthirsty.

George: Realistic, and operationally, not different to where we're likely to end up anyway.

Alannah: True. The real question is: which plan is most likely to succeed? We're back to making guesses about their security measures and status.

Natalie: Shouldn't we be hurrying at this point?

Lourdes: There's no way they could spot us here. It's only getting later - I reckon we're good to chat before we commit.

Alannah: We know they've only just scrambled. All the

concentrated assholes on the Bowline payroll are coming here, along with most of the contraband that they're not prepared to abandon. Specifically that stuff is either en route, or has *just* come here. So inside they should have chaos. I'd expect furious, overtired activity inside, leading to maybe a big downtime in a couple of hours.

[Coughing, muffled by a hand or elbow, but heavy and bassy in the microphone]

Alannah: The real question is, what was already here two days ago? This place has to have been more than just a shell - this has all the signs of a well-executed long-term backup plan. The computing, the labs, the security, all the basic infrastructure... It's been here a long time. So just how much disarray might we expect?

Lourdes: One reason for following George's plan and hitting the garage first is that we'll have a bound on how many people are here. No-one would have given the game away and come by helicopter. However many seats are in the vehicles in that hangar should be an upper estimate.

Alannah: ... what do people think?

Natalie: Maybe the side door on the garage is unlocked as well. That's where I'd expect more actual guards, though.

Lourdes: ... try both? Two recon teams?

THAT'S WHERE THEY LANDED. And then they chose groups, and started creeping forward. Sensitivities on the mics were turned up high, so they could communicate with a quiet whisper, but almost nothing was said for almost an hour. I sat and paced, and stretched, rustling and breathing in my ear. I'd heard of 'hurry up and wait', but I'd never signed up for it.

ALANNAH: We're at the door now.

Natalie: George and I are nearly there. Hope this speed is OK, but we don't want to be caught out here.

Alannah: Listening.

[Thirty seconds pass]

Alannah: Going in.

Natalie: Us too.

[Forty more of the longest seconds ever. Clicks, shuffles.]

Alannah: Clear. A bunch of store rooms, a bedroom and a door at the end. That one sounds like it's the server room. Checking the bedroom first.

Natalie: Door was locked. Turns out George has skills. Big garage. Internal doors, and no people... Twelve cars. Big ones. So, minimum 12 on site. Maximum maybe seventy.

George: The other two cars are here as well as Hordones', so that makes a maximum of about fifty-five. We'll start by pulling the charges on the cars and repurposing them. You got that Patrick? Fingers well away from those buttons. Remember, I'm your favourite.

Me: You're my favourite?

George: I know, but it's not cool to just say it on an open channel. Think of the others.

Alannah: Less chatter, please.

[Rustling sounds. A few distant mechanical sounds. The sound of tape unwrapping? Was that the explosives being detached?]

Lourdes: This is Gannt's room. I know that smell. Nothing useful here, though. He must have brought it all to the server room to get it all back up and running. Shall we go slag it?

Alannah: He'll probably be there working, since he's not here. Might be guards as well. Let's not think about hardware until we've dealt with that.

Lourdes: ...I'm amazed at the fact that I'm okay with this. Well, not okay, exactly, but...

Alannah: We've got to stop them. We just have to. We've agreed to do it non-lethally if we get the chance, but be sure you've made your decision before we go in there. Hesitation won't just kill you and me... Right?

Lourdes: Right. I just wonder if I've changed because of the process, or...

Alannah: ...or if you met your first monster, and recognised that they're irredeemable. I feel as weird about it, but we have a duty here, and that's enough for me.

Lourdes: Me too. Right.

Natalie: OK, those charges should strand everything in this garage. The anti-pursuit part is covered. We're going to look for the armoury. If we can do the same for their main supplies, the resulting bang should be pretty majestic.

Alannah: Listen at doors. We are always winning if we're undiscovered.

Natalie: Right.

[Sounds of a door opening.]

Unknown man (distant): Hey!

[Several pounding sounds, and a large cracking sound. A second of scuffle and then a heavy crash.]

Another unknown male voice (also distant): Who...? Oh, it's you.

Lourdes: Slowly raise your hands where I can see them, Mr Gannt.

Adam Gannt (still faint): Did you just kill them? Have you come to kill me?

Alannah: I'm not sure. I hit them pretty hard. Don't make us hit you.

Lourdes: We *have* come to stop you. How could you do this? Kidnapping people is bad enough, but killing them? How did you ever think that was OK?

Gannt: I didn't kidnap anyone. Or kill them. I'm just a programmer.

Lourdes: Stand up. Now! Now, go sit over there... Don't give us any shit about 'I'm just a programmer'. I have copies of your notes, you fucking psycho.

Alannah: This one's alive, I'll restrain him.

[Sounds of a tape roll]

Gannt: Really? You got my notes?

Lourdes: Next time you build a critical computer system, try for a high strength password, even on an intranet. What the hell were you thinking with 'oOOooGanntMusic'? Oh. I've never said it out loud before...

[Coughing.]

Lourdes: It's still stupid.

Gannt: So if you have my notes, you realise how amazing this was. The parameter space was unsearchable. Even to optimise around a lucky strike took...

Lourdes: You can shut up about your bullshit genius, asshole! Did you know I was kidnapped with my best friend? Did you know she *died*? Is there any part of you that thinks about people?

Gannt: People are very interesting, yes. So, if you had all my notes, you must have had a copy of the neural net as well. Did you bother publishing that somewhere, along with all the rest? We haven't seen it.

Lourdes: Of course not. We want this to stop, not go open fucking source.

Gannt: That's good. (Louder) Yes, shoot her!

Alannah: Lourdes, he's...

[Four sharp gunshots, almost on top of each other.

Three from assault rifles, and one from something else. For three full seconds of silence, I managed to keep myself from shouting.]

Alannah: We're OK. Did you guys hear that?

George: Couldn't tell for sure. It was so loud in the earpiece, even with the clipping. Certainly not a big sound.

Natalie: The AC insulation of the server room might well help with sound as well.

Lourdes: Oh hell, I fell for the 'look over there' trick.

Alannah: Don't worry. I saw him pull it, and still missed with the first shot. We've got to move fast now. Can you check him while I finish this guy?

Lourdes: Yep, I'll... Ergh... Oh, he's dead... Right. Let's get to the machines.

Natalie (whispering particularly quietly): There are two guards on those double doors. I think that might be the heavy stuff. Any ideas, George?

George (also very soft): Not really. Clear line of sight, so we can't sneak up. We could shoot them, but everyone would hear... Oh shit. Approaching! Nat, in here!

[Rustling, indecipherable sounds for fifteen seconds.]

Natalie: Bad news. Four guards went past. Our two got relieved, and then two more went in your direction. Lock any other entries to that place, and it's go time!

George: We've got to pull back. Through the garage - it's the only route where we know what we're doing.

[Shuffling, clanging.]

Alannah: How are you doing, Lourdes?

Lourdes: The EMP will go first, which should frag all the computers and SSDs. In this building, at least. Won't do much through the sheet metal walls. Anyway, then the incendiary will finish the job for the magnetic media.

Gannt's laptop is there, too. It's a small setup. I think we've got it all. How long?

[Slamming sounds]

Alannah: Better make it short. Forty seconds?

Lourdes: 'Kay

George: Right.

[Running sounds. Door slams.]

Natalie: Patrick, hit the detonator as soon as you hear the other explosions go.

[Overlapping running sounds. Two more door slams. An alarm bursts into life, with four slightly different overlapping delays. Then another one, that sounded like a car alarm.]

Natalie: George? We don't have time to drive out!

George: Just grabbing a bag of contraband on the way out.

IN THE DISTANCE, I heard another copy of the station alarm, this time with my left ear. It was weak at that range, but had no competing sounds in the dead of the night. I swiped the menu to the page accessing the charges, and saw the icons glowing red and pulsing slowly.

I heard the explosions through the earpiece, and having not heard any instructions to the contrary, I hit the detonators. The button press was almost instantly rewarded with sound of much larger explosions over the earpiece. About five seconds later, I heard them outside the van. The alarm went silent.

After a few minutes I started the van, turned it around, and then left it idling as I jumped out and opened the side door. Perhaps six minutes after the explosions, the four of them leapt over the fence and jumped into the van. George came last, toting a huge duffel bag. The door slammed closed, and I took care not to spin the wheels as we hit the road. This time, I used headlights freely, and took off in the direction of Sydney at the highest speed the van could manage.

"I CAN'T BELIEVE you stopped to pick up loot bags from the garage on the way out!" puffed Natalie, as she struggled to get her breath back.

George just chuckled, her own recovery coming in a little faster. "We know those cars were used to pull cash and contraband from the house. Figured it was a high value target. Wanna see what we bought with the gamble?"

Without waiting for a verbal answer, I could hear her rustling with the buckles and straps. I couldn't see the big reveal, but I heard all the gasps.

"What is it?" I asked.

"How much cash is that?" asked Natalie. Her voice had moved a little beyond breathless to hushed.

"At least a million," said Alannah. "Although a lot more if it's all cash."

"Why didn't they carry that up tonight?" asked Lourdes.

I could hear George rustling around in the bag. "It was shoved to the side, and it's surprisingly heavy. It would have taken two of them to move, I suspect. Maybe they made a few trips, and left this for tomorrow."

"Makes me sad we didn't get the other bags," said Lourdes.

"Wow," said Natalie. "It really is all cash."

"Not quite," replied George. I could hear her digging

around, and then hefting something out. "Looks like there's some gizmos at the bottom. What are these?"

"Let me have a look," said Lourdes. She puzzled a minute or so, and then said. "I just don't know. Pass me the aluminium foil, would you Al?"

There was some crinkling sounds as Lourdes wrapped the unknown devices up. "Active or passive, no signals going out or in," she announced. "We can figure out what they are later."

"So that's why you brought kitchen supplies," commented Alannah. "For making the equivalent of little tin foil hats."

"Also for leftovers," said Lourdes.

Natalie laughed. "Haven't been any leftovers that I can remember. Haven't found the meal large enough to make 'em." Then her stomach growled on cue.

There was a general laugh at that, but it died quickly, as exhaustion started to creep in. The conversation hit a lull, and we were all lost in our thoughts for a while.

"THAT'S IT THEN, RIGHT?" asked Lourdes. "They don't have what it takes to restart Project Lycan again, and we can report a major explosion out there. Might be enough to put them under. Now we keep our heads down until that happens."

"Might have to be a while," Alannah said, "but I think you're right. They have no records of the successful trials, and it was luck that got them started in the first place. Without a successful sample, they've got nothing at all."

Then George asked something that took the edge off my feelings of relief. "Don't *we* count as successful samples?"

Chapter 10

THE BRAIN THAT CRIED WOLF

T he next hour was a bit fraught. We pulled into the nearest town, and Lourdes went into the pub, where she managed to borrow a phone, claiming her battery was tanked. After reporting to the local police, federal agencies, news and the fire services about seeing a huge explosion just out of town, she felt that she'd made enough fuss to draw several different kinds of helicopters out to the scene. Lourdes then thanked the kind local, and bought him a beer.

Upon her return, discussion centred around the core question: how long would it take, if ever, for it to be safe for them to return to normal society? George's question had somewhat reframed the possibilities in our minds.

On one hand, one could imagine the Bowline empire falling convincingly, leaving no-one to try to take up the kidnap-and-experiment legacy of Project Lycan. At the other extreme, one major disadvantage of telling the world what Bowline had done, even if the details of the experiments were redacted, was that now the whole world had some idea of what they'd done. It had been advertised on the black market as an extraordinarily effective physical enhancement program, and at least some people believed it was based on epigenetics.

Even with the brains trust of Bowline taken down, a sufficiently curious and amoral entrepreneur might decide to investigate what they were doing with all their guinea pigs. We didn't want anyone to replicate that project, even in the absence of the key original players. Not that they were all out of the picture.

Gannt was dead, but that still left Wüster, who had the best chance of anyone to reproduce his original serendipitous discovery. One positive was that he seemed to have been relying on the data that the Valkyries had destroyed. Would he stay quiet? Would he be caught? Or would he flee successfully to another fall-back position, with a burning desire to get his hands on us as samples?

"Not to mention, he knows about Kirsten," noted Alannah. "She'll be the main target if they go for that approach. It would make sense to do it quickly, if they were going to do it at all."

"That," I said, "is why I'm driving at speed back to Sydney. We'll be ahead of any people heading from that base, but they will have people back in town, and might be giving them instructions."

"You right to keep driving?" asked Natalie. "We need to get there in one piece, as well as fast."

I took a second to think about it. "As long as I eat soon," I concluded. "Seem to be holding up rather well. I'll tell you if that changes."

"At least we have cash to buy proper food now," said Alannah. "Have you counted yet, George?"

"About two and a half million," she said. "Or to put it another way, forty thousand pizzas each."

"That," declared Natalie, "is a ridiculous amount of cash to leave in the boot of a car. Heavy or not, I just can't believe that was left unguarded."

"I once saw a photo of a narc bust in South America," said Alannah, "where they found a billion US dollars in a room. Just kind of stacked in a huge cube. We've got to remember that this was a multi-billion dollar company on the reported books. You'd have to assume that the off-books stuff would at least rival that, or else why would they ever consider doing it? They'd just performed an all-night evacuation, and had unloaded nearly everything. Were they organised to the point of knowing where to put everything? Plus, they must be used to handling much larger transfers of cash all the time. It makes me angry to think about those assholes thinking about millions in cash as an everyday experience, but it probably was. Is."

"Still seems like a lot to me," said Natalie.

"Maybe, but it's not much of a retirement package for five people living under the radar," commented George. I could picture the subtle little shrug that went with the tone.

"Let's take things one at a time," suggested Alannah. "We don't know how all this is going to shake out."

The food purchase came soon after, and it was mighty. Pizzas didn't come quite fast enough, so I replaced a couple of my forty thousand with four hamburgers and large serves of fries. After a couple of hours, I felt a little greasy, but my energy was staying surprisingly level.

Dawn broke over the grizzled horizon as we reached the outskirts of Sydney. We slipped into a large all-night supermarket, and the four Valkyries swarmed it with a shopping list they'd constructed. Once inside, they found that it sold clothes as well as food. There certainly weren't many sartorial options, but they bought a lot, with the idea that we needed to look a little respectable and largely unrecognis-able in the middle of town. Back in the van, they delivered fruit, some tracksuit pants, a t-shirt, a fleece and a hoodie. Also some toiletries and deodorant. Maybe it was just my imagination, but were those last items delivered with a certain attitude? I suspected it wasn't my imagination, but I said nothing.

With a second shopping trolley full of other stuff, they poured back into the van, and we headed towards the US embassy.

"What now?" I asked.

"We're assembling our disguises, and you get us there," said Lourdes. "Then we scout for trouble."

"What are you going to do if you see it?" I asked. "I don't think there's a disguise in existence that will let you wander around with assault rifles."

"We will stop those bastards with pistols and knives," Natalie declared.

"...and force of personality," added Lourdes.

I considered suggesting that she go easy on the deodorant if she wanted her force of personality to be at full strength, but then decided to just grin briefly at my own joke. As we made our way under the harbour, I yawned.

"Think I'm going to need to crash in the van," I said. "Did any of you get any sleep at all?"

"We all got an hour or two," said Lourdes. "However, we're going to scout in shifts so that we can get a little more. George and Alannah are heading out first. Are you good to sleep in the front?"

"Sure," I said, and only a few minutes later, I pulled into a multi-storey car park in the CBD, and went to an unpop-ular corner of it. I heard the sliding door open, and George and Alannah got out. They came around the front, and looked for my reaction regarding their disguises.

"Looking good," I said agreeably. Their faces were clearly a little disappointed. Alannah was dressed in the splashiest winter fashions that could be assembled from a suburban supermarket. A huge hat and big sunglasses framed her face, and her stockinged legs went up a long way before they were covered by any kind of skirt. Her sleeves and shirt were frilly and puffy, and covered by a delightfully tight woollen top. She had a large handbag hanging on one elbow. I was most impressed by her boots, which I wouldn't have thought she'd have managed to get in the clothes aisle. She later explained that there was one of those busker-like leather stalls in the shopping centre just outside, and they'd opened crazily early.

George had done a magnificent gender flip. Whatever she was wearing around her waist was disguising her hips, and her chest was bound tight and flat under some comfortable layers and a quite nice looking men's leather jacket. Little touches here and there turned her undeniably female figure into a male presentation. I think there was a little makeup involved, but there was a lot more to it than that. Her short hair was brushed differently. Even more important was the change in her walk. I'd have clapped with sincere appreciation of the art of it, but that would have involved looking fractionally less cool.

"Long live the king!" I said, giving the faintest of smiles. I received a manly smile in return.

As my exhaustion finally started catching up with me, my brain was sliding from its default galvanised state to something more 'alarmed, but not alert'. I could feel my libido scratching to take over, but shielded inside my sealed cabin, it was but one thought of many. I gave them a little wave, and started setting up the front cabin as a bed. Once they were gone, I cracked open the window for air, and sank into the white noise of dreams, and then the depths beyond.

I WOKE TWICE, and had water and snacks. When the traffic started coming in to the car park, I closed the windows again. The third time I woke, it was with a significant headache, and a knocking on the window. Lourdes was dressed much like Alannah had been, and there was rustling in the back of the van behind me. As I struggled back to coherence, Lourdes tapped her ear pointedly, and I put my earpiece back in. It chimed as it registered where it was, and powered back up.

"Nat saw what she thought was probably a van doing a scouting pass," she said. "We're all heading out, in case this is a grab."

Somehow, I managed to clear my mental cobwebs enough to function. They shredded away easily, as I felt my slightly recovered brain become overwhelmed by its Lycan chemistry once more. "What about gear? Are you taking much firepower? Where's Natalie?"

"She's still there, so we have eyes if the van comes back," said Lourdes.

"I can't see it," came Natalie's voice. "No wait, I can. It's looping around the block. Call it four minutes worth of lights."

"Can't take anything too visible," said Natalie. "There'll be plenty of guns in the building in the hands of the officials, and if the Bowline goons attack the embassy, there might be police involved very soon. If we go in with rifles, we risk being shot by people we'd rather not shoot back.

Both on the way in, and then again on the way back out, and then once we're outside. Instead, we're going to be unexceptional members of the crowd outside. They'll bring Kirsten out, and we'll catch them by surprise, at short range."

"Makes sense," I agreed, "but I really don't like where the final plan ended up. The guns are still in play, just not for quite as long."

Probably unreasonably pessimistic of me, but as usual, my mind was constantly screaming that something was wrong. I had to fix it. I had to *act*. The urge was not quite overwhelming, but I wasn't even sure I should be resisting.

One of the problems with incessant, undiscriminating panic and paranoia was that it forced me to ignore sensations of alarm. But what if I really *ought* to be feeling alarmed? It was just like that classic story: The Brain That Cried Wolf. I took a deep breath and released it slowly. All plans seemed awful. This plan, specifically, also seemed awful. There were so many ways they could be hurt.

"Look after yourselves," I breathed.

Off they went. The pressure to follow them was palpable. I leaned back and closed my eyes. There was a sense of personal responsibility that was self-evidently delusional. I hardly knew them, and they hardly knew me. These were people I'd conversed with for a handful of hours during a particularly stressful period in all our lives. Nearly all of that short exchange was done at a considerable remove, due to my rather distressing physical reactions to them. They probably felt my existence was a burden they didn't yet know how to put down. Couldn't fault their manners to that point, but politeness is not the same as friendship.

I found myself crying lightly into my hands, but it was far from cathartic. Rather than release, I found myself getting more worked up. A couple stopped in a small blue car a few places away. When when they got out, I saw them slide into each other's arms and melt together for a kiss. The joyful contentment on their faces burned itself into my brain. Then, the dark-haired one looked over her shoulder and saw me watching. Suddenly shy, my distant presence was sufficient to break the moment. Embarrassed, I pretended to rummage around in the hamburger boxes at my feet. When I came up again, she'd led her partner towards the stairwell by the hand, and they glided away.

I sat, alone, shy, and ashamed in the front seat of a van. Memories of similar fragile, beautiful moments flitted past like they happened to someone else. Now I was so unsuited to them, that I could spoil them with a glance, at a distance. I sat alone, with my large, oafish hands and ungovernable passions that must be written across my face. The van smelled of grease and sweat, and so did my new clothes. When their chatter started up again, I felt like a voyeur listening in from another world.

Natalie: There you are.

Lourdes: OK, we're ready to rock. Any sign of the van?

Natalie: Not yet. It's taking them a while.

Alannah: Just find a natural reason to be hanging around. Don't attract attention. We need to be close to the door without hovering.

Natalie: OK... Where's George?

George: I'm across the street, buying some bagels.

Natalie: Come on, they might be here any second.

George (quietly): And if they come round the corner, I'll remember something and come over. But if they take a while, I'll have a lovely, delicious alibi lunch...

George (much louder): Oh hi, can I have two pulled pork subs, a caesar salad with chicken, a fruit salad, aaaannnd-ddd... what would you recommend? ... OK, I'll try that.

Alannah: They would have done the loop by now. That's the second set of lights since I've been down here.

Natalie: Maybe they were just passing, and they're off doing something.

George: Thank you!

Lourdes: Phones make the perfect loitering tool. How did people look distracted and casual before them?

Alannah: With ease. For me, it's these damn boots. I think there's something in them. Which gives me a chance to sit down.

Natalie: So where are you? Damn it... OK, I've been stood up by someone, and I'm cross and late. See? I'm peering down the road, and looking at the clock on the building over there. Nailing it. Also, genuinely interested in people coming down the road. Traffic's not that heavy.

George: Well, I've got lunch, and I can sit on this bench next to the pretty lady and have some.

Natalie: That sounds good.

George: You're cross and over there. I'm the one on my lunch break.

Lourdes: You've got food for more than one person there. Can I be your friend that comes over to have lunch too?

George: Since you asked nicely. Unlike 'Ms. Come-On-They-Might-Be-Here-Any-Moment'.

Natalie: Seriously, do you think they're coming back? Should we go back to taking it in turns? What if nothing happens? How do we manage it?

Lourdes: I like how you make it look like you're muttering angrily to yourself when you're talking.

Alannah: Let's give it a few more minutes. Settle in, but stay alert. I can't believe it was a coincidental drive-by.

George: No worries.

[Sound of a couple of people munching, and a non-verbal murmur of assent from Lourdes. Distant and nearby traffic sounds in the city. Buses and brakes. Honking SUVs and sirens.]

ALANNAH: Did you hear that from inside?

Lourdes: ... no. What was it?

Alannah: Shouting?

[Siren getting closer.]

Natalie: Why do I have a bad feeling about that ambulance?

Alannah: Oh shit, what a great extraction if you have people in the right places.

George: They're in the foyer. I'm chatting with you, Lourdes, but I'm also curious about the siren in a naturally nosey kind of way.

[Siren gets extremely loud, and then stops. Doors slam.]

Natalie (very quietly): I don't recognise any of these guys. Could they be legit paramedics? Is the catch at the hospital, or is this it?

Alannah: Shit. I don't know. It's a real ambulance. They either got hold of one, or called one.

Lourdes: There's a lot of variables in calling one with random paramedics. I'm betting this is the grab.

Natalie: So we...?

Alannah: We jump in at the last second?

Natalie: I'm game.

Lourdes: It's going to look very weird.

George: Could we intercept as if from the Embassy? ... Consulate General? Shit, better get the name right.

Alannah: I'm not sure we...

George: We're getting in either way. Remember your American twang, and try to come in behind the handoff.

[Distant shouting. Through half-voiced comments, I hear that the paramedics go inside, and then emerge soon after with an unconscious Kirsten on a stretcher. The wheels of the stretcher make a lot of noise, which gets louder as it is approached.]

~

UNKNOWN MAN (DISTANT FROM MICROPHONE): Clear the way, please! Clear the way. Thank you.

[A loud clatter as the stretcher trolley folds into the ambulance.]

Second unknown man: We'll take it from here. Thank you.

George (passable east coast American accent): This patient is to be escorted at all times. We are assigned to follow.

Second unknown man: You can't -

[Doors slam. Then a clicking sound. There is a thumping sound and a sudden expulsion of breath. Then a strange hissing.]

Alannah: What's that?

Unknown man: Our best case scenario. Five of you? You're too... kind...

[Another loud thump. The front door slams, and the ambulance moves off. The siren starts, painfully loud inside the vehicle, even through the microphones.]

Alannah: Why did he...? Shit! Hold your... uhhh.

[Frantic rattling of the door, which fades rapidly. Several thumps.]

Lourdes: Patrick: Al, George and I have got one of the trackers each. We...

[One more crash. The door rattling ceases. The siren continues.]

THE SIREN in my right ear continued for a long time after it could be heard in the street below.

Chapter 11

CLARITY

Shock, as I've said, can be very adaptive. It certainly quietened my demons. One moment I was literally shaking with repressed desire to leap from the van and burst into action. The next, there was a wonderful cessation of the conflict as I leapt from the van. All five of them had been taken, and I was going to have to drive with the tracker thingy in the front seat.

I jumped into the main part of the van with the intention of grabbing the electronic gizmo Lourdes had shown me from the back, but when I went in there, I decided to take a moment to get other things I might need in a hurry at the other end. I surveyed the chaos. There were still explosives left in the pile, but the lessons I had on using them were blurred and indistinct. That hadn't been a very focussed day.

The assault rifles had also been left behind. They were simpler than detonators and charges: they loaded from a magazine and had a safety and a trigger. Basically point and shoot. But how do you manage single shots? Or bursts? Maybe I had a better than even chance of being able to use them properly first time. Not much better than that, though, and I'd never practised firing them. I knew just enough to know that there were things I didn't know about trigger discipline. Or something. Was that important? Damn.

In the end, I demoted my firepower ambitions to the remaining pair of handguns. Again, I could imagine screwing up, but they seemed simple enough, and came with the benefit of several loaded magazines. I familiarised myself with them once more, and grabbed a blanket to wrap them loosely so they wouldn't bounce around. Then I grabbed the tracker doohickey and a large bag of dried bananas.

A tall man in a sports car pulled in next to me, and gave me the look over as he stepped out of his car. As I bundled things in the front seat in my leisurewear and gumboots, his face developed a superior sneer. The urge to murder him was there, and possibly righteous, but in that moment it was distant and irrelevant. I had a legitimate mission now, and it was letting me dismiss concerns that would have bedevilled me only a few minutes ago. Starting the van, I marvelled at this discovery. Then I backed out quickly, causing him to have to dodge, and I left the carpark to the sound of him screaming angrily behind me.

You should control your anger, mate, I thought. *It's not healthy to be so uptight.* Then my full attention was required to follow the trackers. The tracker widget gave direction and range, but I couldn't easily find something with a map, so I was constantly glancing down at the paper map, and trying to translate. Of course, the problem was much, much worse in a city plagued with one-way streets and complicated traffic flows. Fortunately, by the time I'd gotten out of the car park, the ambulance was far to the north. That meant I needed to take the tunnel under the harbour, which meant I didn't need to check again until I was there.

When I did check, they'd lost connection. Back up on the other side, I simply stayed on the main highway, and soon they reappeared on my screen several kilometres ahead. The gap kept widening for some time, but luckily they must have not been using their siren to cheat traffic. I suppose that would have brought too much attention. Instead, we both crept through the city. I still had no sound in my earpiece, but I wasn't sure about its range limits. Visions of the five of them being killed by the gas plagued me, but surely the fake paramedics would not have been so sanguine if it had been lethal.

If it weren't lethal, and it had been brought as a contingency, then the goons probably had gas masks and some method of securing the women. They'd probably done that right away, so I couldn't expect the Valkyries to free themselves. Instead, I'd have to follow them all to wherever they were going, and deal with whatever I found. This led to kilometre after kilometre of speculative planning. There wasn't going to be a lot of thinking time when I arrived.

If George had been right about the effectiveness of the explosion she'd engineered at the garage, then no-one from that black site had driven to Sydney that night. And helicoptering out would have been ruled out by the swarming news, police and emergency services. So chances were that the kidnappers in Sydney were either Bowline people left behind in key positions, or some kind of contractors. Someone from the Bowline inner circle would have to avoid anything known to be connected to Bowline. Their secret backup option had already been outed as well, so they would take them somewhere improvised. Chaos to the enemy.

On the other hand, if the job had been contracted to some external organisation, then they were probably better prepared. They'd go straight to an appropriately discreet and guarded base of operations. In either case, I wasn't going to be able to just drive up to their destination and achieve anything.

Other than dying, that is.

The tracker kept telling me to stay on the highway, so that's what I did. North and east, up out of the city and along the coast. Potentially hours of driving lay ahead of me again, so I stocked up hard in the petrol station. Over the course of a long drive, the cityscape was thoroughly replaced by tree-covered coastal hills. It was beautiful by any standard, and when there were houses, you could almost smell the money. Little personal piers with several boats on them replaced the standard ostentations of Sydney harbour.

I managed to close the gap on the trackers a little, but the dwellings kept getting sparser and larger, so I didn't push it too much for fear of accidentally following them up a private driveway. As I drove past a densely forested headland, I finally lost the signal entirely. Pulling off the road, I saw that the last known location placed them right on a property a couple of minutes drive away. Picking a parking place off-road, I crept a little closer, threw all my food in a bag, and then went in at a light jog. It might have been better to start even further away and come in more stealthily, but it didn't seem like time was on my side.

The soil was rocky, and the vegetation was classic Australian eucalypt-heavy scrub. I followed animal tracks, and soon got turned around. In the end, to avoid going around in circles, I made my way towards the sound of waves, and came out on a tiny beach made entirely of smooth grey pebbles, with trees going right to the edge of a jagged, rocky headland on either side. I made my way over the rocks, enjoying the fact that my gumboots were finally a decent choice of footwear for the terrain.

Waves slammed against the sharp and steep boundary to their world, spraying me a little as I clambered above them. Beyond the point was another tiny dent in the coastline, not qualifying as a beach or a bay. There was just enough of a point on the other side to break my line of sight. Twice more this happened, and then I saw a proper beach, perhaps five hundred metres long, with whitish sand, and its own little jetty. Two fancy-looking yachts were moored there, but there was no activity. A little sandy path worked its way from the beach, to where the map showed a very large residence, but my eyes showed me only trees.

Perhaps on a moonless night I'd have risked the beach, but I could not risk being seen, and I couldn't wait until then. Unfortunately, this meant going through the bush. I backtracked a little until I found a gap in the dense, tangled bushes that lined the cliff edge, and then I climbed up. Gumboots had reasonable edges, and I found the rock was solid, and held my weight reliably. Once at the top, however, the gap in the bushes turned out to be quite shallow, and moving was both slow and distressingly loud. I persisted, without moving too quickly, and soon found myself far enough back that there were paths through the trees.

Not too long before, I'd been contemplating both total reclusion and/or suicide. Being unable to trust myself not to be a danger meant that all company had to be forsaken. The last few days had teased me with a little taste of post-Lycan sociability, albeit with unique companions and under odd conditions, but ultimately, they had also tended to confirm my initial assessment. The beast inside me really wasn't safe.

The last few hours felt different. For once, my own cold-blooded assessment agreed with the beast. Action really was imperative, and if it came to it, violence was absolutely an option. In fact, I should emotionally commit to it before-hand, as hesitation on that front was suicide. Even with full-forward momentum, failure was likely. In that case I'd prob-ably die, and the Valkyries were all likely to be seed experi-ments for a new program that required no less than human sacrifices to progress. On the other hand, if letting the beast out allowed me to rescue them, hundreds of strangers would also be saved. That simple necessity of my actions gave me an unaccustomed clarity, although when I thought about the stakes too much, my composure threatened to crack.

So I simply didn't think about them. That too, became necessary. Instead, I thought about strategy.

Was this going to be a stealth mission, where I picked off the guards one by one? Probably not. Those are best done in films, in some kind of montage. Guard stands, alert: hands emerge from the bush behind him and pull him out of sight. Figure guards a doorway: just the torso of an upside-down silhouetted figure descends from above, snaps his neck, and rises out of sight. Three armed guards stand in a key vantage point: three silenced shots ring out, and all three figures drop without a cry.

If films were realistic, then most of those montages would end in the sudden, random death of the main charac-ter, as some piece of luck went against them. Maybe this rescue had to rely on some measure of luck, but a complete series of secretive surprise attacks would be best left to fantasy. Should I then capture the boss and exchange hostages? Try the element of surprise, and attack in a berserker frenzy? Frankly, no approach seemed *likely* to succeed, so in the end I decided to try to gather a little more information before committing. Summoning the spirit of the hunter, I crept closer to the hidden mansion.

~

UNKNOWN MAN: Hello! Hello! Report, please!

Alannah (distantly, quietly): We've taken them out, we can't.

[Slapping sound.]

Second Unknown man (distantly, Scottish accent): Shut it, bitch.

Unknown man: Hello! Can you hear me?

~

I HADN'T TAKEN out my earpiece in all that time on the off-chance that I'd be able to communicate, but obviously they'd been discovered. Slowly, I reached up and removed it from my ear, taking care not to bump or rub the microphone. It had a small button for switching channels, and one to mute. I checked the latter, and replaced it in my ear. Ahead, I could see the first signs of a clearing. I crept forward, placing my feet to make minimal sound, and watching for the first signs of humans.

~

UNKNOWN MAN: Is no-one listening? Well?

Alannah: They're short range. The four of us used them to talk.

Unknown man: Did you now? And who else has one?

Alannah: Bowline - we took them when we left. But

they're paired with each other. Bowline couldn't listen in even if they were here. Not until they reset them.

[Scratching sound close to the microphone. The man talking is unshaven.]

Unknown man: We saw the footage of the four of you running from Bowline's little bolthole. We picked up number five with you... So where's the sixth one? Or the man you pulled from the hospital?

Alannah: We dumped his body in the ocean. Should have been eaten by now.

Unknown man: Yes, you are bloodthirsty little sluts, aren't you? Can't believe you managed to kill two of my men even after they got the gas going.

[A mighty slap resounds in the room. From the echo, it sounds large. Lots of hard surfaces. I hear Alannah moan, and work hard to clear my mind.]

Unknown man: However, I asked about the sixth one, and you will tell me now where she is.

Alannah: She said something about having family in Australia.

[Another punch. There is coughing.]

Unknown man: She is English, and has never been here before.

Alannah: I don't know them. Or her, really. Maybe they visited her once. Anyway, she said she wasn't going to 'risk her neck' with us.

Unknown man: Is this true?

Natalie: Far as I know. She chickened out, and left us to fight you assholes by ourselves.

[Another punch. This one sounded like it might have broken something.]

Unknown man (almost cheerful): Spirited! I like you. Don't talk like that again, though, or I'll cut off your fingers.

Scottish man: Mr Silver, I just had a text from Hordones. He said he'd be another two hours, and he'd like to be on the ship as quickly as possible.

Mr Silver: Maybe we should put these packages on board, then. Get five of the guys to switch the new shipment over to the *Ladybird Special*, and make sure the *Buoyant Bride* is fuelled. Then get these bitches in the hold. And tell the Bradys to watch out for Hordones. We don't want any surprises when he gets here. We get paid in full, or he fucking goes in the hold with them, and we look for another buyer.

Scottish man: Yes sir.

Mr Silver: I'm going to have a drink and watch the footy. Call me when he comes.

Scottish man: Yes sir.

[Sound of the earpiece being removed roughly, and tossed onto something hard. Footsteps.]

Lourdes (distantly): You're not going to leave us back here? It's a much nicer view of the water.

Scottish man: After what you pulled, if I had me way, you wouldn'a woke up.

[The footsteps went silent as the earpiece decided it wasn't in the ear any more, and shut itself down.]

THE CLEARING WAS grassy to the left, and stony to the right. On the far side, I could see the dirt road that led out to the highway. As I got closer, I could see several buildings to the right. The first building I saw through the trees was massive, and utterly ridiculous. You know those oversized houses that spring up in certain new suburbs, where the owners just wanted more, more, more? Where they paid no attention to the fact that the floor plan practically reached the boundary of the plot of land in all directions? Plus they made sure to have a grand front entrance with columns in one style, and then a balcony off to the side in another style? This was like two of those had been built so close that they just said "fuck it", and merged them.

Behind that was a giant warehouse with a gabled roof that was the size of a couple of decent barns. The short stretch of road down to the water went past that. Looking in the dozens of windows, I expected to see goons moving, but the first signs of humans actually reached my nose before I saw them. Men. Sweaty and stinking of stale cigarettes. Turning upwind, I squinted. I finally spotted them when I heard one of them move when he received a text on his phone. They were high up on a platform built into a tree. Like a cross between a treehouse and the crows nest on an old-fashioned ship. The position was perfect - it would be very hard to spot when coming in by car, but had a great vantage over almost the whole site, including that side of Chateau de Silver, the warehouse, and the road to the water. I counted four of them up there, and though I didn't see any, I assumed they had rifles. Were they perhaps the 'Bradys'?

Thanking Quob's noodly appendages for my luck in spotting them before crossing the open area to the house, I backed around to the side. Lourdes had either fortunately or cleverly mentioned that they had a view of the water, but I was still loath to use that knowledge by running around to that side of the house and attempting to free them immediately. There were a lot of nasty, armed men around here, and the best armed and most ready for trouble were presumably watching over their hostages.

Still, I had to make a move at some point. Within a fairly short time, the Valkyries were going to be moved to one of the yachts over to the east. My choices were to try to free them before, during, or after they were moved. Aside from the obvious pain of delaying action, striking after they were installed in the yacht sounded the safest. There, they would presumably be locked in somewhere, and therefore guarded by a smaller contingent of thugs. If I could get to the yacht itself, there'd be plenty of chances to sneak around as well, I imagined. Although it might be a bit cramped for anything too fancy. I could probably sneak around this crazy house as well, but with many times more people to deal with, that seemed like a bad option. The Valkyries themselves would be most mobile when being moved, but that would mean no chance for surprise, and no cover for any of us from being shot.

A variant of the wait-until-they're-on-the-yacht plan would be to stow away properly, and just deal with Hordones and his goons once we were under way. That sounded best, but it relied on the yacht being large and complicated enough that long-term hiding was possible, and the ship didn't seem quite that large when I glimpsed it from the shore. Still, I could wait until I got to the yacht before choosing between that and busting them out before Hordones arrived. Decision made. The goal was to get to the shore as fast as I could. I was considering whether to go back via the shore or to go bush, when there was a zipping sound, and tree next to me was hit by something hard. Less than half a second later, I heard a cracking sound from the house. Looking up, there was a goon with a handgun, sighting down at me.

～

So. The plan I'd just made was in tatters, and all the other options were gone as well. If this turned into a big firefight, would the girls be executed?

I don't have a clear memory of moving. The next thing I was aware of was being in the open, going at a terrible speed across the line of fire of Goon-With-Gun. My feet spent very little time actually touching the ground. The Goon was standing on a balcony one floor up, and he got off three more shots as I closed the distance. There were many windows, a wooden door and a sliding glass door to choose from at ground level, but I didn't try any of them. Instead, I leapt for the edge of the balcony.

I knew I was going fast, and I knew I was stronger than anyone I'd ever heard about, but I still wasn't expecting to get so high. My left hand reached right up to one of the horizontal bars of the railing, and it bent as I pulled myself up as part of the same movement. From the Goon's point of view, he failed to track me as I'd sprinted, and then vanished beneath him. His head had just begun to lean forwards towards the edge, when I was suddenly in the air in front of him. The gun started to move, but my right hand grabbed his shoulder to complete my leap up onto the balcony. As I went up, he went down. I heard a cracking sound in his shoulder, and his gun jerked wildly to the side. My left hand came free, and I added a cracking sound to his neck as I landed. I prised his gun from his hand, and ran inside the open door. Somewhere between five and seven seconds had elapsed since the first gunshot. Everyone would be moving now, so I simply had to move faster.

Inside, the decor was a fusion between beach house and Wall Street penthouse. The walls were white and wood, and the furniture included materials such as dark polished wood and wicker cane. A set of glasses and a crystal decanter sat tastefully on a small, heavy dresser, and on the other side of the room was a large screen television. The only other door opened into a short, open corridor with several other doors, and stairs leading down to a large entry hall. Through the cordite, I could smell the tracks of countless men. I could hear footsteps and yelling. My best guess was that the women were down and behind me to the right, but from the doorway, I could see two more burly men with guns coming up the stairs.

The gun in my hand felt useless. In all likelihood, I couldn't hit someone with it. That takes practice, and I'd fired a handgun once in my life. I knew just enough to know that I didn't know enough. For example, I didn't know if it had one bullet left, or a dozen. There was no chance to rush them, so what I needed was something I couldn't miss with. My head spun back to the room I left, and in two big steps I had the dresser. The delicate crystal decanter and glasses were launched into the air as I snatched it up, and then three more quick steps got me back out the doorway. It just fit through sideways, which was fortunate, because imagine how stupid I would have looked if instead it had jammed me in the door frame and I'd been shot. Way too embarrassing.

The two men were appearing over the lip, and brought their guns to bear as I lunged, and threw the dresser as hard as I could. Exactly two shots went off as I rolled back along the corridor. The dresser tumbled through the air, and hit them both hard. There was a lot of breaking sounds as they both went aerial. My balance was coming back, but I didn't feel like following them down into that open space. I could hear a lot of people down there, and I'd run out of handy dressers. No, it was time to be somewhere unexpected again, so I burst through one of the doors in the corridor behind me.

Inside was a bedroom with the same confused decor. A

large window with a view of the ocean and the pier over-looked a queen bed and a built-in wardrobe. On the wall above the bed was a kitschy painting of a nude, and on the opposite wall was a wall-mounted screen. The room stank of some man, but was empty. I crossed it, threw open the window and jumped out with one hand on the sill.

On the way out, I surveyed the surrounding area. I could see the warehouse properly now, and I could see goons rapidly shutting the huge corrugated iron doors. The path to the pier was empty, as was this side of the house. I managed to slow considerably from my grip, and then let go as my arm straightened. Absorbing the shock of landing with a deft bob of the knees (thank you, childhood gymnastics), I saw that below was a set of open sliding doors. I'd landed squarely in front of a huge room full of armed goons. At least two had snub-nosed submachine guns, and many had handguns. Most had their backs to me, as they were looking towards a room further inside the building, where a dresser and a couple of their colleagues had just made a consider-able bid for attention. That meant that the first clear face I saw was Lourdes, who was liberally duct-taped to a wooden chair.

Her eyes widened as I landed behind the two machine gun-toting men who had just entered the room in front of me, and had conveniently left the doors open. George, Alannah and Natalie were similarly trussed next to her, modern-day mummies in shiny black. There was blood and bruising on their faces. Alannah's right eye was puffy and half-closed with a big welt. Anger welled up in me, and for only the second time in my life, I gave myself over to it completely.

Still spring-loaded from my landing, I turned that energy into a leap that took me into the air above and behind the two closest men. I could just reach both their heads, so I brought them together as hard as I could, as my body followed. From the feel of that impact, I knew they weren't going to be a problem again, so I shifted my attention to the next closest goon. Landing was awkward with the bodies in my hands, but I managed to get my feet back in under me. The next closest goon was still craning past the others looking inside, but three more of them behind him were already starting to react to my arrival. They were all reacting and moving very slowly, but even so, it was clear that time was going to be tight. I was pretty sure there was no way to avoid taking shots point blank.

Part of the need for haste was that I needed to move at least four metres to reach the ones that had noticed me, and another part of it was that the closer goon was blocking the way. I decided to use that as a feature, and use him for cover. That plan didn't survive landing, however, as my right foot snagged slightly on the hip of the body below me, so as I leapt sideways, I accidentally tumbled a little to the side. This meant that I first grabbed the guy by his gun arm rather than his torso, and was twisting past him. The charge wasn't going to work any more. Fortunately, this became clear long before those handguns started coming up. With a violent, anger-fuelled wrench, I simply used my goon as a missile instead. In a move reminiscent of high-school attempts at the hammer throw, I leaned into a half turn and released.

One of the least significant things that changed in Project Lycan was that I grew taller. One of the more dramatic physical changes was my weight, which approximately doubled. With all my forward momentum, I managed to whip the goon up to a decent speed. He rag-dolled across the room as I staggered backwards.

It worked much better than I expected. By the time I'd got my weight forward again, he'd hit two of them pretty hard, and had kicked the other in the shoulder. They were starting to fall as I ran to the third and punched him hard in the chest. I noticed blood on his fist as I did so, and thought of the blood on the faces of my four companions. Maybe that coloured my decision making, but even in hindsight I think that taking his gun would have wasted at least a second, maybe two, and I didn't have that kind of time. I'd already used about three seconds in this room, and any advantage of coming in from a surprising direction had been well and truly spent. I decided to replicate my success with the human missile, and grabbed him by the head and belt. Once again, it didn't feel like his body did well under the sudden acceleration, but he went flying acceptably.

That's when the first shot was fired, but I wasn't staying still. Shouts echoed through the house as I raced into the bodies ahead of me. It wasn't subtle, it wasn't skilled, and it wasn't pretty, but my attack was unbelievably effective. I may have only been a little larger than them, but they were half my weight, and less than a quarter of my strength. Most of them a lot less. I pulled limbs and heads, I snapped whatever joint I could reach. At one point I picked up a chair and used it as a monstrous club. Then I slipped on some blood, and scissored with my legs like a mad breakdancer. I leapt over obstacles, and despite all that, I would have been shot dead at least twice if it weren't for the help I received.

Lourdes had been the first to see me as I landed on the ground floor. I saw the flash of hope in her battered face, but there was no time to even think about freeing her. Every fraction of a second counted. My initial incursion into the room had been away from the side of the room where the girls were trussed. This had the effect of drawing all the attention away from them, and as the melee started in earnest, I saw George stand up. The duct tape didn't give way, but the chair she was taped to was wooden, and when she flexed hard, it simply came apart. The goons had taped her legs to the legs of the chair, and her forearms to the arms of the chair. That meant that when she stood and the chair shattered, she had armour on her back, clubs attached to her arms, and her legs were almost entirely free.

One of the men that had been covering her with a gun had swung it around in my direction. The fact that he stood a good chance of hitting some of his fellow goons didn't seem to deter him from taking sight. It also didn't make me feel any better about being shot, so I was very glad when George hammered her arms down on his shoulders. Her upper arms were still partially stuck to her chest, which gave her a comical T-Rex kind of look, but the wooden splint still slammed hard enough to visibly break the man's clavicle. She followed that with a kick to his lower back that sent him into the man next to him, who was also busy bringing his submachine gun into play.

Two goons later - call it a longish second - Natalie, Lourdes and Alannah tried to copy George's move. They each managed it after a few wrenching tries, but only Natalie managed to land on her feet. Alannah's twisting method dropped her to the ground, but it did also free her arms a lot more, and she grabbed a gun. Ten seconds later, the hand-to-hand phase was over, and everyone but George had a gun. I grabbed a knife from the floor, one that seconds ago I'd liberated from a bald-headed man who had tried to plant it in my right eye. While Alannah and Lourdes covered the two main exits from the room, I cut George's tape so that she could get a gun of her own.

"Thanks," I said.

She looked at me oddly. "Buy me some flowers later," she said, and then busied herself with looting some spare weapons.

Alannah and Lourdes also needed some extra help with some recalcitrant duct tape. While I was doing so, Alannah stepped to the side, and opened fire. I spun and saw a goon with a huge gun diving for cover behind a low, rendered wall. "I'll take some flowers too," said Alannah, and sent a couple of small bursts at the wall while we backed out of the open room. We needed to find somewhere more defensible.

The next room was really just part of a large open space that included a kitchen, a bar, a dining area and the front entrance. I could see that the windows on that side would afford good lines of sight for the four snipers I'd seen up the tree.

"Not safe that side!" I called, and ran around the interior wall. In the middle of the front entrance was a smashed up dresser, and a still body. There was a blood trail leading up the stairs behind me, but before I could turn properly, I was shot.

The pain and the noise were in different places. The *sound* of the explosion of the gunshot was up and to my left, but the actual explosion was in my forearm. I threw myself out of the way on instinct, and I rolled across the floor to the other bannister. Behind me there was a brief, deafening exchange of gunfire, and I saw Natalie shoot the injured goon who'd been crawling back up the stairs. She advanced up them, and delivered another round at point blank range.

I was still thinking clearly, to the point that I realised that I could only do that because of shock, and that my clarity probably wouldn't last very long. I chose not to look at my arm to prolong that window, but there was considerable blood, so I pressed hard on the injury with just a brief pause to pull off my shirt in order to fashion a temporary bandage. A small part of my attention was thinking about important diagnostic questions, about whether the bone was broken, or whether it had ruptured an artery. I was of the impression that both answers were 'no', largely because I had any doubt. My best guess was that it was just a grazing flesh wound, and that it was going to be fine if I simply ignored the pain and pushed on. Simple. Especially since not pushing on would rapidly be fatal.

"Why was he going up the stairs with a serious injury?" I asked out loud, although I was really just talking to myself. "Was he going away from something... or *towards* something?"

In the absence of gunfire, I suddenly became aware of the sound of sports commentary, and a distant, weak crowd noise. A television, upstairs. "Mr Silver," I said, indicating the noise.

The others were well ahead of my line of reasoning, and were hunting up the stairs, guns at the ready. I wound my shirt around my forearm. The very tiny fraction of my brain that had any perspective was noting how much fuss everyone would make over an injury this bad in any normal circumstance. Instead, we were wondering how to survive through the next few minutes.

Chapter 12

STATISTICS

Wooden floors made it hard to be silent, even for Alannah and Natalie, who were barefoot. The floor creaked as we passed. The door to the room with the active television was closed, and we crept up to it. I assumed that as the firefight broke out, some of the goons must have come up to protect him. As we got close to the door, we could smell that our suspicions were correct. Natalie sniffed for a moment, and then looked over her shoulder at the rest of us.

"Three?" she mouthed silently. Alannah nodded.

The pain was really setting in from my arm wound. I tried flexing my hand, and it worked, though it was extremely painful. Pulling the hand back was a lot worse, but I decided that I could safely ignore it.

George seemed to have an idea, and she slipped back to the stairs, then came back with the body we'd left there. Pointing at the door, she nodded encouragingly to Natalie. We all stood well out of the way, and Natalie reached from the side and threw the door open. There was no burst of gunfire, just a resounding crack as the door slammed into the wall, and started slowly swinging closed again.

A second later, George held the body out with one arm, and pushed it into the doorframe like a puppet. Several shots slammed into it, and she pulled it back.

"What the fuck do you think you're doing, you fucking sluts?" she shouted.

There was a considerable pause, and then Mr Silver's voice came out: "You're gonna fucking die, you bitches! I'm gonna fucking kill you!" His voice went high, and he sounded slightly deranged.

The five of us were making eye contact, rather desperately hunting for a plan. Charging in was suicide, and leaving them armed behind us was pretty close. I leaned in to whisper. "Where's Kirsten?" I asked.

The answer was in Lourdes' eyes before she opened her mouth. "She didn't make it," she replied quietly. I thought of the gentle caterer's assistant, and felt a little dissociated.

"'Mr Silver', I presume," I said.

"Who the fuck are you?" came the response. It was a comfortable snarl. Maybe he was back on familiar ground being sassed by a man. Lourdes used two fingers to mime sneaking away and raised her shoulders questioningly.

"I'm just asking some important questions of each of your employees," I said. "Would they rather die than shoot you in the head and surrender? May I say, the others sure have been loyal. Wow."

We looked for an alternative place to go. I thought about trying to go bush, but there were too many people trying to shoot us on both sides of this crazy McMansion to make it across the cleared area.

"Fuck you," came the response from inside the room.

Alannah pointed at the other doors up on this level, and then slunk off to investigate. A standoff was bad for us. We were far too exposed here, but exposure was even worse downstairs. We were flanked, and needed to create a safe direction.

"I mean, I *think* I asked them first. Did I ask them first? Shit, maybe I forgot. OK, I'll ask you guys. Would *you* rather die than shoot this asshole in the head for me?"

"You fucking threatening me, dickless? I'll cut your dick off, and piss on the hole," snarled Mr Silver.

I decided not to point out the lack of self-consistency there, as we were doing a silent inventory of our liberated weapons and ammo.

"I don't think you can threaten someone to shoot *themselves* in the head, moron," I laughed. "This is just a last chance for your cronies."

Alannah came out of one room holding a handful of plastic-wrapped bricks of some white powder. Depending on the powder, it was probably worth enough on the street to buy a luxury car, or a mansion. Her body language suggested that she was pissed that there wasn't anything useful. There was a clatter downstairs, footsteps, and chatter. Whatever move we were going to make, it was time to make it. I held out my hand for the drugs, and Alannah passed them over with a quizzical look. I indicated the activity below, and motioned that I was going through the door, then I quickly opened the packages, slicing the tape with my new knife.

"You do *not* know who you're dealing with," came Mr Silver's voice. It seemed he'd heard the sounds below as well, and was getting ready to be the rock to their hard place.

"I'm hoping that's basically the *only* thing we have in common," I said, catching George's eye, and miming throwing the powder into the room, and then indicating for her to pass me the body afterwards. Looking to Alannah and Lourdes, I flicked my head in the direction of the stairs. They were coming.

Then, without waiting for confirmation or clarification, I mimed taking a big breath, and then used a half million dollars of powder to fill the doorway, and then pegged the others in to slam against the walls. A shot rang out. George obligingly released the body when I grabbed it on my way into the cloud-filled room. I had to close my eyes as I entered the explosion of white, and I heard a sneezing spasm to my right. On the threshold I probably couldn't be seen clearly, but I knew that wouldn't last as I went further inside. Trusting to my meaty shield, I used the wall to change direction fast, and continued the charge.

Five shots slammed into me. Or maybe the body I was holding like a shield. I felt the kicks as I burst into the room. Inside, it was almost like a studio apartment, with a bed and sitting space. Three men had positioned themselves as spread out as possible, so they all provided crossfire to the doorway. The window was huge, with yet another amazing ocean view, and I regretted that I hadn't tried that entrance instead.

The guns all tried to track me. As I travelled in, I moved in front of the one to my right, and that meant that he had a clear shot at my unprotected body. I needed to move fast, so I threw the body at the gunman to my left, and leapt at the one to my right. He was still pulling his gun around to point at me when I reached him.

My forward momentum carried me into his chest and belly, and I added an upward strike to his nose with my elbow as I swung my legs to give another big jump. I grabbed him as I moved, and threw him instead. The wall next to my head exploded from a bullet impact, and chips of wood punched into my face, but he cartwheeled through the air at the muzzle where I was aiming, and that blocked the next shot. As I started to move, George appeared in the room, and shot the remaining two men. She was much, much faster than them, but it took her seven shots to land two hits on each. They went down, and she finished them while I staggered. That shrapnel from the near miss had hurt the side of my head more than I thought.

Natalie came in, and inspected the room. There was an exchange of gunfire outside, and she called out "clear to come in", as she went to the window. After replacing her empty weapon with those from Mr Silver and his loyal troops, George looked over at me, and her eyes flashed wide with momentary fright.

"Patrick's been shot in the head!" she told the others as she came over.

I brushed her away. "Just shrapnel," I said. "We've gotta look for an exit."

Lourdes came in, and obviously there was still a lot of whater-it-was in the air, she hadn't held her breath enough as she came through the doorway. She sneezed, and then sneezed again, and then coughed.

George's hand was firm, and my gum-booted foot slipped on some blood on the floor as I tried to move.

"No. You've been shot in the head, you dumbass," she said. "Let me look properly."

I reeled a little. "I'm OK," I insisted. "Let's keep it that way by finding a way out of here."

Natalie pulled back from the window. "It's swarming down there. I counted three at least, and one of them saw me."

"That's a pity," I said, "because the other side is where the snipers are. That's pretty much our only clear direction, unless we want to hold out here."

"Not an option," said Alannah. "They'll have weapons other than guns, and if we're pinned, they can blast us out with impunity."

"Can we sneak out?" asked Lourdes. Even though she was holding it in well, an edge of hysteria had crept into her tone. Nothing wrong with that. I think that really spoke to all of us.

"It's a really big house, but it's just a house," said Natalie. "We might be able to surprise, but there aren't enough options to get us around secretly. We're going to have to fight our way out."

George was trying to investigate my head wound, but again I shrugged her off and wiped the blood out of my eyes with my bicep. "They're still better shots than us," I said, "with the possible exception of Alannah, and this is a gun fight. So far we've used our strength and speed to make it a brawl, but even that didn't go great. Do we have any advantages that we haven't used?"

No-one came up with any. The sound of footsteps in the corridor told us we had company outside. Alannah and Lourdes took aim at the doorway. We were bleeding, trapped animals, and we'd been lucky so far.

"Don't you goons want to know Mr Silver's new orders?" I asked, trying to peer through the window. There wasn't anyone in view, which probably just meant they'd had time to find a position to shoot at the window from cover.

"We know enough to kill yer," came the reply.

"Scottish guy!" I said. "Wondered where you were. How about we settle this with a contest of strength? Man to man?" The window was easy to open, and I did so. Outside air came in, clearing my head considerably.

"Sure," he sneered. "Put yer guns down, come on out and we'll do that."

I whispered almost under my breath, and tried to orient the others by pointing at a sequence of directions moving clockwise. "Snipers. Warehouse. Pier with two yachts. Bush-bashing to the coastline. The van, parked off road on this side, south of the turnoff."

Louder, I said: "You're Scottish... What do you think about dwarf tossing?" I accompanied the question by picking up Silver's corpse, and throwing him as hard as I could into the corridor. It smashed dramatically into the far wall. "...Or is that uncool? I can't help feeling like it might be a little insensitive."

Lourdes whispered quietly. "I reckon I could jump cleanly out of here to the ground and be ready to go."

We looked at each other with interest, a hopeful flash coming across many faces. The ability to be somewhere unexpected quickly might just save us.

"It's so sad we don't have to take his orders any more," came a voice from outside that I didn't recognise. "If you come out I'll thank you personally for the promotion." I suppose I had plenty of entirely valid reasons to hate all of these drug smugglers, but something about this guy's voice made my skin crawl. I was still facing George and Lourdes when he spoke, and I saw a visceral reaction flicker across their battered faces as well.

Lourdes and George started moving to get as broad a view out the window as possible. "Can't see anyone down there," whispered Lourdes. "Maybe we could get out fast enough?"

I shook my head, and pitched my voice for the group outside. "You're not worried that there'll be disagreement about who gets to step up?" I asked. "Do you and Scottish guy need to have a conversation? We could always leave you alone to sort that out safely, if you like." It sounded like I was afraid, and looking to deal, but that was only half true. I wasn't stupid enough to expect any deal to be honoured. Or even offered, really.

Alannah didn't look away from the doorway she was covering, but she pitched her whisper for us. "Still take several seconds to get to cover. Won't make it if we run."

Natalie, by her side, agreed. "Be safer start to a fight down there than going out this door, though."

A clatter of footsteps came up the stairs. Perhaps three more arriving, although it might have only been two. They whispered very quietly, but weren't aware of our increased hearing, so we all heard the exchange:

Newcomer: Here they are.

Self-promoted guy: Not tear gas?

Newcomer: This was faster to put my hands on.

Scottish guy: We gotta clean up the place anyway.

Self-promoted guy: On three...

I WHISPERED. "LOURDES' plan. All down together, guns first. Just go hard, keep moving fast. Shoot them from somewhere they don't expect, and get to cover."

George, Lourdes and Alannah nodded, but they hadn't even whispered their count outside, and it must have been very fast. Before we had time to get out, there was a clatter of metal, and three grenades bounced inside the room. George and Lourdes had already leapt out with some measure of control and planning. Alannah and I had to accelerate suddenly, and we also had to turn around and make a two-stride sprint through the window. My gumboots and her bare feet had decent traction, but I was still half twisted as I basically exited the building horizontally. There was a tiny flicker of deja vu, but I was busy.

I didn't know much about grenades, but movies and games had led me to believe that we had about three seconds, which seemed ample. On the way out, I saw one grenade come much further in than the others, and it passed Natalie as she followed us. Reflexively, she reached down and flicked it back out the doorway before leaping. It was part of stooping for the jump, so it couldn't have cost her more than a quarter of a second. Unfortunately, it cost her balance. Like Alannah and I, Natalie came out of the window head first, but unlike us she was still tumbling, and arced into a slow forwards somersault that looked like she would land on her back.

There was gunfire from both George and Lourdes. Just before landing, Alannah had even managed to spot someone and get a burst off with her submachine gun. I didn't spot who they were firing at, and didn't have time to do so. I was trying not to land awkwardly myself, while simultaneously tracking Natalie's descent. At the ground, I had a thrill of fear as I hit hard, and I had to execute a roll. Lourdes' prediction was right, though. I hadn't really adjusted to my body's heightened capabilities, and it was disconcerting how easily I handled the landing. As I rolled, I saw George and Lourdes running for the trees, spraying shots on either side of the little courtyard. Alannah was rolling with me, one arm bracing the impact, and the other tucking her gun inside a circle. It gave me a flashback to my childhood judo lessons, which used to happen at the police academy.

Then my feet gained traction as they hammered over into the grass. Natalie was indeed coming down more or less on top of me, but awkwardly. "Catching you!" I called, and then attempted to do so. She was heavy, and coming in fast, so I overbalanced and we went down in a tangle of limbs. Nothing was badly hurt in the process, however, and I wasn't even shot. That was the moment that the grenades went off.

A cluster of explosions rocked the house above and behind us. There was at least one scream as well, so maybe Natalie's flick had exposed someone. Perhaps more usefully, it distracted Lourdes' opponent, and she got close enough to land her shots. Natalie, Alannah and I scrambled up, and we all sprinted for the bush. Bullets flew past on the way, but the advantages of distance and speed meant that no-one was hit.

As we got to the water's edge on one of the tiny pebbled beaches, all of us were the worse for wear. I was feeling light-headed and woozy, and as I tried to lead us south in order to work back around to the van, I staggered a bit. George caught me.

"Let me have a look at your head," she said.

She said it rather firmly, but I tried to shake it off anyway. She was really, really strong, though, and I found myself standing with my feet in the sea, and my chin turned so that the sore part of my head was pointing towards the sun.

"Too much blood in the way," she muttered, and scooped up a handful of seawater. It stung like chilli juice in the eyes as she poured it on, and it took a large effort of will to act like it didn't. The second one was worse, and her hand started wiping dried blood from my cheek and neck. It was an intimate touch, and would have felt gentle and kind if it weren't so absolutely agonising. Her expression was genuinely concerned as she peered carefully at the part of my head I was trying to ignore. I waited for the prognosis, suppressing a flinch at each touch.

"It's bled a lot, but I think it's pretty shallow," she said, half to herself. "Shouldn't be making you wobble. What about the arm?"

When she reached for my blood-soaked shirt wrapped around my arm, I couldn't stop the flinch. She waited a second, and I controlled myself. Alannah and Natalie stayed at the edge of the vegetation line, listening carefully for pursuit.

The shirt that I'd used as a bandage had partially stuck to the wound, so unwinding it was simultaneously hellishly painful, likely to reopen the wound, and important in terms of proper care. She softened it with seawater, which also stung a little, but the pain was already near a kind of local maximum. After a few moments, George muttered: "This needs proper bandaging, so I'm going to leave this here until we make it to the van. Can you hold it together?"

"I fine," I assured her, quavering a little from the pain. "I mean: I'm fine."

I bit my lip. "It hurts," I admitted.

There was a brief moment where I let myself feel a little relief that it had gone as well as it had. Seeing the four of them standing on the beach, battered, bleeding and thus far victorious, I felt a little smile creep on my face.

"So you're all pretty awesome," I noted. "You'll certainly have a decent honour guard when you finally head to Valhalla."

Then I remembered. "What happened with Kirsten?" I asked soberly.

Lourdes stopped washing her face for a moment. "Whatever they gave her to fake a medical condition, she just never woke up. We woke tied up in the van, and she was dead on the stretcher."

I couldn't think of something to say about that, but it seemed like it demanded some kind of acknowledgement.

"Poor Kirsten," I said. "She didn't deserve that."

Nothing else that jumped to mind seemed to fit. I decided, without mentioning it to anyone, to learn how to make brownies and bread in her honour.

"No she didn't," agreed Alannah. "And neither did the rest of us."

The waves crashed against the rocks, and the water came up to our ankles. The sand melted away from under our feet as the water pulled back, and we sank a little into the beach.

"Well, let's get to the van," said Alannah.

I nodded, and led them south. "We better circle round. It'll take another ten minutes, but it'll keep us out of their search radius," I said. "Assuming they're searching."

Once off the rocks and up into the scrub, we broke into a fast jog, and before too long we got to the road just south of where I pulled off. I heard a car to the north, and we made it back to cover. It stopped before it came past, however, and we moved forward carefully. We kept to the trees, except where it was quieter to slip onto the road briefly. A lazy afternoon easterly breeze whispered in the trees above.

"I smell the van," said George, quietly. Just after she said that, I did too, along with exhaust fumes, and several men. And cordite.

A faint voice in the distance, perhaps four hundred metres through the trees: "They'll be coming here. Prime those, and set up two sniper nests. Maybe they'll be worth something dead."

The subsequent clicks and shuffling suggested that there were more than a dozen men buzzing around the van. The van that represented our method of escape. With first aid supplies, and food. With weapons. And, considering long-term concerns, the van with a huge bag of cash.

The van that was being wired to explode.

I crept over to Alannah. "Any chance you've got some bomb disarming experience?" I whispered.

She shook her head.

An inventory of expressions told me that no-one had a good idea. I indicated that we should back up, so that we could talk. Perhaps a kilometre further away, we huddled. "Let's list options," said Alannah. "I see rushing over there and trying to shoot them all dead, going back to the mansion and shooting them all dead, or trying to hike back to civilisation. Are there any others?"

"That hangar thing," suggested Natalie. "I think it's got serious hardware in it. If we took that, we might be able to kick it up a notch."

"The yachts," I suggested. "There's two of them at the pier, and one of them is being prepped for Hordones. I understood that you were going to be put on there as cargo, and he was going to escape to wherever villains make their evil lairs. My original plan was to hide on that and try the rescue at sea, though I nearly wussed out because I thought it might not have a suitable hiding place. Would have been more embarrassing being shot dead while hiding in a cupboard."

"You looked ridiculous enough doing a He-man rescue in gumboots," noted George.

"Fair point," I conceded. "Anyway, they were moving valuables from the yacht Hordones was taking to the other one. I forget which was which."

"The *Ladybird Special* was the one they were keeping, and the *Buoyant Bride* was the one we were going to be shipped in," said Lourdes. I raised my eyebrows, impressed at her memory. "The name of your slave ship does tend to stick in the mind," she shrugged.

"OK, they'll have first aid supplies and they'll be a fast way out of here," noted George. "How long do we have before Hordones is due?"

I shrugged. My sense of time wasn't great on a good day, and this didn't count as one of those.

"About an hour," said Alannah. "Should be plenty of time to get round there."

The boat plan seemed to win the meeting, so we back-tracked. I felt a little woozy again, and pulled from my zip-up pants pocket my emergency backup fudge. Focussing on it, I counted the pieces. "Only three each," I said, and opened it up, "but they're pretty big." Looking up, eight eyes were tracking my right hand with a sudden, fierce, reverence. Resisting the urge to wave it and watch them sway, I passed the bag to George.

"I told you we should keep him," she said solemnly, and took her share. The bag went around, and the contents were disposed of efficiently. "Let's move out."

Going back was quicker, as we didn't fall for any false paths that ended up in barely passable scrub. Once again, we were helped by our sense of smell, which guided us along our previous path. We jogged alone in a line, with Alannah in the lead, then Natalie, Lourdes, me and George. As we came back to the beach yet again, we had more width, and had to negotiate the rocks more carefully. Alannah and Natalie slowed a little for the sharp parts in their bare feet, so George and Lourdes piggy-backed them. I followed just behind Lourdes.

"So," she said quietly, "you seem to be doing a lot better than yesterday at being near people. How are you feeling?"

We skipped from rock to rock across the point, finding flat surfaces, avoiding slimy rock pools.

"It's... still all there," I managed, only really noticing it for the first time. Every reaction I'd ever suffered under these changes was still pressuring me. If anything, that nameless drive and fight was the source of my energy at the moment, just as much as the fudge. "It isn't bothering me as much, though, you're right. Maybe it's better because I've got something to do."

"Makes sense," Lourdes replied, as we came into view of the next tiny bay. It was the micro-beach. We scanned the edges of the vegetation for lurkers, and then plunged on. "Just give us a bit of warning if you need anything, right?"

"Sure," I replied, though my instinct was that it didn't really work like that. So how *did* I think it worked?

Before too long, the five of us were peering around a pitted rocky wall at the large open beach that led to the jetty and the yachts of the drug-runners. A couple of armed guards stood at the jetty, watching keenly for any intrusions from the bush.

"So rush them, snipe them or sneak?" asked George.

"Can't rush them - they'll see us for ages before we can get close," said Natalie.

"Can't snipe them with pistols, or subs," added Alannah.

"Can't sneak for the same reason we can't rush them," said Lourdes. "Unless... we go by water?"

It was more than four hundred metres from the point to the yachts, and we'd have to go out to the darker water if we wished to be hard to spot. The thought wasn't attractive in winter, as the water was numbingly cold. Even the sea breeze on my dry skin was a little chilly, and I'd been jogging for the last half hour.

"I don't suppose the guns would be much use after that," I asked.

"No," replied Alannah simply. "We'd have to leave them behind."

"Well that's unappetising," I added. "I've quite enjoyed the bit where you were able to shoot back."

"Better ideas?" asked George.

There weren't, and so after a brief pause, she backed off to the beach, stripped off the rest of her now-tattered costume, and tucked it and her weapons under a bunch of ferns. She had bruises across her torso and several on her legs. Without fanfare she dived into the sea, and began swimming out beyond the point. The others started copying her, and I found myself watching them for a moment in their underwear, with predictable results. I blinked and quickly added my gumboots to the pile, and then pants. I left my shirt tied on my arm, and raced for the freezing water. I got there seconds after George.

The seawater was not just cold, it stung. My bruises enjoyed it, but my scrapes flared with pain. By the time my shot arm went under water, the pain was intense. Part of that was the water pulling on the fabric that had become bound up in the early clotting, and part of it was the water in the wound itself. Fortunately, my mind was soon distracted from that pain when my head went under water. Unfortunately, the distraction consisted of lancing pain where water washed on my head wound. I briefly worried about whether the blood would attract sharks, and wondered whether I should have tried to bring the knife after all. Probably would have dropped it when my head went under water, anyway.

As I got out to the level of the rocks, I started spending more time under water, surfacing only to take a breath. This made me harder to see, and also made it easier to negotiate the waves. Following George, we made our way out far enough that the waves were breaking just past us, giving us cover. As we got deeper, I found something quite distressing - I could no longer float. Whatever else changed, my density must have gone up considerably, because with no effort I was sinking disconcertingly fast to the bottom. With a very full breath it wasn't too hard to swim up to the surface, but my mind rebelled at the change, and it made me flustered and upset.

Perhaps it seems silly, after all the obvious wrenching changes to my self-identity, that the ability to float even registered. But once upon a time, Patrick Arthurs had been a very good swimmer. For some reason, realising that was never going to be true again made me mourn him. It was a surreal feeling.

Perhaps the others experienced somewhat similar buoyancy changes. They were diving deeper than they needed, although none of them seemed to be pushing off the sandy bottom like I did whenever possible. Water clarity wasn't great, but I saw a fuzzy blob where George was, and I could see two more behind me when I turned my head. After a few minutes, the blobs behind me went overhead, and I was at the back of the chain. Rather than feel unmanned by this, I simply kept working hard not to drown.

Sometimes when I surfaced, I'd be behind a wave, and that was good for being sneaky. Sometimes I'd be able to see the yachts and the shore, which was good for staying on course. On those occasions I took care to breathe fast and deep, and get down again quickly. Once we reached level with the yachts, we turned and came in towards the shore. When we got close, I found that it was less effort to walk along the bottom for some of the way, and then jump up for a breath. We reconvened under the jetty, hands grabbing onto the horizontal supports underneath as our heads huddled together. I was tired.

"So which yacht?" asked Lourdes. "Or should we sneak up and take care of the guards?" She indicated the heavily armed group down at the end of the jetty.

"Sneaking around with those guards in earshot creeps me out," I said, "but taking them out would announce our presence, which means that we'd have to leave in one of these yachts right now. On the other hand, if we leave those guards there, we have a lot more choices. For example, we could hide on a yacht or just leave all together." I tipped the water out of my ears. "Of course, they might hear us anyway if we screw something up."

"There's a lot of risk attacking them, even from behind," replied Alannah. "Plus, we don't even know if we can operate either of these boats. Ships? Whatever. I vote for checking them out quietly."

Alannah looked around, and saw shrugs and nods. We decided to split up. Alannah and Natalie joined me on one ship, and George and Lourdes went to the other. The vessels looked a lot bigger up close, and after some puzzling, we reached them by climbing up the underside of the pier itself, and then slipping across under the gangplank. Rather than going up over the edge, which would unnecessarily risk being seen, we spent an extra couple of minutes to traverse around to the far side, holding the side of the ship. This told us that we were on the *Buoyant Bride*, as we passed the name on the hull, and it also had the side benefit of letting us dry in the breeze. When we went up on deck we were merely damp rather than sodden.

I have no idea how much a ship costs. This one had a larger floor-plan than an oddly shaped house, and it had several stories. It seemed expensive. I wouldn't have been surprised if it cost millions. Running drugs and people seemed to be a very profitable business. Who knew? Then again, the Bowline people were buying it and a cargo of kidnappees with cash, so...

I didn't really have a 'so'. I just felt depressed as I slipped past beautiful, weather-resistant exteriors, and opened a door onto tasteful luxury. Whoever had designed the house had not been let loose here: the interior was amazing. Wood and white, functional, simplistic, efficient and elegant. We made our way to the cockpit, where I immediately felt intimidated. The navigational systems looked complicated, and although the other controls were simpler, I felt like I could easily miss something important.

"What do you think?" I asked. "Not sure I could manage it. Do you think Hordones is bringing a captain?"

"Doubt it," replied Alannah. "He likes gadgets and exotic travel. He's rated on small and medium aircraft. I'd bet he'd know how to run this thing."

Natalie was looking over the navigation equipment. "Is there a transponder or anything?" she asked. "If we stole the ship, could they find us?"

"Probably," I replied. "But if they are taking this thing long distances and smuggling drugs, they probably know how to fake things like that." I looked at the multiple systems. "Not that I do."

"OK," said Alannah, "let's move fast and look through the rest of the ship. We said we'd meet Lourdes and George back under the jetty in five minutes." The next few minutes showed us a glimpse of a life that only a chosen few ever experience. I'm not sure which was my favourite area: the bar, the spa (on a boat?), the entertaining area, the exquisite sleeping quarters... Maybe it was just the sun deck, which had nothing fancier than a view and some comfortable seats. If I owned the ship, I think I'd move around frequently, as the lazy days wore on, and we hopped from island to island.

The fridges were stocked, but otherwise the ship was empty. I noticed a few smells in the storage rooms down below that reminded me of the cloud of white powder back at the mansion. Also the unmistakable tang of gun oils and ammunition. There must have been a lot of it at one point. We scouted for possible places to hide ourselves, and nothing stood out. There was plenty of space, but nowhere that we could feel sure wouldn't be used or investigated before Hordones and his crew left the dock. For example, those ample storage spaces. We could hide there, but presumably Hordones would be bringing his own stores on board. Alternatively, we could all try hiding in bedroom closets, but then if a single goon put away some pants, we might all be discovered.

I imagined Hordones making a brief tour of the spa room where he discovered that the human specimens he thought had got away had instead delivered themselves. Luckily, the odds were too low to think about risking it.

A little less than five minutes later, we swung over the edge of the boat, and went hand over hand round to the gangplank. A little more than five minutes later, we were back under the jetty, hidden and silent. Without George or Lourdes. Several minutes went by.

I leaned to Natalie and whispered: "Surely we'd have heard if something went wrong?"

She shrugged. "Maybe someone came, and they're waiting."

Approximately four more minutes passed, although I didn't have a watch or a phone. Or an absence of a throbbing head injury. We heard footsteps coming over the gangplank, too loud to be George or Lourdes. They were moving at a brisk walk, so at least they weren't involved in some kind of pursuit. We heard a brief discussion as whoever it was passed the guards on the end of the pier, but the breeze heading away from us made it hard to make out entire sentences. It sounded like they were 'ready'.

If there were goons looking this way, it certainly explained the delay. Sure enough, a couple of minutes later, Lourdes and George surfaced next to us, having swum under the other ship.

"Nearly got seen," Lourdes whispered with a hint of excitement. "We were checking out the storage bays down below when they arrived. Luckily they were carrying weapons, so they didn't come into the money bay."

George slipped down into the water. "I vote we take that one," she said, eyes twinkling as she indicated the other ship with her thumb.

"Money... bay?" asked Natalie.

"It wasn't full," said Lourdes, with some relish, "but let me put it this way: we *did* hide behind the money, in case they opened the door."

I tried to imagine the block of cash that would provide cover for the two of them, but my head hurt too much, so I had to pinch the bridge of my nose.

"The drugs one was full, though," added George.

Lourdes nodded with relish. "I reckon they're planning a trip to distribute, and then to buy more stock. Or maybe they're planning to buy a second yacht, now they're about to be reduced to just the one. Makes me wonder what's in that fucking warehouse."

Lourdes drifted off into her imagination for a moment before continuing. "Anyway, they were carrying something for the room with all the weapons. I suppose that's an armoury, but it was just another one of the storage bays. They've got ammo, guns of every shape, and they just brought in some rocket launchers."

Alannah's eyes narrowed. "They had explosives and equipment to booby-trap the van as well. This operation goes well beyond narcotics..."

"I'm glad the boat's full of exciting contraband, but can we actually move the thing?" I interrupted. "The controls in the cockpit in the *Buoyant Bride* didn't look too bad - apart from the navigation stuff - but there were no labels on half of them. I'd hate to start the engine and then have to sit there for ages as I figured out how to pull the anchor, or something."

"No, it wasn't too bad," said Lourdes. "My family has a boat, and those controls looked fine to me."

"Don't need a crew?" asked Alannah.

"It's not a sailing ship. I could do it myself given time. Quicker with help, but it's basically just untying," she replied. "Mind you, it'll take a minute or so of noise before we get moving. And it'll start pretty slow.

That wasn't good news. Then, snatches of conversation reached us, coming from the west. I held up a finger to forestall more discussion and listen. Again, it was quite indistinct at that range. They were a lot further away than the end of the jetty, but I'd heard it because there were a lot of them, and they were having a very loud and heated discussion.

"Could that be Hordones already?" asked Natalie.

"If it is, we need to be on the far side of the ship," I said. "We can't sneak aboard on this side if there are people on the jetty."

"Why not just let him go, and take this other boat?" suggested Lourdes.

"This has to end," Alannah replied darkly. "I'm with Patrick."

I started climbing. "We can always choose to let go and swim back to here. We can't do the reverse," I argued, careful to keep my voice low. Lourdes was holding onto the cross beam, looking extremely conflicted. "Stay," I said. "We could easily wind up needing someone on this side anyway."

This didn't seem to bring much relief, but she nodded thoughtfully, and climbed a little higher into a more comfortable and hidden position. The other three followed me, hand over hand, and then a quick traverse in the shadow of the gangplank's walls, until we were on the far side.

"So do we just hang off the side?" I asked. "Or try hiding on board?"

"Traditionally," noted Natalie, "one hides in the lifeboat, under the cover."

Yes one does, I thought. *Should have thought of that originally.* "Will we fit?" I wondered out loud.

"Yes," said Alannah. "It'll be tight, but we can make it work."

It was easy to get to a lifeboat without being noticed. There were two of them situated near the rear on either side, and the one on our side was hidden from the jetty by the upper deck cabins. The lifeboat was covered by a rubberised tarpaulin with ties that were unsurprisingly easy to remove. We popped open the tarp on a corner, and slipped in one by one. I went in last, and then spent a tense minute trying to reseal the tarp from inside. When it was smooth and attached, I lay down to avoid distorting its shape.

The lifeboat itself was built to take perhaps fifteen people at a squeeze, but in order for us to hide inside with the tarpaulin back in place, we all had to lie down length-wise along the boat. My back pressed into the edge of a wooden seat just above my bottom rib, and my injured arm was being stabbed with each heartbeat. Even facing the side of the lifeboat, I could feel George's body heat behind me. My nose quivered.

By this point, I could easily identify my companions by scent alone, and I even fancied that I could sense consider-ably more. There was plenty of anger and fear in the air, but also relief, and even a hint of excitement. Maybe I was wrong about the latter, but I carefully pushed my focus towards more urgent matters. My own anger and fear had unfinished business.

Having the ability to affect my choice of focus was a posi-tive development in itself. It was only a few days earlier, back at the farm, that I'd come out of convalescence. Then, as I'd fore-shadowed with my rescuers, my mind had been overwhelmed by its new Lycan chemistry, making me utterly unfit for human company. A few days later, I was lying in the adjacent dark, our shared crisis filling me with energy and intent. My breathing accelerated once more, and my whole body started to quiver.

I thought perhaps the vibration was just a hallucination, but George spoke up.

"How are you doing, Patrick?" she whispered with a slightly wary concern.

I tried to hold my breath and calm down, but my gut clenched and I shook lightly. Having a sharp focus was very different to being calm and in control. A few days before I wouldn't have trusted myself with this level of proximity, but for now, I didn't fear it in the slightest. Though I did have a physical reaction that just wouldn't...

"What do you need? We could split up?" George suggested.

But then I made a quiet 'no' under my breath and we fell silent, ears straining to make out the approaching throng of male voices.

Chapter 13

SHOWDOWN

They were arguing. Footsteps heavy, sounding clearly through the hull of the boat itself. From the cadence, I guessed that they were carrying a heavy load. Before they even left the jetty, it was possible to make sense of their muffled, strident voices.

UNKNOWN MAN: ...I'm not saying the package is perfect, I'm saying that this ship was always the core of the deal. You may not have those bitches, but you've got a clean getaway here. In style. The deal was forty million and ten percent. I figure you can have a million dollar discount for every one of those missing sluts.

Familiar voice: I was very clear in my deal with Archie. Those 'sluts', as you call them, were each ultimately worth more than Archie's entire operation...

"Fᴜᴄᴋ ᴍᴇ," breathed Alannah, her voice carrying clearly in the confined space, even from behind an intervening pile of women. "That's bloody Paul Adams! He's here!"

Pᴀᴜʟ Aᴅᴀᴍs: ...and the only reason we have any kind of deal at all is the body of the dead one.

Unknown man (yelling): Don't you compare your bull-shit mess with *my* operation! I'm not the one who...

Paul Adams: Marc.

[Sounds of two gunshots. Then a heavy thump, and silence.]

Paul Adams: Is there anyone here who can do business?

[A long pause.]

Deep-voiced man: The ship doesn't go cheap. He shoots again, and maybe we all go down. But you go down first. *And* the rest of your men don't get five hundred metres from here. Understand that, and we can do business.

Paul Adams: Twenty million for this fucked up mess.

Deep-voiced man (laughs): This ship is ten million on the open market. Thirty million and the agreed ten percent.

Paul Adams: With a cold corpse, we'll be lucky to make anything out of this project. Twenty two million flat.

Deep-voiced man: If it's ten percent of zero, then that don't cost you nothing, does it? Let's say twenty five million and let's keep that ten percent.

Karl Wüster: We'll have to rebuild the database anyway. Having only one starting sample will slow us considerably, but don't sell it cheap, boss.

"IT's..." started Natalie, before she was shushed by Alannah.

"Hordones is the quickdraw, as well," I said. "It's the full set!"

Then I was poked into silence. The group seemed to be stationary for much of that conversation. Perhaps this was taking place at the foot of the gangplank.

∿

PAUL ADAMS (COLDLY): Be quiet, Karl.

Deep-voiced man: Let's all hope he's right. You want a clean move of operations, and you'll want to use our connections later. That'll be easy if your success is our success. Think of this deal as investing.

Paul Adams: Twenty five, and ten percent for five years. If we're getting along so well, that gives us a chance to rene-gotiate.

Deep-voiced man: Ten percent of gross, and you've got yourself a new start.

Paul Adams: Simon?

∿

IT SOUNDED like they made an exchange right then and there. So the presumably heavily armed quasi-military group that marched onto the *Buoyant Bride* after that must have been carrying the remaining fifteen million in some form. Plus Kirsten's dead body, and all the knowledge and personnel necessary to restart Project Lycan. A couple of trucks drove up within earshot, and the goons took multiple trips to fetch and stow all their equipment. In hindsight, hiding in the storage bays would indeed have been a terrible choice.

We could hear the occasional snippet of conversation all across the ship. Most of it was merely logistics, but we did hear Karl Wüster complaining to Hordones about all the setbacks. Hordones was snappish, and told him to stop whingeing, and focus on getting things back on track. Perhaps fifteen minutes went by, and then the engines of the ship started up.

"What's the plan?" asked Natalie in a clipped voice, showing the strain. "Lourdes is still off-ship. Are we leaving her behind and trying to take over tonight? Or do we go soon?"

The idea of waiting was maddening. Just imagining it sent skitters across my nervous system like small animals fleeing the storm.

"They must have brought explosives," whispered Alannah. "How about we rig it to explode, and then jump off?"

"That would require doing it in daylight, with people everywhere," noted George, "or else jumping off into the middle of the ocean."

"Yeah, it's basically go now, or go at night," I agreed.

To my dismay, we agreed to wait until nighttime. I wondered how stable my equanimity would be after several hours of simulating a reasonable and patient man. So I admit to a tiny, fleeting flash of relief when we heard the shouting, and the gunshots. Then I thought about Lourdes, and panicked.

We heard Hordones demand a report, and then one of his men told him that one of the bodyguards had seen something moving under the jetty, and when they ducked to look properly, they saw someone diving underwater.

Hordones sounded professionally excited. "It's got to be

one of the missing subjects, and where there's one, we'll probably find the whole lot," he barked. "They all came for the Williams bitch at the Consulate. If we can capture them, we might speed this whole thing up by a year or more. But go careful. You know what they can do. Search the boat, top to bottom. Teams, fully armed. Dead is fine. I'll call the Silver Dragons."

So maybe Lourdes was fine. But we weren't.

"WHY DOES HIDING NEVER SEEM to work out?" I complained.

"Get inside or underwater quickly," Alannah advised, ignoring me. "They're armed, and we're not, so don't give them clear lines of sight."

The lifeboat's cover was secured against storms, and designed to be undone from the outside. Exploding into action wasn't an option. Instead, my damp, cold, clumsy hands had to poke around the edges for the hooks. Any moment, I was sure, bullets were about to rip through us. My panic-flooded brain urged me to rip, tear and scream, and forcing myself to stay low and search systematically felt both torturous and lethally slow. Then I finally found the clasp for the corner. After popping the first tie, the others came easily.

I leapt out, wearing nothing but a shirt on my arm and some wet underwear. There was no-one on this side of the boat yet, as the action started on the other side. Lourdes would have had to choose to head for one of the boats for cover. I couldn't guess which. Not that I could do much with the information.

I tried to place all the goons running around by listening carefully, while Alannah, Natalie and George clambered out of the lifeboat. The goons were making plenty of noise as they yelled and clumped about, but the topology of the ship's cabins made it impossible to tell exactly where the sounds originated. Alannah's advice about avoiding clear lines of sight made sense, and I headed inside. Although I didn't like the idea of getting trapped in there, diving off the edge and swimming seemed worse. I'd be a sitting duck every time I came up for air.

The nearest doorway led into a narrow corridor that linked the two sides of the top deck of the ship, and also gave access to various rooms via another corridor that ran from stern to bow. The main room I remembered from this level was the large space up that corridor towards the bow, where there was a spiral staircase into the body of the ship. There was no point going in without hunting for the big three and their bodyguard. They'd likely be heavily armed, but if you're going to grab a snake with your bare hands, it's important to get your grip right behind the head.

I opened the door, and the other three followed. We were all trying to be as quiet as possible, so none of us said anything, even in a whisper. So I'm not sure if they'd come to the same conclusions as me, or if they were just trying to stay together. Once inside, I could smell the tangled web of scents from new people. They all seemed quite fresh, so it wasn't enough to track them. Just enough to trigger the rage I now associated with other men.

Even that biochemically-induced hatred felt different than I remembered. It was like the fury itself was part of my body, and I was floating above. It wasn't exactly the same as being composed, but it was close enough. Maybe I was kidding myself. Were my thoughts and feelings really so separate? Or was the dissociation just what being high on adrenaline felt like? Maybe I only felt self-possessed because I was acting on an abundance of perfectly rational rage, and was feeling wholehearted about my decision to kill these human-shaped cancers.

Maybe my demons and I were just going in the same direction, and if I tried restraint in the future, it would again struggle against madness. I grimaced. Better to worry about that later, in the distressingly unlikely case that there would be an opportunity. In the moment, it was only important to be quiet and fast.

We padded down the centre of the main deck. The main room was, like all the others, beautifully appointed. Lots of open space, and wide sliding doors on each side to the deck outside. White walls and ceilings, with modern lighting. A large screen on the wall towards the bow on one side, with chairs and tables set out to face it. Tables and more chairs were stacked behind a half-open screen at the back. As well as the spiral stair, there was another straight and wide one that led to the rear. This was the hub by which people and things tended to come on board.

To the left we heard sounds of one of the patrols coming close, and then the sliding door started to move.

The four of us were quiet enough, but standing right in the open. I went for speed, and in a couple of steps I made it to the doorway just as it began to reveal a man. Unlike the drug runners, this man was wearing full tactical gear. Probably Bowline. They'd left their half-exploded clandestine base in the middle of the night, but they'd obviously had time to fully equip on the way out. Maybe they carried a lot of it. Maybe they managed to use one or more of their vehicles from the garage after all. Or maybe some of their supplies hadn't made it in, and had been intercepted at a distance. Whatever the source, I could see half of a man wearing the same gear that the Valkyries had been wearing when I first met them, all those busy hours ago. Back when they'd been Amazons, wearing matching full-visored helmets and tactical armour. I also saw the barrel of an identical assault rifle, which the leading soldier was holding with one hand as he slid open the door with the other.

Well before he'd had time to react to seeing my right shoulder, I reached forward and snatched the barrel of the rifle. It was uncomfortably hot, probably having been one of the ones that had fired a minute or so ago. It wasn't my plan to hold it for long, however. I pulled hard, and felt something brittle give as I suddenly had the soldier's gun. Maybe his wrist?

Grabbing the centre of the gun with my other hand, I used it as a pile driver to deliver back to his neck. The face would have been better, but the visor looked really strong, and I had an intuition to put as much pressure on joints as I could. Really leaning into the abrupt thrust, I found out that my footing was better than I thought, and his whole body flew back into his partner. I quickstepped through the small opening in the doorway, and repeated the action on the other soldier. The second one had a little more time to react, and started to shout, but he couldn't bring his weapon to bear through the still-falling body of his comrade, and he wasn't fast enough to duck a second jab from the appropriated weapon. It came at him with breakneck speed, at first figuratively, and then literally.

The half shout would attract others, so I took just enough time to liberate the second assault rifle, and then stepped back inside and closed the sliding door. I passed the weapons to Alannah and Natalie.

"Thanks," said Natalie with a slight quiver, teeth bared as she took it. "Bridge?"

Now that we had weapons, it might be worth a shot, I

thought, and we moved towards the bow. I heard some voices, but they went quiet, presumably as they listened for more sound of the ruckus we'd caused. A short corridor led from this open space towards some forward storage areas and the cockpit. We advanced, and found the door closed. George raced back, even her bare feet hammering the deck, and we heard the sliding door open. A couple of seconds later it closed again, and she returned holding two grenades.

Alannah grinned, and we prepared to crack open the door and throw them in. The door was steel and solid, as were most of the walls of the ship, making it perfect for shielding us from any forthcoming gunfire or explosion. Still, we rapidly organised ourselves to be as far out of the firing line of the doorway as possible. George pulled the pin on the grenades, and then nodded to me. I reached across the doorway, grabbed the handle and pulled. It didn't budge.

I pulled harder, to no effect. Being so much stronger and faster than before, I still hadn't properly recalibrated what was possible, so after a couple of failed attempts, I braced myself against the frame of the doorway. This involved offering more of my body as a target should I succeed in getting it open, but it wasn't a time to get precious. Gathering all my strength, I heaved. My joints felt like they were about to rip out themselves, when I started to feel the metal warp. With every gram of my strength I heaved, and then the metal gave way. I flew into the side corridor, and bumped into Alannah, the tortured handle in my hand.

But the door remained closed.

"We know how fast you are," came Marc Hordones' smug, muffled voice from inside. "But I assure you that if you'd managed to move that door, you'd be dead now."

I puffed on the floor. Looking over my shoulder, I saw

George looking at the grenades in her hands and snarling with frustration as she looked at the door. The handle had snapped rather than the locking mechanism, and there was absolutely no leverage we could apply to open it.

"Then you could open it and kill us," tempted Alannah, as I rolled over and started clambering to my feet. Natalie switched from readying a shot through the doorway to covering the corridor back to the main top-deck area.

"Happy to wait," said Hordones. "Without surprise, all you are is fast. You're not trained soldiers, and you're not equipped."

"You might be surprised," George muttered, looking to see if she could find the pins on the floor.

"Oh I know what you can do," came his greasy reply. "We've been planning what could be done with those talents for years now. But I also know your limits. You've all been tested so extensively I could predict your performance in things you've never even tried."

Thinking back to that testing, I wasn't so sure. I didn't recall ever pushing myself to my limits in any of those exercises. Why would I? I gave the veneer of obedience, but was hardly committed to the cause. A natural curiosity regarding my physical changes combined with a primal, intrinsic urge to push myself, but my repressed anger also drove me towards rebellion. Anything to mess them up, so long as they didn't realise I was doing it and punish me.

Even if I had been trying hard, it might have taken a long time to figure out my body's new potential. I heard once that under general anaesthetic, even stiff, elderly people were able to perform amazing feats of flexibility. Even things like the side splits, which most couldn't even do when they were young. And then as consciousness returned, they'd tighten up and become inflexible again. A lot of our supposedly physical limits were apparently just functions of our neural maps, and mine were trained in a pre-Lycan childhood.

All of which boiled down to the fact that I thought that maybe we could surprise him. If only we could get in there. However, warning him about potential secret advantages didn't seem either wise, or a good way of taunting him. I turned to Alannah to see what she was thinking, and tossed the door handle on the floor.

"So you're saying we've got nothing to lose, and might as well just burn the boat down even if we can't get off it?" she said, with a mightily fey tone.

Burn the boat down? I mouthed. She shrugged.

There was laughter inside, and some whispered conversations. Outside, there was a sound of booted feet.

"Good luck burning down a metal boat," Hordones laughed. "Hope your half-tonne of thermite didn't get wet." He then muttered some quiet, indecipherable instructions, possibly on a phone.

"If you've got bars, look up a magnesium fire," said Alannah, moving into a position to join Natalie in covering the corridor. "It's something you should see, once in your life."

I moved over to Alannah, and whispered in her ear. "Magnesium? It'd be steel, wouldn't it?" I asked.

She just shrugged. "Probably," she said. "Confusion to the enemy. Any ideas?"

I did not have any ideas. A lot of thoughts, but nothing that didn't sound like suicide.

I could hear running and scrambling outside. Direction was impossible to discern, we could hear an increasing number of people running around the ship, and then a lot of shouting outside.

"That's either a bluff or a mistake," came the silky voice of Paul Adams from the bridge. My hackles literally went up.

I'd heard the phrase "hair standing up on the back of my neck" before, but I'd never felt it happen. In real life it's particularly creepy, because it's not just the back of the neck, it's the whole spine. Alannah startled as well, naked hatred flashing across her face.

"Doesn't matter which," he continued dispassionately. "So if things go as we all expect, you'll all die, and we'll probably have casualties too."

Natalie snarled over her shoulder. "So we've got nothing to lose."

"Precisely. So let's talk options. I point out that we *all* win if you give yourselves up."

"We all win if you let us go as well," pointed out Alannah. "We get to live, and you get less damage to your lovely boat and operation."

"You're wrong on two counts there," replied Adams. "First, even dead, we'll be able to back out the induced variations. Given that..." he paused, and consulted briefly. "... Patrick Arthurs is the only male specimen still in existence, that makes him indispensable. We need him, and letting you go is absolutely not an option."

"However," he continued in a calm, parental tone that I found maddening, "the only reason there's any threat to your lives at all is the choice you're making. You know perfectly well why we want you, and you know that it doesn't require anyone to die. Or even be uncomfortable."

Natalie was enraged. "So *that's* your offer? Surrender ourselves, let you build your evil empire off our body chemistry and more murders, and assume you'll be nice to us? Are you insane? We're here because we'd rather die than help that happen! And as for *trusting* you to treat us well..." She sputtered to a stop incoherently.

Adams continued undeterred. "Your suicide won't stop

this project. We have one sample, and there are two living samples who aren't on this boat that we can still track down. We'll find Brooke Provan, and take her alive. All we really want from here is the body of Patrick Arthurs. This stand you're taking isn't some noble crusade. You're just saying that you'd all rather die than live."

Natalie fired a single shot as someone tried to slip a mirror around the end of the corridor. The mirror pulled back.

George looked at the grenades in her hand, looked down the corridor, and then back at the sealed doorway between us and the bridge. Her eyes were wide and almost tearful with frustration. I wondered if Adams were right. Was that all we were doing? Trading our lives for maybe a few dead soldiers that Adams and his inner circle would never think of again?

"We must be worth more to you alive, or you wouldn't be talking," I said.

"Quite," said Adams. "It should enable shortcuts that would save us many months. I might point out that it would also save a lot of lives, so as well as surviving yourselves, you could also take them off your consciences."

This was too much for Alannah. "Murders you don't commit don't win you any virtue, motherfucker," she snapped in a voice strangled by anger. "And murders you commit don't have anything to do with *our* consciences."

"I won't argue the point, but it's incontrovertible that your actions here could easily prevent them. Thought that might be worth something to you."

It was possible that he was just buying time for some kind of local attack, but looking at the three of them, sweating and ready to die, I came to a decision.

"Adams," I announced. "If I'm the only one you need,

and alive is better, then I'll offer myself in exchange for letting the others go. That's a situation upgrade for you, provided we can organise it."

"No!" hissed George. "Shut up."

"Good decision, Mr Arthurs!" called Paul Adams.

"This is not your decision to make, asshole!" growled Natalie. "We're not damsels in distress here."

"Yeah, that's not a deal," agreed Alannah.

Adams' voice called out firmly. "Take a moment to sort things out with your, ah, colleagues, Mr Arthurs, and I'll see if we can figure out logistics."

He immediately began murmuring with Hordones, but I couldn't make out what they were saying over the vehement disagreement from the Valkyries.

"You're insane," said Natalie. "There's no way we can trust him."

I held up my hands, palm forward. "Couldn't agree more," I said, pitching my voice down, trying both to keep our conversation private, and lower the tension a little. "Let's see if he can come up with a method that doesn't require trust. I imagine he'll try to betray us as soon as he can, and I expect you to do the same."

"You can just get off your white horse, anyway," said Alannah.

She went to say more, but I cut her off. "Knock that shit off, Alannah. This is not a hormone-fuelled melodramatic gesture. I'm the only one who can make this deal, and face it - it's a better deal than we have right now. I'm all for killing that fucker and his team, and I'm resigned to selling my life for that if I have to. But if I'm selling my life, I damn well want to buy something with it!"

"You know how bad it will be if he takes you," Alannah replied, pitched low, finally.

"Yes I do, and I'll take that over being shot as soon as these fuckers get organised," I replied. "Especially if I can get you clear in the process. Where there's life there's hope."

I thought I made out the word 'tranquilliser' from inside, and a burst of chatter on a phone. Also, more people coming on board. There hadn't been any shooting outside for a while, which might have been a good sign for Lourdes.

"If we're discussing knight errant rescues, I won't object if you organise one," I added quietly. "Just take the time to make sure it goes smoothly, because I can imagine they'll be all out of patience."

Alannah didn't look back at me, as she kept her attention focussed forward. There weren't any more instant denials or refusals leaping to her lips, however. I looked to Natalie, who was the same. Then to George, who was looking at me. She was pissed.

"No," she said, very quietly. "Fuck."

I wiped my eyes a little, and I could see her better. I shrugged, helplessly, and succumbed to a little shaking fit. "Still taking ideas for better plans," I said, even softer, and then starting pacing involuntarily, my chest squeezing hard. There wasn't much room to move, so I just went a few steps forwards, spun and then went back. Before it could become too irritating, I stopped and started investigating the storage cupboards.

The engines started.

"No deal then?" I called out.

"What?" asked Hordones.

"You're setting off without letting anyone off, so I'm assuming you're bailing on the plan?"

"No, this is part of the plan," replied Hordones. "We can't just offer free passage onto the jetty: I have a strong feeling that the Silver Dragons would simply shoot you. So we need to move away from here to make this work. We've got all our people on board, and so we're setting off."

Where was Lourdes? Not on this ship, I was fairly sure. The anchor would have been the only way up, and surely that would have had guards. Her situation was therefore probably independent of where the *Buoyant Bride* was, whether it was dire or manageable. There was a small shudder, as we cast away and began to move. It was a pity we couldn't see outside.

"How do you want to do this, then?" I queried.

"We clear out the main deck, and go a short way up the coast. You go check that we're out of the way, unarmed. Then you lock yourself up with a set of handcuffs that we'll leave, in view of the camera above the television. The others go out on your signal, and can dive off. We have you alive, they are free."

"What's to stop you just shooting us from the ship?" asked Natalie, incredulous.

I actually heard his sigh. "We are prepared to leave one of the lifeboats, motor running. You should be able to make good speed. That's the best we can think of."

I lowered my voice and asked, "What do you think?"

Natalie chewed her lip, and Alannah blew out a slow breath.

Then Lourdes spoke up.

Chapter 14

WITH ALL HANDS

"Hello there," came Lourdes' voice over the radio, wreathed in a little static. "This is the emergency channel, but I think we all agree that the situation is definitely fraught. Who out there wants to try gloating?"

None of us in the corridor knew what to do with this development. I spent the time pulling out life jackets from the cupboard. Under the reasoning that swimming would be a little easier with them on to compensate for my unusual non-buoyancy, I slipped one on. Then I started putting one on George. She looked at me like I was completely insane. She might have been right, though if I'd been forced to keep doing nothing, I strongly suspect I would have snapped.

A little scrambling inside, and Hordones called back. "Ms Bowen, I believe. So you have commandeered the other ship of the Silver Dragons. And you are calling us in the hope of getting back off alive?"

"Something like that," came her reply. "One of the goons here explained to me a couple of minutes ago that you were taking my friend's body. Seemed unnecessary to stay here and die if you were just going to start your unholy project back up again anyway."

Hordones' smug, lying grin was *audible*. "Great to hear one of you making sense -"

"One of us? What have my other friends been saying?" interrupted Lourdes.

As Hordones started to reply, I shouted: "Hey Lourdes!" as loudly as I could.

"Is that Patrick?" came the tinny sound of Lourdes' reply. "How fun!"

"Yes, your friends are alive," said Hordones, "and if you want to keep enjoying the same status, I can send a group back to fetch you. Better be fast, though, because if we don't call the Silver Dragons quickly, I wouldn't rate your chances."

"Oh, they're getting a lot more cautious for some reason. So, I can hear that Patrick's alive in the cockpit. Are the others in there with you too?" Lourdes asked. It sounded a bit like she was hunting for reassurance, feeling vulnerable and isolated. To me, it sounded like she was feeling less vulnerable, and carefully hiding that fact. Acting more on instinct than anything as firm as a hunch, I administered life jackets to Natalie and Alannah. They tried to resist so they could focus on providing covering fire, but I was quick, minimally disruptive, and managed to convey wordlessly that it was important.

"Sorta," I called out lightly, "we're all locked out."

"I can hear him in the background," said Lourdes. "Did he say that all four of them were locked out? Or did he say locked up?"

Hordones had started organising things on his cell, but he retorted on the radio one more time. "I'd worry more about myself than them if I were you," he warned.

"We're free as can be!" I cackled happily, as he finished his sentence. "For now!"

"Thanks Patrick!" came Lourdes' buzzing voice. "Good to know."

Then there was a huge, incoherent shout outside, and a couple of seconds later, there was a terrible explosion towards the rear of the ship as the first rocket hit.

THE SHOCKWAVE through the ship was minimal, just enough to wobble our footing slightly. The sound, however, was incredible, and it seemed to come from all directions at once. The engines stopped immediately, and there were a few moments of inaction from all sides, while we tried to figure out what had happened. There was another explosion in the far distance, and then another, much, much larger one. Like the finale of a fireworks display, it was followed by a series of overlapping explosions. The only two places I could picture in range were the other ship and the drug runners' warehouse. Given the greater distance of the warehouse, if that were where the sound was coming from, then it would have to have been a truly startling amount of stored explosives going off.

Then our ship was hit again. And a few seconds later, again. From that point on, I didn't speculate about distant explosions and gunfire, because things started to get intense.

Ever so slightly, the deck seemed to tip down towards the back of the boat. The ship was going down. George looked at the grenades in her hand, and rather than wait for an opportunity to get both of them into the cockpit, she decided to use one of them to expedite an escape. She leaned out behind Natalie, and rolled it down the corridor. We all pulled back out of the field of view. There was a solid click as it started, and then it bounced, bounced down into the open area, eliciting a cry of "Gren-" before exploding. There were screams, and then we were on the move.

Anticipating our charge, a burst of gunfire slammed into the end of the corridor before we reached it, which brought us all to a halt. Given the fact that the only avenue of escape was through the main deck area, the soldiers knew they had to defend it. George thought about using the other grenade, but we didn't have any vision on our targets, and they were likely using cover by this point. I nudged her and pointed back at the closed door behind us. If this were our only exit, it was also likely their only exit. She nodded, and kept an eye looking back.

The shouting outside was referencing the lifeboats, and they were obviously being prepped and released. We'd hardly had time to move, so I doubted we were far from the beach or the dock, but perhaps all those soldiers were not keen on diving into the water wearing full kit. Thirty-plus kilos will put you at the bottom, and I had recent personal experience as to how hard it was to swim against that kind of weight. Still, they had the option of shedding mass, and I didn't.

There was perhaps a half minute of scrambling, which I used to consider charging forward anyway, wondering how I was going to handle being in the deeper water myself, and wondering how Lourdes was going, assuming she was the source of the explosions. Had she said something about rocket launchers? How many rockets did she have? And how hard were the launchers to reload?

I grabbed another couple of lifejackets each, and passed them around. I managed to slip another over me, although it looked more like a neck brace with delusions of grandeur than a lifejacket.

Reloading time: approximately half a minute. A burst of distant gunfire was ended with another explosion.

"Go!" I heard outside, and there was a splash as the port lifeboat hit the water.

"All on! Does anyone have eyes on the launcher?" came the call.

The replies came back negative, but I heard a lot of people decamping into the lifeboat. Then the other one splashed down.

Alannah said quietly: "Do we rush them now? Will there be a point when they won't be covering us?"

"I'm not sure," said Natalie, "should -"

There was another almighty explosion, this time not quite connected to the boat, as evidenced by the more directional nature of the sound. It was very nearby, however, and there was a smattering of shrapnel on the port side of the ship.

"Don't load the other boat until we take out that fucking launcher!" came a scream from that side.

The angle of the deck was getting steeper, and it was clear that there was a real limit to how long anyone on the ship was going to be able to wait. There was a deep, base rumble as water poured into the ship. I thought I heard gunshots from the cockpit behind (and increasingly, above) us, and the shattering of glass. Perhaps they were finding another way out. There was a sudden jerking movement, and the ship tipped another five degrees suddenly, and was then definitely moving down in surges. I could see water down below, black, foamed, and churning. There was a heavy thump against the cockpit door, and both George and

I, who were looking that way when the surge came, almost lost our footing.

"In three," announced Alannah, taking a few very deep breaths. "Two..."

The cockpit door opened, and two figures leapt through. A glimpse of the bridge windows and the sky behind them showed it to be black with smoke. George threw her other grenade hard past them. The leading soldier dodged it, which dropped his weapon from readiness, and it bounced off the shoulder of the rearmost figure, who I thought was Hordones. The grenade then disappeared into the chaos of the cockpit, bounced several times, and then exploded. Natalie was turning around with her weapon, but before anyone could get to firing, the ship lurched, the deck went to perhaps forty or fifty degrees to the vertical, and we were all suddenly falling.

A huge wall of water came up as we went down, and I tried to control my movement by running down the deck instead of tumbling. Chairs and tables boiled in the foam below. As we came into the open space, the windows making up the majority of both sides were crazed with cracks. I could see the water line through them, now slightly above the open, sliding doors on each side. Water was torrenting in through those doorways, making a maelstrom in the middle, where we were heading.

The only good news was that no soldiers were visible, though there may have been some under water for all we knew. Alannah saw that the side doors were the only exits, even if they were against a ferocious current. She used what little purchase she had on the angled deck as she plummeted down, to run towards the starboard wall. We all followed her. The first soldier behind us came tumbling down and landed in the water. The second, which was definitely Marc Hordones, managed to keep his footing, and went for the other side. It looked for a moment like he was going to be able to take a shot, but he hit the water hard, and went under.

The only reason I had time to see that is that I'd landed on Natalie, and she'd slowed my own fall momentarily. Alannah had turned her descent into a dive at the end, and she'd carved into the open doorway with enough force to pull herself through. Natalie had tried the same, but didn't quite have a clear line, and so she'd stalled against the force of the incoming water. Then I helpfully came down feet first, looking the other way, and assisted her with an almighty shove to her legs and buttocks. As I plunged in down to my hips, I swung her and she managed to catch the edge of the door with one hand. She then started pulling herself through.

George had managed to find the best balance back in the corridor, where she was looking 'up' and braced accordingly. She was therefore nearly a full second behind me, and after I elegantly expedited Natalie through with my feet, she heartlessly crashed into my shoulders with hers. The fact that I was immersed in water helped cushion the blow considerably, although my feet were only just above the angled deck. When George landed, I suddenly had weight on my feet again, and used it to push myself doorwards. Like Natalie, I managed to slip a hand around the doorframe. I reached back and grabbed George's thigh as I pulled down. She came with me, and in a moment I had her down holding the door frame as well. Then I pulled through.

I promptly began to sink. I couldn't see where Alannah had gone, but Natalie had somehow gone up. Earlier, swimming upwards in the ocean had been hard enough. With the ship going down and producing a swirling downward current as well, it was too much. Struggling with a gasped lungful of air, I resorted to climbing the sides of the sinking ship itself. Despite how dramatic it seemed inside, the ship was probably only sinking at a dozen metres per minute, so I scrambled hard, and soon broke the surface. Then I went further, and ended up climbing up right onto the bow of the ship, gasping to get my air back. From there I saw the madness.

Thick black smoke filled the air, and more was boiling up from an oil fire spreading from the broken vessel. Many pieces of the ship were floating, but it was more than half under water. We were further from the jetty than I expected, a few hundred metres, and definitely in much deeper water than I could use the walk-along-the-bottom method of transport. Deep enough that this ship was going to completely disappear soon. One lifeboat was sitting in the water, and despite the order to stay off it until Lourdes was stopped, most of the surviving soldiers were inside, keeping under cover. They were searching with scoped rifles, but apparently either reluctant to leave their remaining colleagues, or reluctant to move out of the cover created by the remains of the ship and the oil fire.

The bridge below was empty. An emergency exit to the outside had been forced by shooting out the side window, and the door was swinging open, with no-one remaining inside. We'd only seen Hordones and a soldier leave by the door, so Paul Adams, Karl Wüster and any others must have come out this way. Scrambling around, I couldn't see where they were. Most likely they'd dived into the water or made for the lifeboat already, and either way I wasn't going to see them. I'd never seen Paul Adams, but I knew Dr Wüster's amiable face quite well. An unassuming man with short-cropped dark hair and glasses, he looked like an accountant, and talked like a professor who was obsessed with his research. Adams would likely be with him, as he was the goose that could lay the golden eggs. Making sure the two of them didn't make it was probably as important to our long-term survival as getting safely to shore.

The boat kept moving, however, and I started to focus on our short-term survival. I was currently wearing two life-jackets, but I had no capacity to judge whether that was enough to enable me to make it. Lifejackets were supposed to enable exhausted people who could *almost* float unaided to stay up with their head out of the water. The way I plunged down to the bottom made me rather reserved about trusting them to help with the 'safely to shore' part.

Unfortunately, the only large floating object in sight was the lifeboat full of soldiers whose attention was fortunately pointed away from this position at the moment. I couldn't see Alannah or Natalie, but I was fairly sure Natalie had gone over the bow to other side of the ship. George was following up from below. Gasping, she came up next to me and put her mouth near my ear.

"See them?" she asked, breathlessly.

Not sure exactly who she was talking about, I indicated the position of everyone I knew. Some of the soldiers below started firing towards the coast as the wind caused a break in the smoke cover. Half a second later, I could see a rocket blazing towards us, drawing a red line as an afterimage in the air. It zipped to the lifeboat, which was then engulfed by a fireball and destroyed with all hands. I'd shielded myself as best I could but felt the shockwave ring my head like a bell as something heavy hit just below us. Without discussion, George and I started moving over to the other side, where we saw a line of figures swimming away from the ship. The placement of the oil fire meant they had to swim a little away from shore and then sideways for a few hundred metres to get around it, and they hadn't made it very far against the swell.

Alannah and Natalie were crouched on a wall that had become an approximately horizontal surface. The two of them had somehow managed to bring their guns on their trip through the water, and Alannah, who was judged the better shot, was firing at those in the water. She aimed at the most distant ones first, and with a few bursts, managed to cause each in turn to jerk and cease swimming. Before she could clear them all, she ran out of ammunition. Three figures very close to the boat were left, none of them yet swimming out.

"Can you see those lifesaving rings?" George said, as she leaned close and pointed into the wreckage of the lifeboat. "Let's go for them."

They were large, orange, and adrift from the wreckage of the first lifeboat, trailing their ropes into the water. The two of them looked like living up to their name. "Absolutely," I said. "I'm just a bit worried about those guys." I pointed to the three figures below us. "Chances are they probably have pistols, at least."

The concern was suddenly vindicated as one of them began firing. Bullets ripped against the side of the ship near George and me, and we threw ourselves back to the other side of the ship. Alannah and Natalie had some cover due to their position, but it would fade as the ship went lower. There appeared to be no surviving soldiers on this side of the ship, but the water was a long way down, and very deep. It would have helped a lot to know whether I would be able to swim to shore if I started off on the other side, but I strongly suspected not.

The ship shifted, and started to move sideways as well as down.

"I think it's hit a sandbar!" George shouted.

It was sliding in the direction of the group with the guns. Probably not quickly enough to threaten them, but possibly such that they would consider swimming away from it rather than treading water with a readied pistol.

"I'm going through those fuckers, and then I'll grab one of those lifesavers by the rope," I said. "Follow me quickly. We need all guns out of the equation."

"How -" started George, but I didn't want to think about it while this possible window closed. Moving like my arboreal ancestors, I clambered over the shifting ship. The ship protested as I treated its walls as a floor, but in a couple of seconds I was back in view of the three swimmers. Two had indeed started drawing away from the toppling, keening ship. The other had lingered, watching the ship's silhouette for our return a little longer. I leapt for him.

THERE WAS time for the man to fire two shots while I was in the air. I was a moving target, the water was choppy and on fire, and he was treading water with his other hand, so it was perhaps no surprise that they missed. Though they were so close that I heard both of the bullets go past. In between shots, I realised it was Hordones. The man whose current personal fortune was based on arming drug runners with gear for covert operations. Whose plans for future wealth involved coordinating the kidnapping, personnel training and the body disposal for a resurrected Project Lycan. He was an expert in weapons, assassinations, and all aspects of the profession of special forces.

I had jumped from the equivalent of a couple of stories above, so even given his gun, my primary concern was making sure I wasn't badly injured by our impact. I flipped in the air before landing on him, and tried to use his shoulders as a springboard.

That didn't work at all.

One foot landed on one shoulder, but he twisted in the last fraction of a second, so my other foot hit mostly water. Hordones was driven down, but the uneven resistance tipped me wildly and I smashed into the water with a splash that left me reeling. A second or two later, and I found that my pair of life jackets were not quite enough. I was sinking. Hordones floated limp just below me, but it took a serious panicked effort to halt my descent and go upward.

The nearby fire lit the water with a hellish flickering light the colour of molten rubies, and I saw the objects above by their shadows. The first was a swimming figure, and the second was the buoy I'd been targeting. The rope trailing down was harder to see, but once I was looking for it, I was able to make it out from the shadows. Swimming sideways as hard as I could, my hands wrapped around it. The slick polypropylene fibres were slimy, but I gripped tightly and pulled. I could tell that something heavy was attached to the underwater end, but the other led to the life-saver itself. As I pulled myself up, I could feel the buoyancy device being pulled down, and thanked the god of over-engineering when it stayed on the surface.

My lungs ached and my muscles burned. My chest kept trying to pump like it was breathing, and it was all I could do to keep from taking a breath of the dark ocean water. The shadowy figure above me was writhing, and then fired down at me. The bullet's path arced towards me like a movie special effect, but stopped near my face after a few metres.

Pausing at that distance was not an option, as black spots were already pooling in my vision. I heaved at the rope, advertising my presence further, and climbing into the danger zone.

I was aware of two more shots coming down. One ripped past my face and continued, and one slammed into my calf like a hot lance. The pain made me pause, and I nearly lost my grip. With a huge splash, something large slammed into the figure, and it was pushed down to me. It was a tall man wearing a suit and tie. The smile lines in his slack, unconscious face seemed incongruous, but my body's urgent need for air didn't give me time to wonder or reflect. I hauled myself upward, and almost made it.

I remember seeing the sky: hazy, oil-smeared and almost in reach. I felt a hand on my wrist as I blacked out.

Chapter 15

FLOTSAM OR JETSAM

I came to in George's arms, tipped over the huge orange lifesaver, with the taste of vomit in my mouth. She'd just cleared my airway, and was trying to position me for CPR, when I jerked and feebly indicated my consciousness by coughing and retching at her.

"Where are the others?" I asked, wiping my mouth.

Turning my head, I could see both of them on the other flotation device. There was no sign of any more soldiers. I took a moment to finish my little bout of vomiting. Must have swallowed a bit too much brine.

On one side, the ship was keeling over at us, and on the other we were only avoiding being covered in flaming oil due to the wind and waves that were pushing us into the flaming oil. Natalie and Alannah used their legs in the water to drive a powerful kick. It wasn't terribly efficient, but got them moving acceptably. George and I put our legs in the water and tried the same, but the rope was tied to something that dragged pretty hard. Pulling it up, we had a broken plank from the lifeboat, and that made a decent paddle.

It took some time to steer around the mess, and then we saw the damage done to the jetty itself. Large chunks of it were missing, and behind it was a serious-looking forest fire that had consumed much of the headland. Many bodies could be seen on the beach. The other ship was relatively unharmed, still moored by anchor and tied to the remaining parts of the jetty.

"Did you see that flash from the side of the other ship?" I heard Natalie ask from the nearby boat fragment. "I think someone's on there with a scope."

"Lourdes, I hope," said Alannah. "It would be a pity if she managed all this and *then* was taken out by those drug runners."

No more bullets came down our way, and as we got a little closer, we saw Lourdes untying the ship from several parts of the jetty that were now under water. Her face lit up as we came closer, and she lowered a ladder.

"Pretty sure I got them all, but let's get this thing out of here just in case," she said. "How are you? Any serious injuries?"

"Couple of cuts and I think a broken rib," said Alannah. "Hurts to breathe, but not dangerous, I think."

"Nothing serious," said Natalie, looking at her leg dubiously.

"Doofus got shot again," said George. "I should patch him up before helping."

Lourdes didn't pause. "Natalie will do to help with this. Alannah, could you watch out for more hostiles?" She passed over the rifle.

The *Ladybird Special* had everything a wounded hero could desire: bandages, antiseptic, painkillers, chocolate, frozen bread, long-life milk, ice-cream, TV dinners, and a small army of ferocious heroines getting us the hell out of dodge. It was good chocolate, too. Fancy-brand dark chocolate in paper wrappers. Drug-runners with expensive tastes. If our tastes got substantially more expensive, we also had a ridiculous amount of the white powder that we used as a distraction back in the drug-runners' McMansion. Or, if we'd rather buy something else, such as an island and its inhabitants, we had the ready cash.

Lourdes got us away from the coast, and into a light squall. We huddled in the cockpit, eating and taking stock.

"So," asked Natalie, after wolfing some microwaved lasagne, "is that it? Are we safe?"

"The data's gone," said Lourdes, who'd wisely opted to start with the chocolate, "so once again we're the only source of data for anyone who wants to go again. Except I definitely saw Wüster fall after I shot him, and not come up again. What does that mean?"

It means we don't have to go back. I blinked a little at how bloodthirsty I had become. Without hesitation or regret. Perhaps it was just shock. Thought I'd have been a lot more upset at everything we'd just done. Instead, I just couldn't raise a serious emotion above relief.

Maybe the judge had been right.

"Gannt's gone. The notes are gone. Adams, Wüster and Hordones are gone, along with their inner circle. Bowline is not a problem any more," declared Alannah. "Though they'll have people paid off in a lot of places, it's not the same." She laid her head back against the seat and closed her eyes. She looked very, very tired.

"I'm still worried about other people trying to capture us to figure out what Wüster did," said Natalie. "And we never checked in with Brooke since we know they found Kirsten."

There was a quiet moment as we all thought of Kirsten,

and then I wondered about the information that Lourdes released.

"What exactly is out in the public domain about Wüster's experiments?" I asked. "You did a pretty complete data dump, didn't you?"

Lourdes shook her head. "Complete in terms of the post-treatment indignities, but I redacted anything that gave a clue about the process itself, patient identities, and even the benefits. Precisely because we didn't want to spark a raft of emulators. We focussed our details on the kidnappings, the deaths and the imprisonment. We mentioned the regularly administered drugs, but redacted which ones. They'd have to start with a completely blank slate."

The mention of the drugs reminded me. "Oh! What about the withdrawals? You four seem remarkably functional for people going through opiate withdrawal. Are you OK?"

Natalie shrugged. "I feel awful," she replied. "Some of that could be withdrawal, but I've had enough beatings to explain it, too. Nothing obvious." She looked at Alannah and George.

George just shrugged as well, and Alannah just kept her eyes closed as she thought for a moment.

"If I am having withdrawals," she said, carefully, "they're no worse than a hangover. Maybe Penny Whitman wasn't quite worth her gold-plated reputation. Or maybe she was deliberately not doing her best work." She subsided, and then mused: "or maybe the changes in our brain chemistry altered that as well."

Nothing but eating for a while, and then the collective unease about whether Brooke was safe resulted in the boat changing course for a nearby town to the south. Thick black smoke filled the sky to the north, and we discussed whether the fire on the peninsula might get out of hand. Natalie expressed her doubts, but in any case it was one problem that we could safely leave to the authorities.

"Speaking of the authorities," I asked, slurring my words as I started to get sleepy, "we need to have a long talk about the future."

Alannah stirred enough to peer over at me with one eyebrow raised. "That we do," she said.

"So can we lay low until after that conversation?" I asked.

"We can," she said, and rolled her head back. The seat was reclined into a position that would probably be fairly comfortable for sleeping. "Shut up now, everyone," she said, kindly but firmly.

I did, and then went aft, looking for a chair just the same.

~

Natalie shook me awake. It took me several seconds to get out of the crazy dream and into the ship full of drugs, cash and weapons. It was dark.

"We're going ashore to get a burner phone and contact Brooke," she said, when I stopped looking confused. "You're on lookout."

My eyes and mouth were scratchy, and my head hurt. I sat up, and the rest of my body complained too. "Who's going?" I managed.

"Lourdes, George and me," she said. "Alannah's still asleep."

"OK," I said, and went looking for some more painkillers and a litre or two of water. "Is she all right?"

Natalie bit her lip. "Think so. You're here for the boat, but you're also here for her. Stay up there?"

I nodded. Natalie passed me a pistol, showed me the safety, and then headed out.

"We'll only be an hour at most," she said. "We're anchored right on the dock, though. If someone comes and hassles you for docking fees or something, just apologise and pay them off."

With that, she slipped out. I went up to the cockpit, and through the grimy windows, I saw them heading up from the dock into town.

I sat there for twenty minutes before asking: "Would you like some water? Painkillers? Snack?"

Alannah hadn't moved, but she'd been awake for about five minutes. "Thanks, but I'll get them myself," she said. "I have to pee."

I assembled the items anyway while she was away, partly because I was making an identical care package for myself, and partly because I was worried about how stiff and sore she seemed when she got up. Alannah left with a shadow of a limp, and took a long time to come back, gingerly, where she settled back into her chair.

"This is surprisingly comfortable," she remarked. She thanked me for the pills, and ate mechanically for a while.

"You're officially dead," she said after a time.

"Apparently so," I replied. "But if somehow I suddenly weren't dead, the most merciful analysis of my status would be 'involuntarily misplaced prisoner'. I'd actually need a lot of help just to go back to my original sentence."

"Yes, you would," she agreed neutrally.

"Only I am now spectacularly unsuited to prison life," I said, carefully. "The only reason I didn't snap before was that I was still numb on so many levels. Now..."

Alannah watched me evenly. "It seems to me that you're basically better now. I never met you before all this, but I could imagine the 'old you' acting somewhat similarly."

"I am absolutely not better now," I declared. Rubbing my forehead, I paced in the small space. "It's not like I thought it was. I *thought* that Patrick Arthurs was basically dead, and a madman was in his place. I thought I'd never be able to interact with other people again, and that the only safe thing to do would be to find some way to kill myself. Better than becoming one of them."

Alannah said nothing, and just listened.

"I saw them raping and murdering, and laughing while they did it. And I felt awful things in me as well. Obviously I wanted to murder them, which didn't bother me too much, except that after a while I realised that I also had an urge to strangle every other man I met. All of them. Scientists, soldiers, trainers, wardens, inmates... I just found myself hating them. The worst thing was that it seemed so natural. I found myself rationalising it, and had elaborate reasons why everyone I met was equally complicit and evil. But I caught myself bullshitting once, and suddenly I realised I was seeing this anger from *their* side. That maybe I was a murderer and rapist waiting to happen."

Still no response, just a steady stare from those light green eyes framed by pain.

"Not that I ever wanted to rape anyone, obviously, but the *drives*..." I figured I was past the point of shame anyway. "Even you and me right here, Alannah. We're shot up and battered, exhausted and briny. But it still takes *willpower*, to... to just keep everything cool."

"You're pretty much the opposite of my type."

Nope, it turned out that there was plenty more shame to be felt. Ouch.

"Anyway, then I started re-examining everything I'd felt to that point, and realised that it was just too mixed up to sort out which feelings came from me, and which ones came with these new instincts. Just because I thought they were assholes didn't mean they weren't, if you get what I mean, and at some level we live by our instincts."

A small nod of encouragement, and I tried to unclench my fists and my gut. The fists part worked, for a moment. "When you were all taken, I just went with it. Decision made, the drive to action was given a green light, and I didn't have to fight myself all the time. Made me feel weirdly normal. And I could tell that Patrick Arthurs still lived at this address." I tapped my head. "I know I can steer in this storm. But I'm not all better. Going on from here without disaster is going to require careful handling of my environment, as well as learning to summon my Buddha nature. Prison will not work out."

So there it was. The plea to a cop, whatever kind of cop Alannah was really, to help keep a convicted murderer out of prison. Worse, the basis of my argument was essentially that I was too bad a person. There were good reasons I became an engineer and not a lawyer.

"No promises," she said. "But I'll try to figure something out."

"Fair enough," I said, figuring that it was better than an outright refusal. "Hey, remember when we looked at each other like this through the windows at Lycan?"

"Yes," drawled Alannah, and it came out a bit slurred. "As I remember, that wazzall right. Intheend."

She sank back, breathed deeply, and closed her eyes again. "So what if the police do come to take you back to prison?"

"I'd run away?" I replied. "If I could, and if not..." I

looked inside, and tasted the idea of killing myself. Would it be better?

After a while, I decided that it probably would, but I didn't think I could. "Convince them to keep me in solitary, I suppose." While there's life there's hope.

Alannah didn't say anything, but she nodded a little, as if to herself.

"I'm going to grab something," I said. "Be right back."

The first aid kit was top notch, and came with a good first aid book. I skimmed the section on head injuries as I picked up some antiseptic and a pad. Under the guise of cleaning a couple of the wounds on her face, I got a much closer look at her eyes. They weren't dilated, which put me into the less upsetting part of the flowchart on the page at the back.

"You get some rest now," I said. "We'll finish this later."

She didn't say anything, but she did sag a bit, and was breathing deeply a moment later. The reek of the antiseptic filling my nostrils shielded me somewhat from my inevitable reaction to Alannah's close proximity. Which, to give my inner beast his due, was almost entirely protective rather than possessive. This time. That cheered me, as even my own inbuilt demon wasn't necessarily pushing me in the wrong direction all the time.

I read the first aid book more carefully while I waited for the others to get back.

NATALIE, Lourdes and George came back talking excitedly. Seeing them coming towards the empty docks arm in arm, I stashed the pistol and put on some tea. Alannah was back dozing.

I heard footsteps on the gangplank, and then the sounds of it scraping. I went outside to help get us going, and saw a big grin on Natalie's face. "Brooke is fine," she said. "Not to mention an absolute genius."

Lourdes bustled past and put us to work, and we were backing very slowly out of the dock a minute later. When I got back to the cockpit, everyone else was there, and Alannah had woken up again.

"Seriously?" she asked. "And the story seems to have legs?"

"Yeah," said Natalie, as Lourdes steered carefully. "Though Lourdes nearly blew it. We were eventually put through to Brooke at the British High Commission, and she was really pleased to hear from us. And then just before we could blow it, she got all serious, and said... What was it?"

Lourdes spoke without turning, putting on a creditable version of Brooke's light middle-class London accent. "Listen, they've been testing my heart and stuff as the enhancement drugs wear off. I'm feeling pretty lethargic, but they say my heart rate is staying super high. Have you all been feeling OK? The doctor told me the level of stimulants we were on, and some of the things I told them I could do while I was all juiced up... They said it was dangerous. There might be cardiac damage."

Natalie jumped back in. "Yeah, brilliant! So Lourdes looks confused for a second, and is about to ask her what the hell she's talking about or something -"

"I was not!" Lourdes denied. "It just took me a little while to figure out what she was doing."

Natalie scoffed. "Sure. So, they were obviously listening in to wherever she was taking the call, and she was giving us the official story. With the principals dead, and the notes gone, it's a really good explanation. More plausible than the truth, really. Fits with what Bowline has been doing all along, and everyone should happily believe that it was a bit of a con game. Long term, as that story spreads, it gets everyone off our back for good!"

I finished making the tea and passed it around. Natalie took a deep sniff of the aroma. "It'll take a little while for all the rumours to stabilise, but we're good to go home probably sooner rather than later!"

The obvious relief was just pouring out of Natalie and Lourdes, and it was impossible not to catch some of their smile.

"So where are we heading now?" I asked, taking a sip.

"Somewhere safe and secret to work out the details," said Lourdes. "How long is long enough to be sure no-one is coming after us, and that we have our stories straight? There's going to be a lot of investigation into this, and we want to keep Brooke's story solid, and preferably make sure we're not sent to prison for murder in the process."

"We could avoid the latter just by shutting up," remarked George. "Lots of shit went down, but no-one could pin any of it on us specifically."

"Not without making the rest of the story sound weird," said Natalie. "We need to go in full victim here. That's not even a lie."

I had a quick little inner montage of all the destruction we'd caused, and wondered.

Natalie appeared to be doing the same, because she wound down rather weakly: "...right?"

We all sipped and thought. Then Lourdes spoke up. "We *are* the victims," she said with an uncharacteristic quiet anger. "I was kidnapped from the side street just outside my hostel, much like Kirsten and Brooke. George had a gun pulled on her in her aunt's house on the afternoon of her aunt's funeral. Alannah was ripped out of witness protection, and Natalie was taken when she saw something suspicious. After that, we were nearly killed with an untested epigenetic process, experimented on, drugged, and threatened and beaten when we didn't comply. Since escaping, one of us was killed, and the four of us have been tortured and resold as slaves. Worse - as laboratory rats."

She locked the steering, and turned around. "We deserve to be able to get back to our normal lives, not go to prison for murder."

Everyone seemed to agree, and then George's brow furrowed, and she looked at me sharply.

"Except, of course", I added, "the one of us whose normal life *is* being in prison for murder."

Lourdes looked a little startled. "For, might I add," I went on, "a crime not that dissimilar from the..."

I counted silently for a few moments. "...many dozens? Of similar crimes that we all just committed. So get your story straight indeed. Escape and recapture, as close to the truth as you can get, and then last minute terrible fight between two groups of bad men, and you swam to another boat and escaped. Please help, I think they're still after me. Get it straight, and get to the authorities fast as you can."

I think we were all watching Alannah for her reaction. She matched our gaze, and nodded. "He's right, fast is important. It's important for your story, and it's important because this ship is full of things no-one wants to see in circulation."

"You'll back their story?" I asked. "Save them and yourself from any fallout?"

"Absolutely," said Alannah.

"*Their* story?" asked George. "Them?"

"Yes," I said. "Because while that's a really good plan, it's not one that works for me. *My* plan is to fill a very large bag with some of the cash down below, and try to find a way to stay out of trouble. Off the grid and out of the way."

I grabbed a small armful of food, and went to the door. "I am now going to sleep in the cabin down the back. Sort yourselves out, and figure me into the logistics however you see fit." With that, I exited, and headed for my overdue bed.

On the way, I heard Alannah asking if they'd brought her a clean phone like she'd asked.

I LIED. The cabin was comfortable, and quiet, but no matter how exhausted I felt, sleep simply wouldn't come. Perhaps an hour later, she came to the door and knocked quietly.

"Come in," I said.

George's black curls peeked through the doorway first, but the rest of her soon followed, lit only by the little round window on the wall.

"I've decided to forgive you," she said gently. Then, looking at me, she went on in surprise. "Have you been crying?"

"Yes," I said. As she came closer, I noticed that she had as well.

"How did Alannah come down?" I asked.

"Don't be an asshole," George replied. "She doesn't care about the cash, and she wants you to be all right."

She sat down on my bed, and I tensed.

"There's precious little 'all right' to be found around here, though, is there?" she asked.

George knew why she was sitting on my bed and what she was doing, but I certainly didn't. In fact, I wasn't feeling sure of anything any more. Emergency finally over, my clarity dissipated, leaving me adrift. George's musky smell and empathetic tone made it hard to steer the beast in the direction of 'protective'. I wasn't even sure I was still holding the reins.

"So we've got to find something out, and I'm sorry, but it has to be tonight," she said, and started taking off her jacket.

My face froze as a wave of abject panic rolled over me. Every signal she was sending was perfectly obvious, and yet utterly incomprehensible.

"Listen, I..." I began, but she hushed me.

"This part is going to be fine," she said.

"I'm not sure..."

"No," she insisted very firmly. "This part is going to be awesome, and somewhere in there you know it. And I don't mean the 'beast' part of you. I mean you, you."

Her jacket hit the floor, and she worked on the button of her new jeans. "What we don't know is what else we might have here. What happens afterwards. That might take a while to find out, but I'm not going back to that empty house to wonder. So stop fighting and try to ride that beast on over here."

SOMEHOW IN ALL MY plans and deliberations, I'd never really considered the possibility of being wanted. Blinking, I watched her for a few moments, magnificent and brave, with that quiet sparkle of a grin.

Then I nodded, and sat up, ignoring the vigorous protest of my injuries. In that moment, a discovery: I wasn't actually wrestling any kind of beast. There was only me.

AND, oh, unexpected butterfly of a miracle, her.

Chapter 16

EPILOGUE

The new house nestled snugly in the green foothills, and the tree line started well above. The wood pile in the woodshed was complete, and I beamed and stretched. The farm life was going to work out a lot better than the place in the city. George's aunt had looked after the place well, but the suburb around it felt too much like a cage. Plus, the three of us had been a bit squeezed in a two-bedroom house. Here there was room to run, and breathe.

I breathed.

Oh. Shower time. Back inside, I met George as she ferried the groceries inside, filling the kitchen with heavily laden bags.

"Can you help get the freezer stuff away while I get the rest?" she asked.

I looked at the time, and saw that we were expecting Alannah in less than an hour. "I've got to shower and then prep the fish," I said, turning on the oven to preheat. Just then Lourdes bustled in, arms also full of bags. George turned to her. "Can you get the freezer stuff away? Stinky needs a shower."

Lourdes wrinkled her nose. "Yes he does." She plopped the bags down and shooed me out. "Go!" she ordered.

"Who's this 'Stinky'?" I asked as I disappeared. "I thought we were just expecting Al?"

LATER, after Al arrived and we were all suitably replenished with my famous Greek-style salmon, I was promptly sent away.

"Don't I get to listen while the grownups are talking?" I asked indignantly.

"Why don't you go see what you can do about the barn gate?" asked Lourdes. "Use your engineer powers."

Relenting, I headed off. Before I'd even left the room, Al turned to the others and asked: "So how are you going with handling him?"

"I'm still right here!" I protested, but they didn't pay me any further attention.

"It's a learning curve," said George, "but we're starting to get the hang of it now. It's easy at home, but when we practise going to town, it gets a lot harder..."

I hurried off to the barn. I thought my dignity might be there.

OFFICIALLY, I was dead again. Every detail of their individual stories had to match each other, as well as the abundant pool of evidence. So simplicity was the order of the day.

The basic story was that the Valkyries escaped with the information that they later released, and Bowline hunted them down to bury the evidence. Bowline came into the hospital with serious firepower, and though I escaped with my fellow inmates, I died soon afterwards as Bowline recaptured the Valkyries. They took my body to remove the evidence, just as they picked up Kirsten's.

For the rest, they simply pleaded ignorance. *Why did the building explode?* Maybe the other inmates got into the armoury, where there were a lot of explosives. *So what caused the explosions at the off-site Bowline operation?* Which off-site Bowline operation? We didn't read the stuff we released in that much detail. Was it on there? *What about the explosions at the kidnapper's base after you were recaptured?* They started fighting, and it escalated so fast. Yelling turned into shooting, turned into exploding buildings and ships. We escaped in the ruckus, and hid in the other ship. We left after the explosions stopped. *Why did they start fighting? …*Money?

A lot of lies in one little package. They used a lot of the truth, though, and the story should have made sense from the criminal side as well. It was all helped by the fact that the more accurate version was frankly weirder. The ongoing investigation rapidly focussed on the details of the criminal organisations. The Valkyries all feigned greater physical distress than they felt, and pleaded mental trauma, which was real enough. They were soon left alone.

It wasn't clear how hard it was for Alannah to manage it. I was grateful. Editing me out of the story like that was still a huge leap for someone in law enforcement to take, and we didn't know each other that well. The official story downplayed the less defensible aspects of her own involvement too, I suppose. As well as the others. The Valkyries had all bonded heavily over their months in the Lycan labs, and I felt like I'd just slipped into the group as they closed ranks.

In some ways, the ordeal had affected Alannah the most. Being kidnapped out of Witness Protection meant that returning to work felt unsafe. Maybe it really was. Every professional friend was now a potential enemy. I know she played her cards very close to her chest. Back on the ship, she had called people on that burner phone, but only to set up a face-to-face meeting. The rest of us helped move a small part of the gear and much of the cash into a national park, where I guarded it for about three uncomfortable days before being picked up by George. No-one saw Alannah much after that, as she was busy wheeling around in a decoy wheelchair and being debriefed.

Natalie returned to her family and the rest of her life. Brooke left the country to do the same. Lourdes and I just sort of stayed on at George's house, and she never kicked us out. Bought a larger place, in fact.

ONCE I HAD the barn gate hung back up on properly braced hinges, I returned to find the three of them sipping beer and chatting casually.

"So how about you, Al?" asked Lourdes, legs tucked under her on the couch, "you never say much about getting back to work yourself."

"Oh, there's a lot going on," she waved airily. "I have a lot of energy, but I have to keep it under wraps. I rarely go into the office any more. Fortunately, my job description is very, well, flexible."

I still wasn't sure where Al worked, never mind what might be in her job description. I did suspect that she had some pretty powerful connections, however. For example, the return to civilisation of a ship full of drugs, weapons, cash and fellow victims had been managed surprisingly quickly and smoothly.

"I know I've never spoken much about my work, besides

the fact that I've been attached to the Federal Police for a couple of years."

She let that hang for a moment, and I could see she was choosing her words carefully. Didn't she say that the original Bowline investigation was something to do with drugs?

"And I know I promised to keep our real experiences off the record, which they are. But there is a *very* small group that knows the whole story, entirely undocumented. When things like this happen, it's incredibly valuable to have someone with influence who isn't blindsided, and I waited to report until I could do it face-to-face with people that I knew could be trusted with our lives."

Alannah tried to read the expressions on our faces, but they were suddenly rather blank. She went on. "They actually already had a lot of pieces of the puzzle. The main reason I was poking into Bowline in the first place is that some intelligence was coming in that needed verification, and a drug-based operation was the only official lever we had."

Sounded like the word 'intelligence' there was used in the official sense. Al sounded like some kind of spook. If she had trust issues with her colleagues, that could make things really tough.

"You're not some kind of clandestine black ops, are you?" asked Lourdes. "I didn't think we had those."

I wondered how an ordinary citizen would ever know whether clandestine organisations existed. Lourdes suddenly frowned and looked into the distance, confused. Maybe she had the same thought. We often did. Of course, most governments are surprisingly bad at long-term secrets. If Australia had something like that, we might have expected to have heard rumours.

"No I'm not," said Al, shaking her head. "This group is

much more ad hoc. You could think of us more like a tiny prototype of Special Circumstances. There's less than a dozen of us, and we're usually just working our normal day jobs. We occasionally organise to perform specific tasks."

"I had no idea that kind of thing could be hidden in our system," said Lourdes.

Al shrugged. "Correct. That's why it's not technically in our system," she replied. "And since it has no official status, it has no visibility. Coincidentally, that also means it has no authority, so we rely on having members with their own. By construction, the group tries to fix problems that can't be done through safe and authorised channels. We're actually supported by a sizeable private endowment."

I marvelled silently at the idea. Having private interests controlling aspects of law enforcement was almost synonymous with organised crime, with results like the corruption that enabled Alannah's initial kidnapping. But what would it be like if the group were more altruistic? That sounded awfully naive, although the possibilities were fascinating. I wondered how it worked...

"Couldn't this group have helped us as soon as we escaped?" asked George.

Alannah winced a little as she shook her head. "Someone, somewhere, ratted me out, and who that was is still an important open question. I couldn't safely contact anyone on open channels, and we didn't have the time needed to improvise anything face-to-face. The inner circle is actually very small. That's very important for maintaining trust, but it does mean we have to be pretty creative with minimal resources, particularly personnel. Given more time, I would have figured out how to get help with zero chance of tipping off Bowline, but this time I hoped we could be our own cavalry."

This was a lot of information to take in, and I wasn't sure I was managing.

"I still can't picture this group," I said. "It sounds like a bit like you're working with Batman. ...or is it more like a *privately funded* double-oh program?"

"If you like," said Al as she shrugged again, "except most of us have jobs and placements within normal public organisations, and we don't have a licence to kill."

George raised an eyebrow.

"...or," added Al, "any kind of licence at all, really."

"That's fascinating," said Lourdes, who fidgeted like she had a thousand questions all trying to crowd through one small door. "but if you're all about secret and exclusive, why on earth would you come out and..." She ground to a halt, eyes wide and staring off into the distance, beer forgotten in her hand.

"Huh," I grunted, and took a swig of mine.

George just sipped, thoughtful. The motion covered what might have been a smile, but did nothing to hide her interested gleam.

Gold all over the hills and trees, gold in our hands and bellies. We turned as a pack, and listened.

AFTERWORD

Thanks for reading! If you liked this book, I'd really appreciate it if you took the time to write a review. Feedback is essential, and I cannot express how much encouraging words can stoke the creative fires.

Writing news will be published on my website: jhopepublishing.com. Upcoming books will be released in the usual channels, but if you'd like to be informed of any future releases, drop me a line on jhopepublishing@gmail.com, and I'll add you to the mailing list.

ACKNOWLEDGMENTS

Thanks to everyone that made this book happen. I don't exactly know how this book happened, so I can't be thorough. Here's a simple attempt. Thanks first and foremost to my family, who took up the slack while I was distracted, with both cheer and supportive noises. Thanks also for everyone who read drafts and made encouraging sounds early in the process, particularly Anne, Brenton, Tim, Janet, and James.

Thanks to the countless authors who have enchanted and intrigued me over the years. Who still do. You are legion, and your example is not just why I am a writer, but also why I am a lot of other things. My decision to become a physicist can be traced to days spent reading and rereading *The Dispossessed*. I spent a decade or two hoping I could write like Roger Zelazny, and hopefully I now don't. I never even dreamed I could write like Lois McMaster Bujold, but it's always worth seeing what can be done. Thanks to Jim Butcher for sharing his story about writing *Storm Front*, which inspired me to put aside my pet project and just get something over the finish line.

I just made the mistake of looking over my shoulder at one of our bookshelves. Suffice it to say, I have climbed this high only by standing on the shoelaces of giants. Thanks everyone, near and far. Time to get to work.

ALSO BY JOE HOPE

Feral

Coming Soon:

Bridge

Printed in Great Britain
by Amazon